Books by Anne-Marie Sheridan

Summoned to Darkness
The Far-Off Rhapsody

SUMMONED
TO
DARKNESS

ANNE-MARIE SHERIDAN

SIMON AND SCHUSTER

NEW YORK

SUMMONED
TO
DARKNESS

CHAPTER ONE

MY PATERNAL grandfather, who lost a leg at the battle of Waterloo, frequently declared that I was, in his characteristic phrase, "a child with a temper as short as her nose and as long-lasting as ice in Maytime." Grandpa may or may not have been correct in his summation of my character, but I have to admit that, of all the things that beset me in my twenty-fourth year, it was Esmeralda who most easily summoned up the hasty temper to which all of us, even the most placid, are heir.

"Meg! Meg, where are you? Confound you, Meg, why are you never about when I need you?"

Her petulant voice came to me from the window of her bedchamber, and there I was—immersed in a novelette of a most sensational character, it being a Saturday afternoon in June, and most agreeably warm, so that I had taken my favorite chair on the shady side of the great house overlooking the moat and was enjoying both the warmth and the gothic delights of my book. Then who should call but Esmeralda—she who had declared that, after last night's ball in Cambridge, she would sleep forever.

"Meg!"

"Yes," I called back.

"Where are you?"

"I'm in the garden."

"Come up, then. I need you."

"You're supposed to be asleep," I reminded her.

"I can't sleep. Come up and talk to me."

I felt a surge of the sharp temper of which Grandpa had accused me. Turned down the corner of the page—a habit that I normally detest—slung my shawl round my shoulders, and went into the house. Bosun, the Newfoundland, was sprawled asleep in the cool ashes of the massive fireplace in the great hall. He lifted his powerful black head. His absurdly gentle eyes quested over me. The thick tail gave a tentative wag. I smiled at him, and he looked relieved, for he was a dog who could gauge to a nicety a human's temper, and he knew well enough what my frown had meant.

"You are a good boy," I told him. "And my anger isn't with you." His tail increased its activity, raising a cloud of wood ash that covered his glossy black coat in a dusting of grayness.

Esmeralda's suite, comprising bedchamber, dressing room, and bathroom, was on the first floor at the back, overlooking the carriage drive and the long avenue of memorial oaks which, so it is said, were planted in honor of the restoration of the monarchy after the Civil War, some two hundred years ago and more. The wide sweep of the staircase was lined on each side with portraits of the Demaurys, in heavy gilt frames. They all put me in mind of Esmeralda, or of her various cousins: fair and blue-eyed all, with petulant mouths. Real Demaurys, not like me. Not dark of hair and green-eyed. But then, I am a Gaunt, related to the Demaurys only by marriage.

I found Esmeralda sitting up in bed, propped against her pink pillows, dressed in the pink negligee that she brought back from her last trip to Paris. Not for the first time, I despaired at her figure and her complexion, both of which owed so little to the artifices of the toilette. Esmeralda, I declare, could rise straight from her slumbers and walk into a ballroom with no more attention than a smoothing down of her hair and a moistening of the lips, and you would think that she had spent the whole day at her hairdresser's and had consumed a chemist's shop full of rouge, powder, and unguents of beauty. I told myself, and not for the first time, that I sometimes hated Esmeralda.

"You look ridiculous," she said. "You've been sitting in the sun, and your face is as swarthy as a washerwoman's."

"I can't help it," I replied. "It's my nature to change color in the sunlight. I know I should carry a parasol always, but it's such a nuisance. Why do you want me?"

"Ponsonby has brought a packet of letters from the village," she said, pointing to the dressing table. "You can read them to me."

It was on the tip of my tongue to ask why she was incapable of reading them to herself, but prudence overcame the impulse. When one is beholden to the tune of four square meals a day and a roof over one's head, one does not lightly make a grand display of independence. Besides, I had as much interest as she in reading her correspondence. I picked up the letters and sat down on the edge of Esmeralda's bed to open them.

"The first one's a bill from Madame Colette in Cambridge," I informed her. "A bill for seven pounds, fifteen shillings, for your new evening cloak."

"Fiddle-de-dee," she said. "What else?"

My heart gave a treacherous lurch as my gaze alighted upon the sprawled handwriting on the front of the next envelope.

"This is from Peter," I told her.

She snatched it from me; tucked the letter under her pillow. "I'll read it myself, later," she informed me. "What else?"

I bowed my head, the better to hide the color that must have mounted to my too-healthy cheeks; paused awhile and made a great thing of examining the exterior of the next communication, in order that my heart should cease its sudden hammering and my breathing become more even.

"Well?" demanded Esmeralda. "What's that, eh?"

"It's from Venice," I told her.

"From Great-uncle Giles! Heavens! He doesn't write to members of the family more than once in a blue moon. What can be amiss? Open it quickly, Meg. Hurry, do."

I had to confess to an excitement and curiosity that equaled her own. Though not a Demaury, I was nevertheless kin to the head of the Demaury clan, that fabulous, almost legendary figure known to the world as Giles Demaury—lover, recluse, multimillionaire enigma.

"It's written by his secretary," I said.

"Well, of course it is, silly," snapped Esmeralda. "Giles is half blind and hasn't put pen to paper in my lifetime. Read it, do, and stop procrastinating. You really are most irritating."

The letter was penned in a neat, clerkly hand and bore the Demaury coat of arms embossed upon the top of the sheet.

Palazzo Demaury
Venezia
Saturday June 13th, 1891

Dear Miss Demaury,

I am instructed by Mr. Giles Demaury to communicate with you, together with the other principal members of his family, concerning his present wishes.

In short, Mr. Giles, finding himself in a state of indifferent health and greatly advanced in years, has decided to make some settlement of his affairs.

It is very many years since he has seen the principal members of his family (I am bidden to add, in your case, dear Miss Demaury, that Mr. Giles has indeed never had the pleasure of making your personal acquaintance, and knows you only from a photographic representation of yourself that was sent to him by your parents on the occasion of your birth), and he feels that the matter of the inheritance can best be settled at a general assembly of all concerned. To this end, Miss Demaury, Mr. Giles requests and requires you to repair to the Palazzo Demaury no later than the 11th of next month, for a short stay.

Perhaps you will be kind enough to signify your acceptance at an early convenience.

I remain, Madame,

Your obedient servant,
Henry Obadiah
(Private Secretary to Mr. Giles Demaury)

"To Venice?" cried Esmeralda, sitting bolt upright, her face a picture of pretty, pink dismay. "But I can't possibly. I am due to go to Scotland next month to stay with Peter's people. Besides, Venice, I am told, smells vilely of drains."

"I don't think you have a great deal of choice in the matter," I reminded her, not without a twinge of malicious pleasure. "If I ever did see a royal command, it was this. You will note that Secretary Obadiah asks you to signify your acceptance. He takes no account of a refusal. Had I not better start packing?"

"Don't be flippant!" she snapped. "It doesn't become you."

"I'm sorry," I said. I could afford to be contrite. It was such pleasure to observe Esmeralda being given orders, for a change.

"Of course I shall have to go," she said sulkily. "After all, I am the head of the senior English branch of the family."

This was true. Her father and mother, who had both been kindness itself to me, had died five years previously of the cholera in India. And I missed them greatly, still.

"He says a short stay," I reminded her. "And you can quite easily postpone the Scottish visit. Peter will understand that it's an important family matter and won't mind your going in the least."

Her baby-blue eyes opened very wide. "Peter will accompany me," she said. "You don't really suppose I would go all that way on my own. He will come. And so will you."

"Oh!" I exclaimed. "Me—to Venice?"

"Of course. You are supposed to be my companion, are you not?"

"But—I've never been abroad in my life before."

"That is quite immaterial," declared Esmeralda.

"But—" I searched my heart for reasons why I did not want to go away with her. And with Peter, of all people. "I have no wardrobe, save the things I stand up in and a couple of changes," I said lamely.

"As a lady's companion, you will not be required or expected to set a tone of high fashion," was her tart response.

So that was that.

My name, as will have already been deduced, is Meg Gaunt. An orphan, like my cousin Esmeralda, I am related to the high-and-mighty Demaurys only by the tenuous bonds of marriage—my mother's sister married James Demaury—and not by blood. Indeed, I called Esmeralda "cousin" only out of convenience, for she was nothing of the kind. My father, a naval officer, died shortly after I was born, and my mother soon after that. Sir Roland and Lady Demaury, Esmeralda's parents, saw to my upbringing; paid for me to be educated at a boarding establishment for the daughters of gentlemen, in Banbury, Oxfordshire; and afterward brought me to live at their country seat, Murchester Hall, Cambridgeshire.

The Demaury fortune, as is well known, was founded in the eighteenth century by the great George Fanshawe Demaury, art collector and man of business. While still a young man, he formed a connection in Italy that enabled him to export large quantities of paintings, sculptures, and other *objets d'art* to England and America for the wealthy and highborn—an enterprise that made him a millionaire before he was twenty-five years old. By the turn of the century and the end of the Napoleonic wars, G. F. Demaury had business establishments in all the major cities of Europe and in America. Through the Demaury galleries and salesrooms passed the most rare and priceless products of the artist's brush: Rembrandts and Rubenses galore, Titians and Tintorettos beyond belief, Watteaus and Bouchers unnumbered. A favored customer at Demaury's of St. Petersburg was the Czar of All the Russias himself, who was so pleased with the principal of that establishment—G. F. Demaury's second son, Arthur—that he bestowed upon him the Order of St. Vladimir. Esmeralda's father, my patron and benefactor, ran the English branch of the Demaury empire in Bond Street, London, and had himself been honored by a knighthood at the hand of Her Majesty. Sadly, it was while negotiating the sale of a collection of Italian Old Masters to the Maharajah of Bangladore that Sir Roland and his Lady both fell victims to a cholera plague; and they were buried out there.

But by far the most renowned of all the Demaurys—outstripping even the founder-father, G. F. D. himself—was the legendary Giles.

The story of the life and love of Giles Demaury reads like an Old Norse saga, or one of the long and involved tales of the ancient troubadours. He was born to the American branch of the family, in Boston, Massachusetts, and it is certain that all the denizens of Fairyland must have been present at his birth, to bestow upon him the gifts and accomplishments with which he was so richly endowed. Devastating good looks, charm enough to move mountains, a sparkling wit, brilliance of conversation, the mind of a poet, and the heart of a lion—he had all these and more. Scorning easy fame as an heir to the Demaury empire, he threw everything aside and traveled to wild and unexplored places of the world: journeying by camel to Samarkand, venturing by canoe up the turbulent Zambezi, trekking on foot across the desert of Nubia. At the age of twenty-five, when he had done all there was to be done, he went back to Boston and took over the reins of the American branch of the family empire. Two years later, he was undisputed head of that empire worldwide. It was then he met and fell in love with Estelle Amor.

Amor was the greatest dramatic actress of her age, perhaps of any age. Her face, which looks out at us from the faded daguerreotypes, gives only a hint of the tempestuous spirit within, only a breath of what a leading American theater critic had once described as "a presence that could silence the clamor of the Universe, or make a marble statue to weep." Five years older than Giles Demaury, and already twice married and twice divorced, she had only to meet his glance and he was hers, and she his.

Their stormy courtship and marriage was the sensation of two continents; their quarrels, both public and private, the scandal of a dozen capital cities. Insanely jealous, Demaury fought a duel for her in Paris, and killed his man. But for the leniency of French law in matters of *les crimes passionels*, he could have faced a capital charge. In London, he struck a noble duke who had the temerity to send flowers to Amor when she was appearing at Covent Garden. At a reception given in her honor at Monte Carlo, they had one of their famous public scenes, in which Giles called her all the names he could give tongue to, and she threw her shoe at his head.

For three tempestuous years, they fought and they loved. Then, one dark and stormy night, the boat in which they were crossing the Lagoon of Venice was swamped by a wave. Next morning, Giles, unconscious and half-drowned, was washed ashore at the Lido. Of Estelle Amor and the boatman, no trace was ever found.

They say that Giles went temporarily insane from grief and never spoke for a year, but remained locked in his study at the Palazzo Demaury, the Venetian seat of the Demaury clan. It is certain that he never again left Venice, and seldom received visitors, even members of his own family.

And now, sixty years after the tragic death of his wife, and himself an old and ailing man, the recluse of the Palazzo Demaury was summoning the clan from far and wide, calling them in from all over Europe and America to attend him. For he was the head of the family, the keeper of the family fortunes, master of the incredible wealth that the Demaurys had amassed in nearly two hundred years as the leading art dealers of the world.

And I—a poor relation by marriage, and a recipient of Demaury grace and favor—was to be numbered among those who were gathered in.

"Do you need me any more, Esmeralda," I asked.

"No, I don't think so." She frowned petulantly. "Oh, yes, will you write to Venice and tell Giles's secretary that we shall be coming? That is to say, my fiancé and myself. And you."

"Do you think we can be accommodated? I mean—supposing everyone brings a fiancé and a companion?"

"Don't be idiotic, Meg," she said crossly. "The palazzo is about the size of Buckingham Palace. Mama and Papa stayed there once and were forever getting lost on the way to their suite. Oh, I have the most awful headache coming on. It must have been all that champagne and dancing last night."

"Lean back and close your eyes," I told her.

"Yes," she said. "I'll have a nap, then I shall read Peter's letter and take a bath."

"You do that," I said.

On the way out of the room, I caught sight of my own reflection in a looking glass on the wall, and had the most disturbing experience of catching myself unawares with an expression of guilt. It was this that prompted me to put on a false, bright smile and turn from the door to say to Esmeralda:

"Read your letter, and I'll see you at dinner."

"I shan't be coming down for dinner," said she. "I really feel as if I shall never want food to pass my lips again."

"I'll tell them in the kitchen," I said.

I left her to her letter, descended the staircase, and crossed the great hall to the passageway that led directly to the vast kitchens of Murchester. The stone-flagged corridor was of such a length, and so devious in its twistings and turnings, that the food brought from the kitchens to the dining table in the great hall was invariably cold and unappetizing—a fact which led to the apocryphal story of the Prince of Wales's comment on the occasion of his visit to Sir Roland and Lady Demaury in the '8os: "Your claret, my dear Demaury, is fit to grace any table in the land, but I would not feed your Brussels sprouts to my son Eddy's pet mouse."

The kitchens, as ever, were hives of industry. Though there were only Esmeralda and myself in residence, the small army of fifteen indoor servants were preparing—as they prepared it three hundred and sixty-five days a year, and an extra for leap year—a full three-course dinner, with entrees and desserts. It was a custom at Murchester, as at all the great houses of the neighborhood and throughout the land, to keep open house and a full table in case of visitors. It is true that visitors seldom came uninvited—but the custom remained. I informed the butler that Esmeralda would not be down: it made not the slightest difference to his arrangements.

I nodded to the cook and to the housekeeper, who were in conclave about particulars of the running of the establishment in the following week. I then went up to my room, forgoing the delights of my novelette; there to throw myself down upon my bed and bring my mind—slowly and with the kind of reluctance that one imposes upon oneself in certain forbidden byways of speculation— to the question of my forthcoming journey to Venice. And, in particular, to the fact that Esmeralda's fiancé would be accompanying us on that venture.

Lord Peter Chalmers was incomparably the most disturbing man I had ever encountered in my life; not that I had had the opportunity to meet many handsome, elegant, aristocratic men with outrageous manners and terrifying ways with women.

Peter had come into Esmeralda's life—and, by association, into mine—during the previous London Season. There, during the succession of balls, dinner parties, visits to the opera, garden parties, and such—in the course of which I mostly sat in corners and made myself look as small as possible, so as not to draw attention to the dowdiness of my costume and the paucity of my smart conversation—a devastating aristocrat was presented to my beautiful cousin. And there and then Esmeralda, who so far had only played with the affections of eligible young men, treating them as grown-up nursery toys to be cast aside when she tired of them, was completely bowled off her feet, as the saying goes.

The following winter, Peter was a frequent visitor to Murchester, staying—for reasons of propriety, Esmeralda being a spinster lady with no male relative on the premises—with a friend of his at a neighboring big house.

On Christmas Day, in the great hall, in the course of a dinner at which I was present, he rose and made the announcement of his engagement to Esmeralda.

It was a week after that, and I know the date well enough, for I noted the whole episode in my diary, that I had my first intimate encounter with Peter Chalmers: he who till then had been a far-off and daunting figure, like a splendid soldier in a toy theater who is really cut out from cardboard, or a picture of a hero from some saga of the Empire.

It was a cold January afternoon, nearing teatime. I was seated in the solar, which was like a conservatory at the rear of the mansion, and there I was working at a piece of petit point. Suddenly, the *click-click* of booted heels on the passage outside alerted me to the approach of company. I thought it to be the butler with a tray of tea. There were no guests in the house. Esmeralda was lying down. Peter and half a dozen others were expected for dinner. I looked up as the door opened, fully expecting to see the rotund countenance of Standish, the butler, peering out from behind a silver teapot. In this expectation, I was gravely wide of the mark.

"Well, bless me, if it isn't the beautiful cousin who's always thrust into the background."

Peter Chalmers entered the solar and closed the door behind him. He was wearing a black riding coat and top boots. His bronzed face, set off by a snowy white stock that banded his muscular neck, and by his mane of gleaming copper-colored hair, had a brutal masculinity about it. And his smile was a predator's smile: white-fanged, assured, under the trim military-style mustache. He crossed over from the door—slowly, with a hint of a swagger—and stood over me, looking down into my eyes with his eyes of incredible blueness.

"Good afternoon, Lord Peter," I said, as calmly as I knew how.

"Good afternoon, Miss Gaunt," he responded, with more than a hint of mockery. "And what are you doing there, pray?"

"As you see, I am embroidering a piece of petit point," I replied.

"May I see it?"

"Of course." I gave the circular embroidery frame to him. On close observation, I could see that his hand was strongly made, and that his fingernails were beautifully kept, and his whole presence carried a tang of cologne water, oiled leather, and the outdoors.

"The design is a coat of arms," he said.

"It's the Demaury coat of arms," I said. "I'm making it into a cushion cover, as a birthday present for Esmeralda."

"The Demaury coat of arms," he repeated. "Of course. And the device upon the shield—three hearts. I should have recognized it at once. Do you know the origin of the three hearts of the Demaurys, Miss Gaunt?"

"Yes," I replied.

"Then enlighten me, I beg you." He smiled down at me, sensuous-lipped, blue eyes crinkled at the corners, ineffably and impossibly arrogant and self-assured.

"The three hearts relate to the first Demaury who was granted arms in the reign of James the Second," I said. "He was Secretary of the Admiralty, and it was said of him that he had three loves in his life: his horse, the Navy, and his wife—in that order." Embarrassed by the intensity of the blue-eyed stare, I let my gaze fall to my hands. "I—I can't vouch for the truth of the story," I concluded feebly.

"And where does your heart belong, Miss Gaunt?" he murmured.

"Sir?" I said, startled.

"I said: to whom does your heart belong?"

"I—I don't understand you, Lord Peter." A poor reply, but the first that came to my head. To my alarm, moreover, I realized that my nether lip was trembling, and he must surely have seen it.

His smile broadened, and he said, "Come now, Miss Gaunt, it isn't as difficult as all that. Your heart either belongs to another, or it's your own. Which is it to be, hey?"

It was on the tip of my tongue to tell him that the state of my heart was no affair of his; but it seemed a churlish thought and, in any event, the tall and impressive figure that loomed above me was not of a quality that one lightly tells to mind his own business. Hindsight—and experience—have taught me that I should have ignored the probing question, passed it off by pointedly changing the subject. I can only say in my defense that I was sadly lacking in finesse for a person of my age—and all through deficiency of experience.

So I answered his question—and was trapped.

"My heart is my own," I replied in a nervous whisper.

"Then it follows that your affections are—available," he replied.

"My affections—available?" Now my hands had begun to tremble in time with my nether lip. "I don't know what you mean, Lord Peter."

"It's very simple, my dear Miss Gaunt," he replied. And then he laid my embroidery frame down upon the side table and—to my great alarm—touched my cheek with his fingertip, very gently. "A lady like yourself, I may say a lady of considerable beauty and attainments, should not waste her heart, and her life, in solitary contemplation of the world outside. You really are a most beautiful creature, Meg."

"Lord Peter, I—"

Rising to my feet, I made to brush past him and leave the solar with as much dignity as I could muster. I got nowhere. His hand was upon my wrist, enclosing it in a grasp that was only gently binding—but binding, no less.

"Don't go," he said.

"Please . . ."

"I saw you first," he said, "at the ball at the Duchess of Almondsbury's. You came down the stairs at Esmeralda's heels. She was like a Rhein maiden: all blonde and silver. You were a dusky queen of old Nile—Cleopatra reincarnated. I have to say that it was to your dark and brooding loveliness that I was first attracted, Meg."

"Let me pass!" I pleaded.

"First—a kiss," he replied.

"How dare you?" I gasped.

"Just one kiss, Meg." His face was very close to mine. All the power and confidence of his maleness seemed to bear down upon me, leaving me defenseless and bereft.

"Let me go, please!"

"One kiss."

"No!"

"Then what is not freely given," he said blandly, "I shall now proceed to take by right of conquest."

Whereupon he slid one hand round my waist and, taking my chin in his other, he drew me roughly to him. The hard length of his body was pressed against mine, and the male scent of him filled my whole consciousness. His lips—those smiling and sensuous lips—bore down upon mine, choking off my breath.

He did not hurry himself, but protracted the kiss to the length of his own pleasure. When he had done with me, he let me go and stood back, grinning with cool and mocking amusement.

"Was that nice?" he asked smugly. "I imagine you enjoyed it greatly."

For answer, I drew back my hand and struck him across the mouth—that insolent, sneering mouth that had so defiled mine.

"You brute!" I cried. "You arrogant, unfeeling brute!"

Fury blazed in those blue eyes: a cold and unreasonable fury that comes from a mind which has never reckoned for refusal or defiance, but has always taken what it wants as a matter of right. For a moment, I thought that he would return the blow—and with interest; indeed, I shrank from him and lifted my hands to protect my face; but presently the fury turned to amusement.

"I should have expected that," he said. "I made a bad mistake, then, to treat Egypt's queen like a common serving wench. Next time I shall be more—oblique and subtle in my approach."

"You will not touch me again!" I cried. "Or I'll . . ."

He smiled broadly. "Or you will—what?"

I had no answer for him, and he knew it. Turning, he swaggered over to the window, looked out across the moat, to the line of trees that bordered the gardens beyond. Then he turned and regarded me again, hands on hips, booted legs straddled, master of all he surveyed, with all the brutal arrogance of a thousand years of aristocratic blood.

"Or you will do what?" he repeated. "Inform on me to my fiancée? I think you will not. No, I don't think you will do that, my dear Meg. Tell me—I am correct, am I not, in assuming that you have no private income?"

"No, I have not," I breathed.

"Nor any expectation of an inheritance?"

"No."

"In fact, one might say that only by grace of Esmeralda's whim are you protected from the hurly-burly of the world outside these exceedingly commodious walls. By the way, have you any hard experience of that world?"

"No," I whispered.

"I thought not," he replied. "And neither have I, not at first hand. But a man may venture where a woman—a gently reared woman such as yourself—would fear to tread, and I can tell you, my dear Meg, that I have observed it to be a hard world out there. I have seen women like you—young, beautiful, and lacking other means of support—begging for favors in the streets. Tell me, what is your honest opinion of darling Esmeralda?"

Taken aback by his sudden change of tack, I could only stammer the first thing that came into my head.

"She—she is very generous," I faltered.

"That she is not," he replied. "Darling Esmeralda, whom I hope with luck to wed in St. Margaret's, Westminster, before the year is out, is anything but generous. Beautiful—yes. Rich—yes. Kind to animals—some animals, mostly of the furry, amiable sort. Has a pleasant singing voice. Paints nicely in water colors and sketches divinely. Is extraordinarily fond of me. Is a compendium of many virtues. But generous she is not. Shall I tell you what would be her reaction to your informing her that I had kissed you in the solar on a June afternoon while she was resting?"

I shook my head, not wanting to hear the awful truth; but he persisted.

He said, "You would be out of this house within the hour, as well you know. Bag and baggage. True?"

I nodded. "Yes."

"As for me," he said lightly, "as for the blame and obloquy that might be laid upon me—why, it would be like water off a duck's back to yours sincerely. My lady would frown and give me cold looks for a couple of days. But, as I have said, darling Esmeralda is extraordinarily fond of me. She is also extraordinarily looking forward to being a marchioness, which in the nature of things she is likely to be when I inherit my dear father's title. Need I say more?"

"You have said all you need to say, and more, Lord Peter," I replied. "And now, will you let me go?"

"One more kiss, perhaps?"

"Please . . ." I felt the tears prickling my eyes.

"Perhaps not this time," he said. "Enough is enough, and there will be other occasions. Yes, my dear Meg, I think you and I will have many happy times together—when friends are absent."

He stood back to let me pass on my way to the door, bowing a mocking bow as I went. The last I heard as the door closed behind me was his laugh: a wild and reckless laugh that put me in mind of the baying of foxhounds when they have closed in upon the panting, hunted creature and are about to make the kill.

I stayed in my room till dinner, brooding over my shame. That I had not immediately packed my bags and left my cousin's house after the incident in the solar was something that I found difficult to live with. I can only say—in my defense, to my own self the accuser—that it was the fear of what Peter Chalmers had referred to as "the world outside" that had prevented me. The Year of Grace 1891 was not a time for a penniless woman of no experience to cast herself adrift in the labor market of Victorian England. As I knew well from the advertisement pages of *The Times*, there would be nothing for me but to join the ever-growing army of "women of refinement" who sought work as lady's companions, governesses, teachers of this and that, even shop assistants—and mostly seeking in vain, as evidenced by the telling frequency of the phrase "wages immaterial," meaning that the poor wretches were reduced to slaving for a roof over their heads and a bite to eat.

So, in fear, I held back what my conscience dictated I should have done. And in so doing I fell into the trap of despair, which fear engenders. I had known some good times at Murchester Hall: times when Esmeralda's parents were alive, and my cousin—two years my junior—had been an affectionate, if demanding, playmate. Even up to the time of the previous year's London Season and her meeting with Peter Chalmers my life had been highly enviable by most standards, for I had gone almost everywhere with Esmeralda, even if only as a mute companion in the background. But from the day of the incident in the solar, I never knew real peace of mind at Murchester. Always there was the image of Peter Chalmers, the menace of his arrogant maleness. I took refuge in avoiding him whenever possible, even in company. When he was in the house, I simply stayed in my room or made sure I was never alone in any of the reception rooms. He never addressed me directly; but I was often aware of his covert glance upon me, along the length of a dinner table or the width of the drawing room. And I shuddered at the remembrance of his unwanted embrace . . .

My broodings were interrupted by the dressing bell for dinner. Having only one dinner gown to my name, the matter of choosing presented no problems. When I descended at the second bell and entered the great hall, I was brought to a halt by the sweep of napery and silver that embellished the long refectory table. Puzzled, I glanced questioningly at the butler, who was posed by the door opposite: the door to the drawing room.

"Why is the table set for six, Standish?" I asked him. "There's only Miss Esmeralda and me in the house, and I have told you that Miss Esmeralda isn't coming down to dinner."

"I 'ave received instructions to the contrary, Miss," replied Standish, who was under no illusions about my position at Murchester, and who treated me, for all that I sat at his mistress's table, as no more than a servant—albeit a senior servant, like himself—of the establishment. "The mistress gave orders for six." With that, he turned his back on me and, opening the double doors of the drawing room, he intoned in his sonorous, professional butler's voice, "Dinner is served, ma'am."

"Thank you, Standish," said Esmeralda, and I saw her—a vision in white satin embellished with sequins and seed pearls at the corsage—rise and gesture to her guests.

There was Miss Harriet Demaury, a spinster lady of around sixty years, who lived in Cambridge. She offered her skinny arm to Bruce Dennison, a gentleman farmer who owned the estate bordering on the Murchester lands, and with whom Esmeralda had amused herself in a brief courtship a year previously. I was surprised to see Bruce as a guest at Esmeralda's table, for they had scarcely spoken since the end of the affair.

A tall figure of a man rose from a chair and offered his arm to a pretty girl in blue taffeta. In doing so, he revealed his profile to me. With a shock of recognition, I saw that Lord Peter Chalmers had arrived!

Esmeralda noticed me and said brightly, "Meg, dear, the letter from Peter was to tell me that he was already on his way down from Scotland and would be arriving this evening." Hence the hastily assembled dinner party of welcome.

"Most kind of you to extend an invitation to your old aunt," said Miss Harriet in her gravelly voice. She flashed me a wink as she passed by on Bruce Dennison's arm. The powder lay thickly among the wrinkles of her haggard face, and her rheumy eyes were rimmed with black kohl. "Hello, Meg," she said. "You grow more handsome every time I see you."

I dropped my gaze before Peter Chalmers' mocking glance.

"Good evening, Meg," he said. "I trust you are well."

"Very well, thank you," I murmured.

"May I present Miss Anne Ackroyd?" He gestured formally to the pretty girl in blue. She smiled nervously at me and extended her hand. "This is Miss Margaret Gaunt," he said. "Miss Ackroyd is engaged to Dennison."

"I hope you will both be very happy," I said, smiling at the girl, then at Bruce Dennison, who was gazing at her fondly. It struck me how well they complemented each other: he the burly, slow-moving country gentleman; she so slight and delicate.

"Will everyone take their places at table," said Esmeralda, with a note of irritation in her voice. "Peter, you at the opposite end from me, with Aunt Harriet on your right and Miss Ackroyd on your left. Meg on my right, and you here on my left, Bruce."

I watched my cousin as Bruce Dennison took his place at her elbow and she treated him to her very special, brilliant smile: the one that entailed a lot of eyelash-fluttering. I had known that smile since childhood. It was the weapon with which Esmeralda had always ensured that she received a second helping of strawberries and cream, the extra half-hour postponement of bed on summer's evenings, the reprieve from scolding and chastisement when she had been naughty.

What are you up to now, my girl? I thought to myself.

"How is Scotland, Lord Peter?" demanded Miss Harriet.

"Even milder than you have it here in East Anglia at this time of the year, ma'am," he replied. "And the salmon are running very well."

"Bruce is a tremendous fisherman," said Esmeralda in a loud voice. She tapped her neighbor on his wrist with her fan. "Do you remember, Bruce, the time you took me mackerel fishing off Lowestoft? The little boat was bobbing like a cork in a tempest and I was quite terrified. And you were so protective, so concerned. Bruce really is such a pet to have around—don't you find, Miss Ackroyd?"

Poor little Miss Ackroyd intimated, by a scarcely audible murmur accompanied by a heightening of the color on her smooth cheeks, that this was so.

"Do you mind if I call you Anne?" demanded Esmeralda.

"No," whispered the girl.

"I feel I know you so well," said Esmeralda. "Though we met only this evening, one is aware of a bond between us, is one not? Almost—how to put it?—a sisterhood, don't you think?"

Anne Ackroyd had no reply for this, but clearly showed by her confused manner that she would willingly have wished the floor to open up and swallow her. Instead, she took refuge in starting on her soup, and fumbled and nearly dropped her spoon in so doing.

I decided that I had a good idea, now, what Esmeralda was up to, and cast a glance to the other end of the table, where Peter Chalmers was smiling into his wineglass with an air that said he had also divined my cousin's intention—and found it all vastly amusing.

"Ackroyd is not a name I have heard mentioned in Society," said the mistress of Murchester. "Nor, indeed, in Cambridgeshire. Have your people been long in this part of the world, er—Anne?"

Bruce Dennison came to the aid of his intended. "Anne's family live in Yorkshire," he said.

"Ah—Yorkshire," said Esmeralda. "That would account for it. You must know the Lawsons of Castle Ilkley, my dear."

"Er—no," faltered the girl.

"How odd. But, of course, you will be acquainted with the Scawboroughs. Deevina Scawborough it was who sponsored my presentation at Court. What, you have never met the Scawboroughs?" She glanced at me and raised an astonished eyebrow. I shrugged my shoulders and addressed myself to my soup. I had no intention of assisting Esmeralda in her cruel game.

"Anne's people don't move much in Society," said Bruce Dennison feebly.

"They would scarcely have to move *much* to be acquainted with the Duke and Duchess of Scawborough," said Esmeralda. "They ride to hounds four days a week."

"Anne's family are not hunting people," said Bruce. His florid, handsome countenance was a picture of concern as he gazed across at the frightened face of his fiancée.

"Not hunting people?" echoed Esmeralda. "But surely they have a place in the country?"

"They live exclusively in the town," said Bruce. "In Huddersfield."

"In—Huddersfield?" said Esmeralda distantly. "I don't think I am acquainted with Huddersfield."

"It is a manufacturing town," said Bruce. "For the wool trade."

Esmeralda made a fussy gesture with her napkin, dabbing her lips and making a pretty moue. "But I am more confused than ever," she said. "Why are Miss Ackroyd's—ah, Anne's—people living in Huddersfield, which is devoted to manufacture in the wool trade?"

"They are *in* the wool trade," said Bruce, letting his gaze slip to his fingernails, thence to his watch fob, then by easy stages to his fiancée.

"*In the wool trade?*" Esmeralda enunciated the words in a tone of disbelief admixed with alarm, and she transferred her gaze to the unhappy, pretty face of the girl in blue, as if for all the world she expected poor Anne Ackroyd to blossom out in wool combings, or start spinning yarn where she sat. For one moment I thought that she would outstep the bounds of all hospitality and dismiss the poor creature from her table there and then, as an offspring of parents who were so lacking in the niceties of polite society as to be actually concerned in—of all things—*trade*.

Anne's eyes were bright with half-shed tears, and it seemed to me that she must leap to her feet and rush from the room. She was saved by Miss Harriet.

"Good for them!" interposed the old lady. "I've a lot of time for folks in trade—speaking as a member of a family who've been traders for nigh on two hundred years."

"Touché," murmured Peter Chalmers from the far end of the table, and he retreated behind his wineglass when his fiancée's angry glance swept down to him.

"The Demaurys are art *dealers*," snapped Esmeralda. "One might almost say merchant princes. There is a wide distinction."

Miss Harriet snorted. "Fiddlesticks!" she grated. "George Fanshawe Demaury, the founder of our fortunes, was more pirate than merchant prince. He bought cheaply from the impoverished Italian nobility left in the aftermath of the Napoleonic wars, and sold at vastly inflated prices to Whig magnates in Bristol and the social climbers of Boston and New York. And we've followed the same principle ever since. The very food we are eating, the very Sevres dinner service from which we eat it (there are no less than two thousand pieces to this dinner set, my dear Miss Ackroyd, and they were a present from Giles Demaury to Esmeralda's parents upon the occasion of their marriage), all of it was paid for by the exploitation of the needy and the gratification of the greedy. Merchant princes, indeed! Fiddlesticks!"

Two bright spots of anger had appeared on Esmeralda's satin cheeks while her aunt delivered this peroration. When the old lady had finished, she burst forth:

"Speaking as the head of the senior English branch of the family . . ." she began.

"That you are, child, that you are," conceded Miss Harriet, nodding her head sagely.

"This seems as good a time as any, Aunt, to inform you that there are presently like to be many changes in fortune among various members of the Demaury family." She paused, as if to let the effects of her words sink in. "Changes, Aunt, which will in all probability affect yourself."

"Is that so? Is that so, indeed?" commented Miss Harriet blandly.

"I have to tell you," said Esmeralda, and I could see well enough that she was enjoying herself greatly, "I have to tell you that I have been summoned—as head of the senior English branch of the family—to Venice. By Great-uncle Giles."

"Have you now?" responded the other, unperturbed.

"For the settlement of the inheritance!" said Esmeralda loudly.

"The settlement! Ah! And you think, do you, Esmeralda dear, that you will greatly benefit by the settlement, hey?" Miss Harriet seemed positively to be enjoying herself, which was surely not Esmeralda's intent. I glanced down the table to Peter Chalmers. He was leaning forward, his eyes flickering intently between the two protagonists.

Esmeralda spread her hands. "It is obvious, is it not?" she asked.

"Because you have been summoned to attend Giles—as head of the senior English branch, as you put it?"

"Of course."

With a tight smile on her wrinkled mouth, Miss Harriet delved into her reticule, which she presently was obliged to upturn upon the tablecloth near to her plate. Out tumbled a pince-nez, a comfit box, several large jujubes, a bunch of keys, a screwed-up handkerchief, some hairpins, buttons galore, safety pins, a small notebook bound in red velvet, a box of vestas, a handful of loose silver and copper coin—and a letter. The latter she opened and tossed down the table in Esmeralda's direction. It was Bruce Dennison who wonderingly helped it on its way to its destination.

Esmeralda picked up the letter, and gave a gasp of surprise to see its contents.

"You—*you* have been summoned also!" she exclaimed.

"As you see," said Miss Harriet smugly. "And from that I infer, my dear Esmeralda, that the changes in fortune of which you spoke just now may turn out to be more sweeping than you had dreamed of. Who knows?" She smiled sweetly at her niece, then transferred her bland gaze to Peter Chalmers. "I am sure, Lord Peter, that you find the discussion of money and position to be insupportably middle class. But then, you see, we Demaurys do not have the reassurances of your thousand-year-old lineage. Do tell me more about the salmon fishing in Scotland."

The dinner party was not long protracted. Her aunt's bombshell had obviously put Esmeralda completely out of countenance, so that she spent the rest of the meal in sulky silence, and rose smartly when the last dish had been carried away. The guests took their departure, Peter Chalmers included, and Esmeralda and I retired to our rooms. She gave no reply to my "Good night."

I slept well and was up early. On my way through to breakfast, I saw a small parcel lying on the hall table by the door. It was about the size of a cigar box, wrapped in brown paper and addressed to Esmeralda. I decided to take it up to her, as much as anything to see if she had recovered from her ill temper of the previous night.

She was awake and lying with a breakfast tray before her,

"Good morning, Esmeralda," I said. "There's a parcel for you. I suppose someone must have delivered it by hand."

"What's in it, I wonder?" she asked, showing interest.

"It's very light for its size," I said, unknotting the string that bound the wrappings and passing it to her.

"Why, it's a little basket," said Esmeralda.

"It must be eggs," I said. "I distinctly felt something rolling inside."

"Plovers' eggs," she said. "Of course, Peter's brought me plovers' eggs from Scotland. How thoughtful of him, the darling. Give it to me, Meg."

She took the wicker basket. It was like a small hamper, about the size of a cigar box, as I have said. There was a hasp holding down the lid: she unsnapped it, lifted the lid, and peered inside.

"Is it eggs?" I queried.

Her scream sounded deafeningly loud in the high-ceilinged bedchamber, and must have been heard all over the mansion. Indeed, it had scarcely ceased before I heard the clatter of running feet crossing the stone-flagged great hall below, that and the sound of Bosun's anxious bark.

"Esmeralda, what is it?" I faltered.

She had stiffened with horror and was incapable of speech. With a convulsive shudder, she released her hold on the basket and it fell upon the counterpane between us. It overturned. Out of it fell a wisp of straw—that and a V-shaped, questing head with boot-button eyes and a flickering tongue. And after it a length of glossy coils, banded with black diamonds. It was an adder, and as big as I have ever seen—a foot long if it was an inch.

I am not one for snakes, but I knew Esmeralda to have a particular horror of them. Indeed, by the look of her you would have thought that her heart had stopped beating from sheer terror. Quickly bunching up the brown wrapping paper, I threw it at the reptile, causing it first to coil itself up defensively, then to make a swift, squirming traverse of the counterpane, to fall off the edge of the bed and land soundlessly on the carpet.

At that same moment, after a frenzied banging on the door, one of the housemaids burst into the room. And Esmeralda found her voice again and screamed shrilly.

The housemaid was followed by a footman, who swiftly poked the adder out from under the bed with the handle of a warming pan and dispatched it with a blow on the head.

Esmeralda turned from screaming to weeping, and from weeping to fury.

"Who could have done such a vile thing to me—who?"

"I can't imagine who could have sent it," I told her. I recovered the screwed-up wrapping paper and smoothed it out. Her name had been written there in anonymous capital letters. It told me nothing.

"It—it might well have bitten me," said Esmeralda.

"Indeed it might," I agreed.

"I shall report it to the police," she declared.

"Indeed you must," I said.

"Have someone cycle down to the village to fetch Constable Waller."

"I'll attend to it right away," I assured her.

The unpleasantness with the snake loomed large in my thoughts that morning. I would be the last to say that my cousin was a person to inspire loving friendship in the hearts of all who had dealings with her, though it was true that she was able to twist any man round her little finger; nevertheless, I was shocked and astonished to learn that there was someone who sought to do her physical harm.

"Is it true, then, that poor Esmeralda's been sent a snake in a hamper?"

Peter Chalmers arrived at midday. Esmeralda had given orders that she was not to be disturbed till luncheon. Her fiancé, despite my careful maneuverings, had run me to earth in the solar.

"Yes, it was delivered by hand early this morning," I said. "The village policeman's been informed, but I doubt if the culprit will ever be traced." I recalled Police Constable Waller, who had listened to the story an hour since, writing it laboriously in his notebook, licking his pencil from time to time, and casting awestruck glances about him at the interior of the "big house," and knew that I spoke truly when I said that the local constabulary would contribute little to the solving of the affair.

"I wonder if it was an undergraduate prank," Lord Peter said. "Did Esmeralda not go to a ball in Cambridge the other night?"

I shrugged. "Perhaps."

"Dear Esmeralda, bless her heart, is somewhat given to upsetting people," he said. "She does it almost unknowingly—you must be aware of that as well as I, or better. We had examples at last night's dinner table."

"Why did she have to humiliate that poor little Anne Ackroyd?" I asked, half to myself.

He chuckled. "Esmeralda's intent was more devious than that," he said. "Not little Miss Ackroyd, not that inarticulate fool of a fiancé of hers, but yours truly was the object of dear Esmeralda's campaign last night."

I had had the notion to brush past him and quit the solar, not wishing to remain for one moment longer than was necessary in his dangerous company; but an imp of curiosity got the better of my prudence.

"What do you mean?" I asked him.

"Simply this," he said. "I have told you that Esmeralda is extraordinarily fond of me. And how could she be otherwise? However, it is a new experience for the poor darling to be so head over heels in love with a man and to dote on him so completely. Despite herself, my sweet intended feels somewhat trapped by the circumstances of her passion. She senses herself to be at a disadvantage, as if I were her jailer, the keeper of the keys to her heart. So she determines to teach the jailer a lesson: to let him know that she has only to snap her fingers and any other man—even a man newly affianced—will come running to her side. Do you follow me?"

"And for that, in your opinion, she humiliated Anne Ackroyd and had Bruce Dennison make cow's eyes at her—to make you jealous?"

"Yes. And I may say she failed dismally, for I was most amused and diverted by the whole pantomime. Did anyone tell you that you have the most beautiful ears, Meg? They are like the tiny pink-and-white shells that one picks up on the beaches of the Peloponnese. Were you ever in Greece, Meg? I must take you one day."

"Excuse me, Lord Peter," I murmured firmly. "I must go and wake Esmeralda for luncheon."

He delayed me for a further instant by touching my arm. Fearful that he would be bold enough to restrain me more forcibly, I paused to hear what else he had to say.

"I understand that we are both accompanying Esmeralda to Venice," he whispered close by my ear. "That will surely provide ample opportunities for you and me to get more intimately acquainted, don't you think?"

I shuddered.

CHAPTER TWO

VENICE! Most serene City of the Doges. Queen of the Adriatic.

We came there on a crisp, bright morning, after a long night's railway journey from Milan. Esmeralda and I had shared a luxurious two-berth sleeping compartment, and she had lain awake all night, complaining of the heat, the noise, the motion of the carriage. In the end, I had given up trying to sleep, and had sat with her till the dawn, playing two-handed whist.

Venice confirmed my every bright hope of what she might be. Esmeralda had the similar and gratifying experience of seeing all her worst fears come true.

"It's dirty, tumbledown, and riddled with priests," she declared. "And as for the smell—*pfui!*" She wrinkled her elegant nose.

"The city's very old," I reminded her. "And after all the political upheavals of the last hundred years, they're terribly poor here. As for what you call the smell, that's just—ozone."

"Humph!" was my cousin's comment.

A large black gondola was carrying the three of us down the curving sweep of the Grand Canal, past high-porticoed churches and fine palaces, past dilapidated tenements where water lapped almost to the very doorposts and large-eyed urchins watched us from open windows. The canal was like a busy street on a market day, with jostling throngs of rowboats and gondolas, and the occasional steam launch nosing its way importantly through the press. Our baggage followed in two other gondolas, but we had long since lost sight of them in the cluster of craft behind.

"I shall never see my things again!" declared Esmeralda. "Those gondola men had the sly look of thieves about them, I thought so at the time. You never should have trusted them, Peter. It was most remiss of you."

Peter Chalmers stood leaning negligently against the canopy of the gondola, a broad-brimmed straw hat tipped forward over his eyes as a shield against the low-cast morning sun, and a cigar gripped between his teeth. He wore a suit of white drill and looked every inch the English gentleman abroad. I looked away quickly, avoiding his glance, as he turned to reply to his fiancée.

"Nonsense, my dearest," he said carelessly. "I gave those fellows half their fare in advance and promised them double when they'd delivered the baggage to the Palazzo Demaury. Hard cash is of more interest to them than baggage. What means have they to dispose of Bond Street millinery?" The idea seemed to amuse him, for he chuckled.

"How long before we're there?" demanded Esmeralda crossly. "I'm fairly drooping for a lie down, after being kept up all night by Meg and her boring card games."

I clenched my hands and counted up to ten very slowly and deliberately—a method of dealing with Esmeralda's vagaries that I had found very useful down the years.

"If you want to see the whole length of the Grand Canal, it will take a matter of another fifteen minutes or so," said Peter. "But a shortcut through the lesser canals will bring us out near to St. Mark's and our destination quite a bit sooner."

"The shortcut by all means!" cried Esmeralda. And Peter gave instructions to our gondolier in fluent Italian.

At the next junction, our man plied his oar in such a manner as to turn the craft out of the moving line of boat traffic and send us between two high buildings, out of sunlight and into shadowed coolness, where a narrow lane of dark water bent out of sight ahead, and we progressed with no sound but the steady beat of the oar and the lapping of water on the dank walls at either side. In this manner, we continued for some ten minutes or so. Esmeralda complained of the smell and the decrepitude, but for my part, I found the byways of the ancient city enthralling to an unbelievable degree: every window and doorway, every humpbacked bridge, the hint of cool greenery behind secret walls, spoke to me with the voice of living history. Presently there was only blueness ahead at the end of our narrow canal. Minutes later a strong flourish of the gondolier's oar sent us sweeping out into the sunlight again.

I gasped with awe and delight.

"Well, I must say," said Esmeralda grudgingly. "That really is quite pretty. From afar."

Ahead, the lagoon stretched to a line of grayness in the distance. Nearer—and so near that in the clear light it seemed as if one could reach out and touch it—was a doll's house of a church on a tiny island of its own, close by the extended arm of another island, also set with domes and russet-red roofs.

"That is San Giorgio Maggiore," said Peter, pointing. "To your left—you can see the bell tower rising up, and the domes of St. Mark's Cathedral beyond it—is the Ducal Palace. And there to your right, across the water, is the end of the Grand Canal, with Santa Maria della Salute and the Dogana, that's the customs house, the place at the tip of the island with the golden ball on the top and the rather splendid steam yacht moored close by. By Jove! Do you see the flag that's flying from that yacht's mainmast?"

I shielded my eyes against the sun. Trailing lazily from the top of the yacht's highest mast was a yellow flag with three red shapes upon it. As I gazed, a fitful gust of wind made the folds straighten out and flutter stiffly, revealing the design upon them.

"The three hearts of the Demaurys!" I cried.

"Good heavens!" exclaimed Esmeralda.

Peter snapped a curt order to our gondolier, causing the fellow to change direction and shape a course that brought us closer to the customs house and the sleek white yacht with its tall brass funnel and raking masts. Its rounded stern was presented to us, and white-clad figures were leaning over the shining rails. One could see some lettering that was painted on the stern. I strained my eyes to read what was there. In the event, it was Peter Chalmers who picked it out first:

"*Semiramis*," he called out. And a moment later: "Boston."

"Humph! The American cousins are here, I see," said Esmeralda. "The flies are certainly congregating round the honeypot!"

·

The Palazzo Demaury was close at hand, just inside the Grand Canal and nearly opposite the church of Santa Maria della Salute. The gondolier pointed it out to us: a terra-cotta and white building rising out of the very waters of the canal, with a broad sweep of marble steps leading from the greeny-blue depths, and a noble row of arches stretching from one end to the other on the second floor. It was by far the most impressive secular building in sight, though it seemed tiny after the massive bulk of moated Murchester.

"Another disappointment!" complained Esmeralda. "What a poky little place, and needs a coat of paint like everything else around here."

I had the misfortune to catch Peter's eye and suffered the embarrassment of receiving his conspiratorial wink.

"Dearest, you will find it much more to your taste inside, I am sure," he said. "In Venice, so much of what appears squalid on the outside turns out to be a veritable Thousand and One Nights within. Bear yourself in patience, I beg you. Well, here we are. And I observe that our arrival has not passed unnoticed. A small army of servitors is issuing forth to do our pleasure. Your hand, my dear. And yours, Meg."

The gondola's black hull gently kissed the marble step of the palazzo, and Peter handed us both ashore. A line of liveried menservants stood ready to receive us, and behind them a row of maidservants in coifs and aprons. The men bowed low, the women bobbed curtsies.

As we alighted, they parted ranks, and a man in black stepped forward to greet us, bowing as he did so.

"Welcome to the Palazzo Demaury, ladies and gentleman," he purred smoothly. It struck me at once that he was like some lean black cat, "Permit me to introduce myself: Henry Obadiah, Mr. Giles's private secretary."

Peter Chalmers offhandedly announced who we were, and the secretary snapped his fingers at the line of servants. "You will be shown to your apartments, Miss Demaury," he said. "And it is Mr. Giles's request that all the guests will please be present to meet him *en famille* in the great drawing room at eight of the clock."

"Thank heaven that will give me time for a nap, Peter," said Esmeralda. "I am so fatigued that I could cry."

"The journey is safely over, my dear," responded Peter, taking her by the arm and gently guiding her toward the vast portal of the palazzo. "And, if I am not mistaken, there comes our baggage."

As I entered at their heels, I glanced back to see our boxes and trunks, and Esmeralda's innumerable hatboxes, being unloaded from the gondolas.

The wide portal gave onto a patio, round which the palazzo was built. It was a place of cool green vines and the refreshing splash of water upon time-worn marble; a veritable haven of peace, shut off from the noise and bustle of the Grand Canal just outside the thick walls. I paused for a moment to admire my surroundings, and was greatly taken by the statue of a laughing nymph who was trying to climb upon the back of a spouting dolphin.

"This way, please, *signorina*," came a soft voice at my elbow. One of the maids—a pretty child who could not have been a day over fifteen—smiled shyly at me and gestured toward a staircase leading off from the patio. Esmeralda and Peter were ascending by another, more important-looking staircase, on the heels of secretary Obadiah.

I followed my little guide, while two burly menservants came after with my trunk and hamper. They contained my few changes of costume, as well as the bulk of my worldly possessions.

"In here, please, *signorina*," murmured the girl, standing aside and bobbing a curtsy by a double door at the top of the staircase. I walked past her, into a vast space of coolness and shadows: an echoing chamber of seemingly illimitable dimensions, whose shape could only dimly be discerned by chinks of light that shone through the gaps of shutters that covered tall windows at the far end. I smelt the tang of ancient must and damp velvets, and could have sworn that something—a mouse? a rat?—scurried away beneath my feet.

"This is great drawing room, *signorina*," said the girl.

"It's in here that we meet Mr. Giles at eight o'clock," I commented.

"*Si, signorina*," she said. "This way, please, *signorina*."

We crossed the drawing room, our footsteps sounding hollowly on marble flagstones; and I looked about me for signs of furnishings but could see little in the gloom save the dark shapes of sofas set against the walls and, above, the spreading magnificence of giant chandeliers. My guide opened a door, admitting us to a passageway and another flight of steps. These we ascended. I decided that I was already well on the way to being lost, and recalled Esmeralda's tale of how her parents had never learned to find their way about the Palazzo Demaury. As if my companion gleaned my thoughts, she treated me to a shy smile when we reached the top of the stairs.

"At last is your apartment, *signorina*," she said, opening a double door for me to enter.

"It's delightful," I said impulsively. "Quite delightful."

I stood within a sitting room: quite small, and decorated in faded rose-colored velvet trimmed with dull-gold braid. Walls and drapes were of the same rose color, and so were all the upholsterings. The golden motif was echoed in the heavy frames of several excellent pictures—mostly of classical subjects—that adorned the walls. And the great delight of all: I had a balcony all of my own that looked out across the Grand Canal.

"Bedchamber is through here, *signorina*," said the girl. "Also bathroom. Will *signorina* require bath now?"

"That would be wonderful," I said feelingly.

"I will see to it," she said. "Here is bedchamber."

The bedchamber was a faded royal blue, heightened with old gold trimmings. The bed was fit for an empress, with great swags of royal blue velvet rising above it, ceilingward, and the underside of its canopy painted in the Baroque manner, with constellations of plump cupids disporting themselves upon and about extraordinarily comfortable-looking clouds. And the bed itself was as soft as sitting atop a hay cart.

The menservants lowered my traps to the floor, bowed, and departed. Through a door leading off into what must have been the bathroom came the sound of running water. So the palazzo had modern plumbing? That was something that Murchester Hall did not possess; back home we made do with water heated in the kitchen copper and carried upstairs in large jugs. Here was luxury, indeed.

The girl reappeared, wiping her hands on her apron.

"Will soon be ready *signorina*," she said. "Does *signorina* wish me to attend her?"

"No, thank you," I replied. I had never enjoyed the luxury of a lady's maid, and it seemed foolish to pretend I had. "What is your name, my dear?"

"Assunta, *signorina*," she replied shyly.

"You are a good girl, Assunta," I told her. "Leave me now. I will manage for myself very nicely, thank you."

Assunta bobbed another curtsy and departed. I heard her footfalls clatter down the stone stairs beyond and fade away in what seemed an interminable distance. A door banged. Silence. I shuddered—as if someone had just walked over my grave.

Rousing myself from a brief sensation of malaise, I went into the sitting room, crossed over to the balcony, and looked out across the canal. To my right, nearly opposite, was the splendid church that Peter had pointed out as the famous Santa Maria della Salute, to my left the Dogana, and a hint of the splendid yacht that lay at her moorings just beyond. As I looked in this direction, a white motor launch with a shining brass funnel came popping importantly round the end of the Dogana, and obviously from the yacht—a fact that was speedily confirmed by the flag that fluttered at the stern of the motor boat: the three red hearts of the Demaurys on the yellow ground.

Instinctively, I drew back, so as to see without being seen. Apart from trim-clad sailors, there were four passengers seated under an awning in the center of the boat: two men, two women. Before I had time to examine them individually, the boat—which was approaching the steps of the palazzo below me—came so close as to shut them from my sight with the top of its canopy. And when the craft was alongside the step, and they were alighting, I had only the clues of the tops of their heads to tell me what manner of folk they were. There was a rotund man, whose pate, when he removed his hat, proved to be pink and bald. With him was a lady of middle years, gray-haired beneath a white bonnet trimmed with an enormous black osprey feather. Following them from the boat came a sprightly moving young man in a top hat. And a young woman in a straw boater. Moments later, they passed from my sight into the palazzo. The American cousins had indeed arrived.

My bath! The water would surely be overflowing—

I raced to attend to it, but need have had no fears, for the bathtub itself was large enough to have accommodated me and a flock of geese to keep me company. It was all of eau de Nil, and the taps were silver-plated. I checked the flow of deliciously soft and luxuriantly warm water, and went into the bedroom to undress, first closing the shutters.

My immediate necessities lay just inside my hamper, and I took them out: soap, talcum powder, some cream that I occasionally use on my hands and face—my only aids to the artifices of the *toilette*. From my trunk, I took out my one and only evening skirt of black taffeta, together with a pretty blouse of fine white lawn sprinkled with tiny red flowers, stockings, underwear, petticoats. These I laid out across the bed. Then, throwing my old blue peignoir over my shoulders, I took my soap and went in to savor the delights of my splendid bath.

The journey had been long; the previous night, a trial of strength against Esmeralda's persistent irritations. The water was warm enough, and soothing enough, to carry me off to sleep almost as soon as my head touched the headrest at one end of the great eau-de-Nil lagoon of a bathtub. I had just let my thoughts drift—somewhat uncomfortably—to the uninviting topic of Lord Peter Chalmers and what his intentions might be toward me in Venice, when I was overtaken by drowsiness. When I woke the sunlight had faded from behind the small blue-glass window at the far end of the bathroom, and it was almost dark. I had wakened with a start—as if summoned by a sound . . .

"Who's that—who's there?" I cried out on the instant.

No response. Silence.

"Is there someone out there in the bedchamber?" I called, with rather less assurance. "Is it you, Assunta?"

I strained my ears for a reply, but none came. Naked and helpless, I lay within the cosseting water, and shivered. The door into the bedroom was ajar, as I had left it. Did my eyes deceive me?

Was it merely a trick of the light, or did I see someone—some thing—flit past the slatted shutters that masked the windows? Dark against light, flickeringly, like a magic lantern show.

Slowly, I exhaled a long and shuddering breath. And when I had done it, *I distinctly heard a door click shut!*

Leaping from the bath and snatching up my peignoir, I was through the door and into the bedroom before I had my arms in the sleeves of the garment. And there I looked about me in the dusk.

Not a sign of anyone.

I crossed over and opened the shutters. The low-cast evening sun painted the buildings opposite in a rosy glow, and suffused my pretty blue bedroom with its revealing light.

Glancing about me for added reassurance that the whole incident had been a figment of my imagination, an extension of my dream, my eyes lit upon something that made my heart turn over.

The pot of talcum powder, which I had laid on top of the lid of my hamper, had fallen—or had been knocked—to the floor. That must have been the sound I heard. But there was worse . . .

In falling, the lid of the pot had become detached, and a considerable amount of the white talc had spilled on the tiled floor. And someone had walked through the scattering of powder, leaving a telltale trail from there to the door!

I knelt to examine the footprints. They were large and obviously male. And the imprint of bare feet.

By the time I had dressed, my mind was quite composed. So much so that I could look at my reflection in the dressing table mirror and tell myself—quite dispassionately—that unless I faced the Italian sun from the shelter of a stout parasol, I should end up looking like a blackamoor or a gypsy. Even the late afternoon's journey along the shadowy canals had heightened my already over-healthy coloration. And my hair, which responds to the vagaries of climate like a piece of dried seaweed, had—presumably through the ministrations of the salty atmosphere of the lagoon—turned quite unmanageable. Not all my brushing could get rid of the kinks and curling tendrils that insisted on unfolding themselves about my ears. But I had to admit that my blouse looked very becoming.

I checked the time from my fob watch, which had been one of my mother's wedding presents and was the only article of real value that I possessed: half past seven o'clock. Time to descend and look about me; perhaps meet the American cousins, and others, before the master of the Palazzo Demaury put in an appearance at eight. Time also, perhaps, to mention to someone—to Esmeralda? or Peter?—that I had had a mysterious barefoot visitor. Or should I say nothing of it? On the whole, I had half decided that this was the best course. The visitation would not be repeated, for I had locked and bolted the outer door and would keep it so in future.

A last, backward glance at myself. A smile to show my teeth were white. A patting into place of one of those ridiculous corkscrew curls. And Miss Margaret Gaunt descended to meet the company.

I found my way easily enough to the door of the great drawing room, but was not prepared for the sight within. That vast and shadowy place was now ablaze with brightness from the massed candlelight that made a million crystal diamonds wink and sparkle from the line of chandeliers. The shutters at the far end were flung open, likewise the windows; but the last of the dying sun could not compete with the great light of the room.

There were about a dozen or fifteen people present, all grouped at the far end of the long room, by the windows. Footmen with white-powdered wigs were passing among the guests with bottles wrapped in napkins, from which they were replenishing tall champagne glasses. The slight buzz of conversation slackened at my entry, and I felt as vulnerable, and suddenly nervous, as if I had inadvertently walked out upon the empty stage of a packed theater.

"Ah, Miss Gaunt. How charming you look—if I may be so bold." Mr. Secretary Obadiah walked swiftly down the room toward me, silent and catlike on neatly shod feet. His eyes, at close quarters, had a luminous, feline quality, yellow-hued in the candlelight.

"Most have assembled, Miss Gaunt," he said, sotto voce, "but I

will not subject you to the embarrassment of a general intro-
duction. Allow me to give you a glass of champagne and attach
you to the outside of a group, from whence you will be able to get
into the swim of things."

There was no one present who was known to me, as far as I
could see. I guessed there would be some of Esmeralda's London
relations, and wondered if, like her, everyone had brought at least
two "hangers-on."

I suppose my unsensational, not to say dowdy, appearance (all
the other women present were in full formal evening gowns and
dripping with jewelry) identified me as a nobody. After brief
glances in my direction, the others returned to their conversations.
No one evinced the slightest interest in being presented to me. I
spent a period of embarrassing apprenticeship as a silent witness
on the outskirts of a group surrounding a stout, bald man who
was holding forth to another man with considerable vehemence.

"That fellow De Lesseps should be guillotined!" he declared.
"Building the Suez Canal did not give him carte blanche to hood-
wink the world with his wild schemes. No one will ever build a
canal across the Panama isthmus."

"It was a perfectly feasible scheme, I tell you," interposed his
adversary.

"It was not, Philippe," responded the other, "and you were a
fool to think so. I tell you . . ."

I never heard the end of that particular argument, for Mr.
Obadiah had managed to catch the eye and elbow of a quite
agreeable-looking young man, who bowed and took my hand.

"Axel von Wuppertal," he said. "I am of the German branch."

"And I am connected—I should say very loosely connected—
with the English Demaurys," I informed him.

My new acquaintance nodded sagely. "Yes, let me see: your
mother's elder sister married James Fanshawe Demaury the Second, which makes you my second cousin by marriage. I am
delighted to meet you, Cousin Margaret."

"And I you, Cousin Axel," I responded.

We raised our champagne glasses, touched them. I decided that
I was prepared to like my German "cousin."

The stout man in the center of the group paused in his argument and treated us both to a slight frown of disapproval before recommencing.

"That is Uncle Bertrand Demaury from Boston," whispered Axel von Wuppertal. "He doesn't like to be interrupted when he's holding forth."

"I think I saw him arriving from his yacht," I whispered in return.

"Quite likely," said Axel. "He does things in tremendous style."

Uncle Bertrand from Boston took a sip of his champagne, which allowed his opponent in argument—who I now saw to be a tall gentleman with an eyeglass—to interpose a remark. It was immediately clear that a new subject was under discussion.

"My dear Bertrand," drawled the tall gentleman, "I can see not the slightest reason why the pretext for our assembling here—the matter of Giles's settlement—should make any discernible difference to the operation of the family business. Not my end of the business, in Paris, at any rate."

"Uncle Philippe Demaury of the Paris branch," came the whisper from my prompter. "Married to a French countess. Very grand."

"Then, my dear Philippe," retorted Bertrand Demaury, "you're a bigger fool than you look. And that's saying something."

"Uncle Bertrand and Uncle Philippe are *not* the best of friends, either in or out of business hours," murmured Axel von Wuppertal.

Philippe Demaury did not take his American relation's insult badly; merely contented himself by removing his eyeglass and polishing it with his breast pocket handkerchief—though I did notice that his long and sensitive fingers were trembling slightly. Replacing the disc of glass in his right eye, he regarded the other with seeming good humor.

"Perhaps you will be so kind as to clarify your assertion, my dear Bertrand," he drawled.

"That I will do," retorted the other. "And gladly. For your benefit, and for the benefit of any other among us—" his eyes circled the faces about him, and I instinctively hid myself behind the upswept hair of the lady in front of me—"who may be of a like, and insane, opinion."

"Pray continue, my dear fellow," said Philippe Demaury. "The floor is yours." He added, sotto voce, "As always."

Bertrand from Boston paused for a moment, till he was sure that he had his audience. By then I was aware that this man, for all his paunch and his baldness, was a force to be reckoned with. His eyes—bright and questing—flashed round the watching circle of faces once more. When he spoke, his stubby finger stabbed straight at Philippe from Paris.

He said, "What this fool knows full well, but is successfully blinding himself to—as he has blinded himself these twenty years —is that Giles owns the Demaury international business enterprise in a very real sense. I'm telling you—and you don't have to take my word for it, the facts are there for all to uncover at the lightest inquiry—that Giles, or his nominees, hold the majority of shares in all the branches of our family enterprise: in Boston and New York, in London, in Paris, in Berlin and Cologne. On every Venetian picture, every piece of Florentine sculpture, every fragment of French Medieval tapestry, every shard of Ancient Egyptian ceramic that comes under the hammer in a Demaury salesroom, seventy-five percent of the commission on that sale is remitted— directly or indirectly—here to Giles in Venice. It then follows that, should Giles decide to settle the inheritance on one person, or even a small group of persons, the recipient or recipients will own the Demaury international business enterprise."

In the long silence that followed this declaration—and it was a silence that spread as ripples spread when a stone has been tossed into a still millpond, throughout the groups of people assembled in the great drawing room—I was conscious of a strange emotion that bound together all the people assembled there. If I had been asked to give a name to that emotion, I would have called it fear.

Then the silence was broken by the opening of the doors at the far end of the room, and in came a small, outlandish figure in a shimmering gown of white tulle sewn all over with rhinestones. Gray hair frizzed and chignoned in the latest Paris mode. White-faced as a clown, with black-lined eyes that looked out at the company with the unwinking stare of an owl. She saw me at once, ignored Mr. Obadiah, who went forward to greet her unctuously, and swept past him like a frigate under full sail.

"My dear Meg," she said, loudly and gruffly, so that all eyes were turned to regard us both. "How are you? I had been informed of your arrival. Come and sit down and talk to me. Obadiah, be so good as to send one of your lackeys over here with some champagne."

"How are you, Miss Harriet?" I asked, kissing the lined cheek that she presented to me.

"Well enough," she replied. "Come . . ."

She took me by the hand and led me over to a large sofa that stood by the wall, between two tall windows. I smiled and nodded to Axel von Wuppertal, who bowed to us as we went past.

"A nice young man, that," said Miss Harriet, with no pretense of lowering her voice. "Make someone like you a good husband, my gel."

I masked my confusion by assisting her to sit down, arranging the train of her outrageous white gown, which, on close inspection, was none too clean and splitting at a seam.

"When did you arrive in Venice, Miss Harriet?" I asked her.

"Three days ago," she said. "Ah, here comes the champagne. Fill up my glass to the brim, fellow. None of your elegant short measures. And you may leave the bottle on the floor beside me. Yes, my dear, I was the first one here. You would have thought, would you not, considering my age and infirmities, and the distance I had traveled at his whim, that Giles would have received me? But he did not."

"You mean you haven't seen him since you've been here?" I asked.

"I have seen neither hair nor hide of him," responded the old lady. "Nor has anyone present seen him, though there's many as would have wished to. Bertrand held a reception on his yacht t'other evening. Very grand affair. The cream of the Venetian nobility redeemed their family tiaras and parures from the pawnshops for the occasion. Bertrand had issued an invitation to Giles, and had us all to understand that he would be present. Well, the night wore on. The champagne continued to flow. The ices began to melt and the flowers to wilt. The orchestra scraped away, but no one could be persuaded to waltz, for they were all on the upper deck, crowding the rails to get a first look at the recluse of the Palazzo Demaury. Ha!"

"He didn't come," I suggested.

"He did not," said Miss Harriet, grinning, to show her badly fitting false teeth. "And pompous Bertrand was greatly put out, I can tell you. Though he still has high hopes of attracting Giles to another shipboard reception that he is holding next weekend, on the Feast of the Redentore. But he'll be disappointed again, I promise you."

I stole a glance toward the object of her scorn. The American was deep in a one-sided conversation with Philippe Demaury, holding on to the lapel of the other's coat as if to prevent him from escaping the full force of his argument. I noticed a pretty girl standing close by, watching this performance with unconcealed boredom.

Miss Harriet tapped my arm with her fan. "That's Bertrand's daughter," she said, "Helena. A spoiled brat if there ever was one, but no fault of her own, poor child. And now they've married her off to a polo-playing sprig of one of Boston's leading families, and she's exchanged a spoiled childhood for a loveless marriage."

"Oh, Miss Harriet, how can you possibly know that?" I chided her.

"Judge for yourself," she replied, reaching for the champagne bottle and replenishing her own glass and mine. "Pick out her husband."

"Not the fair-haired man standing over there?" I ventured. "The one who looks as if he's dying of boredom too?"

"That's him," said she. "Rupert Brayne. They say he never speaks to her from one week to the next. Nor she to him."

"Then why did they marry?" I cried, all my natural indignation rising to the fore at the sight of such a betrayal of the matrimonial state.

"Dear Helena went into the marriage market with a price label pinned to her," said Miss Harriet dryly. "The Braynes, though one of Boston's leading families, are not one of Boston's leading *rich* families. A directorship of Demaury's of America quite compensates young Master Rupert for having to forgo some of his polo-playing for the boring company of his wife."

"I think it's awful!" I declared. "Quite awful!"

"But we *are* awful, we Demaurys," said Miss Harriet, casting me a sharp glance over the rim of her champagne glass. "Surely your own experiences have taught you that. Did you ever know a Demaury who ever did anything that did not directly relate to his or her own profit?"

"Yes," I replied. "Esmeralda's parents saw to my upbringing and paid for my education."

"And provided their minx of a daughter with a companion for her childhood, and an unpaid slavey for life!" was her retort.

"It's not like that!" I said indignantly.

"How much does Esmeralda pay you?" countered Miss Harriet. "Pray don't trouble to dissemble with me, miss. As I am very well aware, you are paid in kind, with a roof over your head, meals, and hand-me-down clothes. True?"

"Yes," I admitted in a small voice.

"It's the Demaury streak," said Miss Harriet. "You know the origin of the three hearts on the coat of arms?"

"Yes, it was in the reign of James the Second. The first Demaury to be granted arms had three loves of his life: his horse, the Navy and his wife . . ."

"Fiddlesticks!"

"But—I've always been told . . ."

"Even the Demaurys have the grace to be ashamed of the quip's true origin," she said. "So they have amended the original, which was made by that wise and discerning rogue King Charles the Second, brother to James. He said, 'That fellow Demaury had three loves—self, money, and power.' And that, my dear Meg, is the Demaury streak. We are all tainted with it. That's why we are here today, at the whim of he who holds the purse strings." Her black-rimmed, rheumy eyes darted malevolently toward the chattering groups before us. "I tell you, my child, there is not a Demaury present who would not gladly see every other Demaury made penniless, if it meant that the accumulated wealth were to devolve upon him. There is scarcely a Demaury present, furthermore, who would not stoop to anything short of murder, in order to bring about that happy eventuality." She paused for a moment, then concluded in a voice that was scarcely above a whisper: "And there is more than one Demaury here in this room who would murder for it!"

"Oh, surely, Miss Harriet!" I protested.

"Where's Esmeralda?" she said sharply. "It's close on eight o'clock and she hasn't yet shown, nor has that handsome and expensive intended of hers. Where are they?"

I smiled. "If I know my Esmeralda, she will be late. On purpose. To make an 'entrance' and sweep Mr. Giles right off his feet."

"Humph!" she snorted.

It was at that moment that Mr. Secretary Obadiah clapped his hands to obtain silence and attention. When the chattering had flagged and died, he said:

"Ladies and gentlemen, we appear to have assembled, or most of us at any rate. May I request that you all please be seated? The footmen will extinguish a proportion of the candles, since Mr. Giles's eyes are affected by excess of light. I will now go and inform my employer that all is in readiness." The secretary bowed to the assembled company, smiled eagerly, and departed.

"That fellow, he grins and bows too much," growled Miss Harriet. "Puts me in mind of a confounded monkey. I half expect to see an Italian organ-grinder lead him away on a chain at the end of the day."

"Would Mr. Giles be the organ-grinder?" I asked, upon an impulse.

"Like as not," was her response. "You are shrewder than you look, my dear." The old, kohl-blackened eyes crinkled with good humor.

A silence had fallen upon the company. Even American Bertrand's strident voice was still. As the bewigged lackeys moved about, snuffing one candle in two, there came no sound but those from the canal below the windows: the murmur of people in passing boats, the occasional tinkle of a bell, a laugh, the *pop-pop* of a boat's steam engine. Presently even these were stilled as one of the servitors closed the windows against the evening and pulled the shutters across. Within minutes the great chamber was totally changed in appearance: what had been a light and airy room was turned to a vast expanse of shifting shadows, peopled with pale faces that peered out from every corner, smelling of newly snuffed candles, redolent with a strange atmosphere of—what? Fear, as I had reckoned it earlier?

"My stays," muttered Miss Harriet, "are killing me."

Someone turned and said, "Shush."

Silence. Total silence.

And then, a creaking sound, as when a farm cart comes down a rutted lane. It came from beyond the open doors of the room, and was accompanied by a shaft of light—the source of which was speedily announced by the entrance of a lackey bearing a candelabrum. He was followed by another who carried a silver salver, upon which was set a crystal carafe of—I supposed—water, and a goblet. Next came Mr. Secretary Obadiah, and after him another lackey pushing an antiquated Bath chair.

The Bath chair was revealed as the source of the creaking sound, which came from its wheels. Seated in the chair was the recluse of the Palazzo Demaury.

How to describe Giles Demaury?

I suppose I had carried in my mind the image of the great lover of the early nineteenth century, the man whose passionate affair with the equally legendary Estelle Amor had been fit to rival the love stories that surrounded the names of Lord Byron, George Sand, Liszt, and others. I had supposed, as one does when one is young and idealistic, that the imprint of a great love remains, like the Mark of Cain, forever upon the loved one's brow. I had imagined, I guess, that Giles Demaury would stand out in a crowd as one who had known a supreme experience, of the kind that is seldom vouchsafed to the normal run of men.

I was entirely correct in my suppositions.

He was—old. That much has to be admitted. How old, I could not begin to reckon. The merest adding and subtracting put him in his nineties, but he could have been more. Indeed, he could have been any age. Or no age. He looked—timeless.

The face was wrinkled like an apple which has stood in a cool, dry barn, and has stayed fresh and sweet when all its fellows have rotted and gone to pulp. The skin was pink, like the skin of a babe—yet wrinkled all over, the way a pair of good old boots will wrinkle, all in a mass of tiny declivities, crazed from one end to the other and shifting with every movement of the whole.

He was entirely bald, yet there was still a vestige of white down over the nobly shaped skull, clear in the candlelight. The mouth was no more than a wrinkled gash, and the nose an imperious beak, more like the prow of a ship.

It was the eyes that told the humanity of what might have appeared as no more than a husk of a human being, a mere doll. The eyes were living blueness, gleaming, alert, revealing, illuminating the soul within. I never truly saw eyes till I saw the eyes of Giles Demaury.

He was clad in a black frock coat with a dramatic cloak worn over all and wrapped tightly about the shoulders, as with one who suffers badly from the cold. His hands, also, were covered in black gloves, and the tiny feet were shod with slippers of Asiatic look, all embroidered with beads of black jet.

Not a sound greeted his entrance, nor did he and his entourage utter a word till the lackey entrusted with the task of pushing the Bath chair had brought it to a position in the middle of the floor, with his master's back to the shuttered windows. He bowed at the seated figure and withdrew.

"I bid you all a very good evening," said Giles Demaury in a high, clear voice.

We all mumbled some kind of response.

"My dear Bertrand, you are putting on weight," said Giles, extending one delicate, gloved finger toward the man from Boston.

Bertrand was clearly embarrassed and angry, but decided to look amused instead. "The pressures of work, Giles," he said. "One does not have the manifest opportunities for relaxation and exercise when one is in harness for twenty-four hours out of every day."

Giles Demaury said, "I have always believed that work—honest toil, performed for honest profit—has an ennobling effect upon the human frame, as upon the human mind. Show me a fat and unhealthy toiler and I will show you a rogue."

Bertrand looked about him, grinning uneasily, hoping that the company would be accepting the dialogue as some kind of jest.

He licked his thick lips and addressed himself back to his tormentor.

"You were ever the one for a joke, Giles," he said.

"If you believe that, you will believe anything," came the unhelpful response. "Do I see Philippe Demaury standing there? Step forward under the light and let me see what disasters time has wrought upon you, my dear Philippe."

The tall and gangling figure of Philippe from Paris loomed out under the chandelier nearest to Giles, casting its long and spiky shadow in all directions. Philippe rubbed his lean, white hands together, smiled and nodded at the figure in the Bath chair.

"Good evening to you, Giles," he said ingratiatingly

"You stand as a living contradiction to my original thesis," said Giles. "A lifetime of ill-applied effort in the defrauding of your few friends and your many enemies has refined you beyond all belief. You carry not a spare ounce of excess weight. Your eyes have the sparkle of perfect health. There is a serenity in your countenance that betokens a quiet and unreproachful mind. In short, you have the appearance of a blessed saint and I confide that you will live to be a hundred."

"Er—thank you, Giles," stammered Philippe from Paris, covering his confusion by the task of taking out his eyeglass and polishing it on a white silk handkerchief from his breast pocket.

"And who," asked Giles, "are you, my dear?"

All eyes turned to see whom he was addressing. I also turned. There was no one behind me. When I looked back to my front, they were all still staring in my direction. Giles also.

"Mu-me?" I stammered.

"You, indeed," said Giles. "Step forward, child."

Heart pounding, I did as I was bidden, and the others fell away, leaving me alone under the light of the chandelier—the suddenly glaring and pitiless light of the candles.

"Well, who *are* you?"

"I am Margaret Gaunt," I replied. And the very sound and shape of my family name—setting me apart, as it did, from the Demaurys—gave me courage. I put my chin up and composed myself.

"Child, as I believe, of Commander Richard Gaunt, Royal

Navy?" said the strange creature in the Bath chair. "And of Elizabeth Gaunt, sister to Maria, who married James Fanshawe Demaury the Second?"

"That is correct, sir," I murmured, surprised that the head of the Demaurys should be so well informed about so insignificant an appendage of that clan as I.

"Come here, child," said Giles Demaury. "Come closer."

I approached the Bath chair. As I did so, he raised his right hand and, reaching out, took my chin between finger and thumb, gently as you please. Gently, still, he turned my profile this way and that.

"Quite charming," he said. "I see, my dear Miss Gaunt, that the passing of your days, whether spent in good works or in evil, has so far laid no mark upon your countenance. You could be either saint or sinner. Tell me—which are you?"

I was fumbling for some suitable reply when the sound of a door opening, and of laughter and footfalls, checked the words on my lips. At close quarters, I saw a spasm of anger and irritation cross the lined face and set a spark in those limpid blue eyes.

"Great-uncle Giles! How devastating of us to keep you waiting. How can you ever forgive me, whose fault it is?"

Esmeralda was making her "entrance."

She came across the room with Peter Chalmers at her heels, her elaborate train making a complicated frou-frou *en passant*. Hands extended. Head on one side, with her marvelous eyes (surely as blue as Giles's) soft and beguiling, and wearing the smile that had served her so well through childhood and beyond.

"Darling Great-uncle Giles. The happiness of this moment . . ."

"Keep that creature away from me!"

The voice rasped out, silencing Esmeralda's unctuous cries, stopping her dead and horrified in her tracks. A lackey stretched out a hand to bar her path; could have saved himself the gesture, for the very words of rejection had done their work. Tears of humiliation and bewilderment were forming in those perfect eyes as she gazed in dismay upon the dark-clad figure in the chair.

"Uncle Giles," she faltered. "I—I am Esmeralda, daughter of Ronald and Frances. Surely you remember . . . ?"

"Your photograph was sent to me on the occasion of your birth," said Giles Demaury. "Even at that early stage of your development, I was able to discern certain—traits. Given the passing of the years, those traits have developed mightily. Go away from me, child. Go and stand at the back of the gathering, and take your noble and upstanding gentleman with you."

I have never felt deeply for my cousin Esmeralda till that moment, but the total and cruel dismissal made my heart go out to her. Reaching out, I seized her by the hand.

"Come, Esmeralda dear," I murmured. "Don't worry. Come and sit down."

I flashed an angry glance at the figure in the Bath chair, and was glad to see an answering flash of fury in those watchful eyes of blue. I guessed that my act of partisanship had made me an enemy.

Hand in hand, with Peter Chalmers at our heels, Esmeralda and I crossed the room to an unoccupied sofa and sat down together. She was crying quietly into her handkerchief.

Her dramatic entrance had badly misfired.

"And now," said Giles Demaury, "you will please listen to me, all of you."

"You are all here on trial!"

That was the burden of his remarks.

The clan had been assembled to be weighed and assessed, each according to his or her merits; to be scrutinized and examined as to fitness to take over the burden of the vast and worldwide business operation represented by the Demaury name.

Some—presumably the despised Bertrand and Philippe were among them, and surely poor Esmeralda also—had already been rejected in very short order. I myself, by openly espousing Esmeralda, had also lost favor; but since my claims to an interest in the family fortunes amounted to nothing in the first place, it scarcely signified one way or another.

"I have not yet decided," said the figure in the Bath chair, "how my fortune will be distributed, whether to one single person or to several. All I can promise you is that it will be settled before you leave here. Till then, you must bear yourselves in patience.

Meantime, the hospitality of the palazzo is totally at your disposal. You may come and go as you please, entertain whom you will. For those who do not know Venice, I would point out that *La Serenissima* is a city that caters to all tastes. You will not easily be bored here. And if you are, may the devil take you, for he—or she—who could be bored in Venice will find the eternity of the tomb a desolation indeed.

"From time to time, in the course of the next week or so, I shall require one or another of you to come and see me in my apartments. There we shall discourse, quietly and alone. I would not wish to raise anyone's hopes by suggesting that such a summons will necessarily mean that the persons so summoned are under any special consideration as heirs to the fortune. Indeed, the reverse may be the case. Any questions?"

The watchful blue eyes, startling in that crabbed and time-worn face, took in the circle of listeners.

No reply: nothing but a muffled sob from Esmeralda. I squeezed her hand.

"Then I bid you a very good night. Dinner will be served immediately in an adjoining chamber. I do not take dinner."

Giles Demaury made a gesture to his lackeys. One of them took hold of the handle of the Bath chair and wheeled it round to face the door. The door was opened. Preceded by Mr. Secretary Obadiah, the small entourage swept out of the chamber, and the door closed behind them to the sound of a massed exhalation of breath and the chorus of exclamations.

"What a shocking performance!"

"Quite insupportable!"

"If I had known, I would not have come!"

"You would have come—and you will stay—even if he pours fire and brimstone down upon your head!"

The last remark silenced all their protests. It came from Bertrand—he who had suffered as badly as any from Giles's barbed tongue. The American looked about him, and, not for the first time, I was conscious of the strength behind his unprepossessing exterior.

He said, "Why do you try to fool yourselves? You know as well as I that there is not one person in this room who will not crawl from here to the Alps for a chance at that fortune. We are in his hands, all of us. I suggest, in all humility, that we make the best shift we can of the time that lies ahead. The answer—our fate—lies with him. There is scarcely anything we can do at this late hour to affect the issue one way or another."

I caught Miss Harriet's profile in the corner of my eye. She was nodding silent agreement to Bertrand's remarks. Back to me came the disquieting assertions that she had made to me a little earlier: *not a Demaury present who would not gladly see every other Demaury made penniless . . .*

And: *scarcely a Demaury present who would not stoop to anything short of murder . . .*

And, more shockingly: *there is more than one Demaury here in this room who would murder for it!*

A hand touched my arm, causing me to start. I looked into Peter Chalmers' bronzed, bland countenance, caught the tang of the cologne water that always pervaded his presence.

"Darling Esmeralda has departed to her room to make some repairs upon her *maquillage,* which has become somewhat ravaged by tears and emotion," he murmured. "She will rejoin us in the dining room. May I escort you there, my dear Meg?"

The company was being ushered out of double doors that led to the upper part of the patio. I could see lanterns in the murky darkness, and a patch of starlit sky above. Unresisting, I let Peter take my arm and lead me outside. The scent of honeysuckle was so strong as to make the senses reel, and from somewhere beyond the rooftops came the sound of a man's voice raised in plaintive song, to the strumming of a mandolin.

We crossed the patio on the heels of the others. Halfway there, my escort tarried, allowing those behind to overtake us till we were last in the line. Finally he squeezed my arm and brought me to a halt beside a screen of honeysuckle. His face was half in darkness and half lit by a lantern overhead.

"Meg," he said. "I have secured the services of a gondola with a most excellent gondolier. Tonight. After dinner. After dinner, dear Meg, I will show you the *real* Venice. Now, how does that strike you?"

"Sir, it does not strike me at all," I replied coolly. "Please be so kind as to take me in to dinner. I am sure that your fiancée will wonder what has happened to you."

"Meg, you are trifling with me," he said.

"Sir, I had thought that it was you who was trifling with *me!*" I retorted tartly.

As well as I could see his face, and it was not too clearly, my taunt seemed to have hit its mark. His color deepened.

"You haven't forgotten our conversation of a while back," he said. "You haven't forgotten your—shall we say—vulnerability?"

"I am well aware of my vulnerability," I said. "A word from you, and I could be out in the street. So be it. Say that word. It will make no difference to my feelings. There will be no gondola ride tonight for you and me, Lord Peter. On the other hand, you might wish to take your fiancée."

I think he might have struck me then. In any event, his hand was raised, though whether to offer an unwanted caress or to smack me across the mouth, I shall never know. As it was, the hand faltered and fell, and he glanced sharply behind him, across the patio, to the shadowy foliage that lay at the other side of the void.

"Who's that?" he cried.

"What is it?" I asked, suddenly affrighted.

"Why, confound it, someone was watching us from over there," he replied. "But they've gone now. Most odd. Damned servant, I suppose. Happily, they none of 'em have a very good command of English."

"If they had," I replied, "the servant in question might well have received a most unfortunate impression of the manners and morals of the British aristocracy!"

And with that, I left him, gathering up my skirts and sweeping across the tiled floor toward the open door of the dining room, leaving him to follow as best he might.

Dinner was the most splendidly presented meal that I shall ever attend, I do not doubt, if I live to be a hundred and mix with crowned heads and millionaires. To begin with, there were no less than three servitors for every guest—two standing behind one's chair, stiff as guardsmen when not performing, and another to carry away one's used plates and glasses.

As for courses: twelve. With entrees and removes. And a different wine for every course. I am not much in the drinking line, preferring a table water or a seltzer to all your clarets and Burgundies, though I have to admit to a slight partiality to the wine of Champagne. On that occasion, I took a little champagne.

Some sort of precedence had been observed in the seating arrangements. The moral ascendancy that Bertrand had assumed from the first was subtly reasserted by his taking the seat at one end of the table and establishing his wife and daughter on his right and left respectively. The wife was a full-blown and handsome version of the daughter, with the same petulant, discontented mouth. Similarly, Philippe from Paris, seeing his cousin's move, had hastened to establish himself at the opposite end, and his lady wife on his right. His French countess looked very grand, and of such superior attainments that she scarcely looked at, let alone spoke to, anyone else but her spouse throughout the meal. She even made no response to Bertrand Demaury when he put it to her—in very agreeable tones—that he was much looking forward to her company aboard the *Semiramis* at the reception to be held on the Feast of the Redentore. I wondered if I, too, should be invited—but doubted it.

As a nobody, I found myself almost exactly in the middle of the table, with—to my distaste—Peter Chalmers on one side of me and—somewhat to my delight—Axel von Wuppertal on the other.

"How are you enjoying the Palazzo Demaury?" the latter asked me, pledging me with his raised wineglass.

"Excellently well, thank you," I replied formally.

"And what do you think of Giles?" His eyes twinkled.

"Very formidable."

"Ah, but you scored a very palpable hit with him, you know."

"I don't think so," I told him. "And in any event, it scarcely matters, for I have no expectations and am here only as companion to Esmeralda."

"Well, I will be frank with you, Margaret—I may call you Margaret . . . ?"

"Meg," I said. "Please call me Meg, Axel."

"I may tell you, Meg, that I have very high and pressing expectations, and only wish that I had commended myself to Giles's attention as agreeably as you have done."

I studied him covertly over the rim of my wineglass. He was clean-cut, healthy-looking, guileless, and in every way the sort of person to whom one would entrust the care of a small child or one's favorite dog. His butter-blond hair was neatly cut and smoothed down behind the ears. He sported a slight, pale mustache. His teeth were well-shaped and gleaming white. Fingernails nicely tended and neat. Yet for all his excellences, he was just the same as all the rest. A typical Demaury. One eye firmly fixed upon profit. It was all very depressing.

"I take it that you work in the family business, Axel?" I said.

"In the Berlin showrooms," he said, nodding. "My specialty is painting of the Italian Renaissance, and my younger brothers, Fritz and Werner, handle works of the seventeenth century to the present day. The three of us have run Demaury's of Berlin since the death of our father last year."

"Is your mother alive?"

"And living in Marienbad, where she takes the alkaline-saline waters daily and flirts with Bohemian light cavalry officers in exceedingly large numbers."

We both laughed. If a typical Demaury in his pursuit of wealth, decidedly a Demaury with a sense of humor—a thought that reminded me of Esmeralda. I glanced to my left, past Peter Chalmers' profile, to Esmeralda seated on his left. She had repaired the ravages caused by tears, but the downward-turning set of her mouth showed that her wounded spirits were not mended. I caught her eye and offered a smile of encouragement, but it won me only a pout. Fiddlesticks to you then, my girl.

"I remember well," said Miss Harriet to the company in general, "how I visited this place in the days when Estelle was alive. That would have been in around 'thirty, for I was a gel of ten or eleven at the time."

A rustle of interest greeted this remark, and conversation died, allowing attention to center upon the old lady, who sat with a battery of half-empty wineglasses. To facilitate her eating, she had seen fit to remove her upper false teeth and place them on the table before her. Even now, with the second course barely started, she seemed far gone in drink, but had lost nothing of her articulateness in consequence.

"One has heard so much of Estelle," said Philippe from Paris. "And, as is the case with people who become legends in their own lifetimes, it is a puzzle to sort the legend from the reality of the person. Tell me, my dear Harriet, what manner of person was Estelle—from your observation?"

All eyes were upon Miss Harriet. Even Philippe's countess so far associated herself with the commonplace world as to submit the old lady to a brief examination through her lorgnette, then to shudder and return to her private contemplations. Miss Harriet, clearly enjoying the attention that her special role of informant afforded her, made no great hurry to reply to Philippe's inquiry, but chewed another forkful of mullet stewed in wine sauce, emptied a glass of champagne, and snapped her fingers for a refill. And then she began:

"Estelle Amor, it should be realized, was an appallingly bad actress. Oh, yes, I assure you. She had the narrowest range of expression with which a leading actress was surely ever blessed, and never played but one role in her entire career: the role of Estelle Amor. She played that role for twenty years on the stage, through three marriages, two divorces—and her own dramatic death out there in the lagoon.

"As to my own observations, I found her kindly, even to the point of overindulgence. She was given to embracing one; and I, a rather reserved child, found it extremely embarrassing. She was, in her last years, of rather voluptuous figure and smelled overpoweringly of patchouli. I can never forget the sensation of being swallowed up in this highly scented mountain of flesh and having kisses rained upon one's lips, eyes, cheeks.

"Her temper was—as legend tells—unbelievably awful. I was present during a luncheon in this very room, during which she took a fancy that the wife of the guest of honor—and he was the Russian Ambassador, no less—had made some slighting reference to her, Estelle's, advancing years. As true as I sit here, Estelle rose and went to a serving table—that one over there by the window, the very same—and took up a large soup tureen, which she then carried over to the place where sat the wife of the Russian Ambassador. And there, before our very eyes, she emptied the contents over the wretched woman's head. I shall never forget the sight of the lady from St. Petersburg, with her mouth open in a scream, and glutinous soup and vermicelli pouring slowly down her head and shoulders."

The unexpectedness of the story, and Miss Harriet's droll manner of telling it, brought a chorus of sustained laughter from us all.

"And what was Giles's reaction to the pouring of the soup?" asked Bertrand presently, dabbing his eyes with his napkin.

"He was furious with Estelle," replied Miss Harriet. "Called her this and that—names that had never sullied my young ears before—and demanded an immediate apology. Estelle refused, bandying names for names. They then commenced throwing things at each other: plates, glasses, anything that came to hand. And through it all, the wife of the Russian Ambassador sat whimpering quietly and all unregarded, with soup and vermicelli falling from her."

"It is true to say," observed Philippe, "that Giles and his Estelle fought and quarreled through one of the great, the truly great, love affairs of this century. Of course, he was never the same again after her passing."

Miss Harriet said, "My father told me that he tried to take his life when they brought him news that she had perished. And, as we all know, he has been a recluse for ever after. They say that there is a room in his apartments on the upper floor of the palazzo which is a museum to her memory and contains memorabilia such as portraits and photographs, her clothing and jewels. I have heard that there is even a recumbent wax dummy of Estelle, lying in a coffin, with candles at head and foot."

"Ugh, how perfectly ghastly!" cried Esmeralda. "How can that horrid old man exist in such surroundings? A thing in a coffin. Ugh!"

Despite the disagreeable impression made by Esmeralda's ill-timed outburst, I was aware—as many others must have been—of an underlying truth in her remark. It *was* ghastly to think that the old man was sitting up there, above our heads, with his *memento mori*. It was unpleasant, also, to remember that Estelle Amor had perished out there in the lagoon. And when, in the silence that followed Esmeralda's outburst, one could hear the night wind moaning in the great chimneypiece, and imagine the dark waters flowing past below the windows, one was brought very close to the realization of life's impermanence.

It was some time and several courses later before the general conversation was resumed. Axel von Wuppertal had been buttonholed by the lady on his right—one of the American entourage, which left me in hazard of being addressed by Peter Chalmers. I did not have long to wait.

"Have you changed your mind about the gondola ride?" he murmured.

"Will you leave me be?" I whispered, casting an uneasy glance past him to Esmeralda, who was speaking to the neighbor on her left.

Peter Chalmers smoothed his silky mustache and eyed me proprietarily.

"You may dodge and weave as much as you like, my dear," he said. "But I will possess you in the end. Come, Meg. Let's not have any unpleasantness. Let's be friends. Later, when Esmeralda and I are safely married, I'll have the money to set you up in a nice villa in Maida Vale. You'll be independent, Meg. All you've ever dreamed of. How's that, eh? Let's have your answer, Meg."

"You disgust me!" I hissed. "And if you persist in your attentions, I shall rise from this table and leave, company or no company."

"By Jove, I think you'd do it, Meg," he said admiringly. "There's spirit in you, and no mistake. I shall have to watch my step or I'll overplay my hand."

"You have already overplayed your hand, Lord Peter," I said. "And by a very large margin. You would not have dared to do so with any woman save one like me—one who is unprotected and without means."

If I had intended the observation as an appeal to his manhood and chivalry—and I had not—it would have been entirely wasted, for the thought seemed to give him considerable pleasure. He grinned broadly and toyed with his mustache.

"You are quite right, Meg," he said. "I have behaved like a cad, and I think that the time has come to bring the matter to a close. I think—" here he gazed reflectively into his wineglass and smothered his grin in an expression of mock seriousness—"I think I shall have to confess to Esmeralda after all."

"What do you mean?" I breathed, greatly disturbed.

"Why, tell her what's been going on between us," he said. "The assignations. The brief endearments. The kisses. All so dangerous, and tending to lead to a clandestine affair under her very nose. Yes, I think I will make a clean breast of it."

I watched him closely. Was he merely tormenting me?

"You—you will do that?" I asked.

"Yes, it's the only decent and manly thing to do," he said. "As I have pointed out before, Esmeralda will speedily forgive me, and all will be well. As for your good self, well, I am sorry, my dear . . ." He spread his hands expressively, and looked quizzically at me from under one cocked eyebrow.

"So you will ruin me?" I said.

"Temporarily," he replied.

"Temporarily? What do you mean—temporarily?"

"I mean," he said, "that Esmeralda will send you packing. Give it three months and you will have learned for yourself that there is no life in the great hard world for a young lady of your attainments. Then you will come knocking on my door of your own accord. How's that for a capital idea?" He sat back and beamed smugly.

I think I could have struck him then. I was certainly within an ace of tossing the contents of my glass in his smooth, sneering, aristocratic face; but my attention was diverted by an excited ripple of conversation that had overtaken the rest of the company. Several were craning their necks to look toward a heavy, carved oak sideboard at the far end of the dining room, upon which stood an array of silverware, pottery vessels, glass, and so forth. And someone was pointing.

"Isn't it the one in the center—the one with the two handles?" asked someone—I think it was Bertrand.

"Yes, that's the Borgia goblet."

"Oh, do let's see it," said his daughter, displaying the only sign of animation she had shown all evening. "It's terribly exciting."

"What exactly is the Borgia goblet?" demanded her husband, in bored tones.

"I will tell you all I know of it," said Bertrand. "Have it brought over here."

One of the footmen went over to the sideboard, and, with the assistance of a chair, reached up and lifted down a large drinking goblet with two handles, and brought it to the table, setting it before Bertrand. On closer quarters one could see that it was of silver, though discolored by age and lack of cleaning. The thing was beautifully fashioned by the silversmith's art, with the head of Medusa set in the middle, and the twining locks of her hair—every hair a snake—gathered up at each side to form the handles. As I looked at the thing, I suffered a strange unease, and gave an involuntary shudder, as if a draft of cold wind had blown across my shoulders.

Bertrand picked up the goblet and revolved it slowly in his pudgy hands, examining it closely as he spoke.

"The Borgia goblet," he said, "was purchased into the family by the founder of our fortunes himself, the great George Fanshawe Demaury. As its name implies, it had former connections with that remarkable family who by brutal aggression allied to political murder set their stamp upon fifteenth-century Italy. The cup may have belonged to Rodrigo, later Pope Alexander VI, but more likely to his son, the notorious Cesare. Even, perhaps, to Cesare's sister, the equally notorious Lucrezia. All three had enemies who died in highly questionable circumstances. Often by poison . . ."

"Poison?" His daughter's eyes were very wide, and her normally petulant mouth was pursed to form the letter O. "You mean, Papa, that the Borgias poisoned from out of that very goblet?"

Bertrand chuckled. "It's quite likely, Helena dear," he said.

"But—how, Papa?"

"Well, that's a matter of some speculation," said Bertrand Demaury.

"If I may be permitted one speculation," said Philippe from Paris. "The goblet is a sort of toasting cup, produced with some ceremony at the end of a feast. It would be filled with wine of a very rare vintage, and then passed round the table, from hand to hand. The—victim—would be sitting next to the person entrusted with the task of actually performing the assassination, whether one of the Borgias themselves or an accomplice."

"And how would the poison have been introduced so as to kill only the intended victim?" The question came from one of Bertrand Demaury's entourage.

"Undoubtedly by means of a poison ring," said Philippe. "This was a hollow ring which, by the operation of a catch, allowed a quantity of poison to fall into the cup. The assassin took the cup from his neighbor, himself drank the toast, deposited the poison in the wine—then handed it on to his victim."

"Who drank, and instantly dropped the cup, clutching at his throat!" cried Helena. "Oh, how awful. How perfectly awful!"

A ripple of nervous laughter, of the sort that affects a gathering where the trappings of horror have been under none too serious discussion, passed round the table. Someone—I think it was one of the people from London—lightly suggested that the cup be filled with wine and passed round the table, from hand to hand, for all to drink; but the idea met with a chorus of disapproval. Nevertheless, the Borgia goblet was passed slowly round the company. When it came into my hand, I gave it smartly to Peter Chalmers, not wishing to retain contact with the hateful-looking thing.

"By Jove, this is a fine piece of craftsmanship," declared Lord Peter, fixing a monocle in his eye and peering closely at the goblet. "The silversmith johnny has got old Medusa to a T. Small wonder that she was supposed to turn chaps to stone at one glance."

"Pass it to me, Peter," said Esmeralda, who appeared to have recovered some of her spirit, and was gazing with some interest at the goblet in her fiancé's hands.

"First I must use my poison ring, m'dear," he replied, grinning.

"Peter, what a perfectly appalling thing to say," she snapped.

"Sorry, old gel," he responded lightly. "Yes, it's a very fine piece, but I'll wager a hundred guineas that it never saw poison, nor the Borgias either. More likely made in Birmingham and shipped out here for the tourist trade. Yes, that's—*ah!*"

He gave a sharp cry, dropped the goblet to the table, and put the thumb of his right hand in his mouth.

"Peter, what's the matter?" cried his fiancée.

"Yes, what happened?"

"What is it, my dear fellow?"

Peter Chalmers took his thumb from his mouth and looked at it in surprised distaste.

"Some part of that confounded cup gave me a scratch," he said. "And not half a scratch, either. Look at that."

He showed Esmeralda his thumb. He showed me. The skin was reddened and swollen, and dark blood oozed thickly from a puncture at the tip, near the nail.

I transferred my gaze to the goblet, which lay where he had dropped it, quite close to my elbow.

"But there don't appear to be any sharp pieces on it," I whispered, in a voice that sounded very unlike my own. "It's quite smooth all over." I reached to take it up, but was instantly checked by a horrified cry:

"No, Meg—don't touch it!"

It was then that Lord Peter Chalmers rose stiffly to his feet. I looked up and was horrified to see that his smooth countenance was drained of all color, and that his eyes were wide and staring, his mouth open as if in a shout—but no sound came, save a hoarse intake of breath. He stumbled and all but fell, and in doing so overturned his chair. It fell with a clatter,

And then everyone was leaping to his feet, and I also. I took him by the elbow.

"What is it?" I asked him. "Are you ill?"

"Peter—Peter!" wailed Esmeralda.

"Brandy—fetch brandy!" shouted Bertrand. "You there, fellow, don't stand gaping. Bring brandy!"

"Sit him down and loosen his collar," suggested someone.

"He's having some kind of fit!"

"We'd best send for a doctor!"

"Peter, speak to me!" pleaded Esmeralda.

Lord Peter Chalmers, eldest son of an English marquess, then gave vent to such a cry as I never hope to hear again in my whole life, throwing back his head and hurling the sound to the ceiling so that it echoed across the room and echoed again in some remote fastness of the great mansion. It was like the roar of some animal in its death agony.

That done, and silence following, he evaded the hands that grappled for him, and fell forward across the table, from whence he slipped, dragging two clutching handfuls of napery with him, and fell slowly to the floor in a cascade of spilled dishes and shattering glass, of candelabra, and the sudden sharp stench of snuffed candles.

Esmeralda was screaming, and I think I must have been screaming also.

CHAPTER THREE

THE DOCTOR CAME: a small man in a very large hat, whom I way-
laid on the staircase on his way to attend the stricken British aristocrat, demanding something to soothe Esmeralda's nerves. He
gave me a draft and some tablets, which I took up to her room.

There was to be no sleep for me that night. I sat by her till the
dawn; till the thin sunlight seeped in through the chinks in the
shutters, illuminating the white-and-gold room in which her
sumptuous four-poster bed was set; till the market boats teemed
past below the window on their way to the Rialto, jostling to be
first there with their produce of vegetables and piled-high seafood,
the boatmen laughing as they plied their oars, the women gossip-
ing across the tossing gray-blue water.

Nor had Esmeralda slept, despite the doctor's prescriptions, but
had lain uneasily dozing, occasionally waking up with a whimper
of sudden fear, crying out for me. But she slept with the dawn,
and did not waken at the tap on the door.

I went to answer it, and there was Mr. Secretary Obadiah, looking as if he had also spent a sleepless night.

"How is Miss Demaury?" he whispered.

"Resting now," I answered. "What news of Lord Peter?"

The expression on his face that greeted my remark sent a chill of
horror down my spine. Hastily I stepped out into the corridor and
shut the door behind me.

"Miss Gaunt," he said, "I have to tell you that . . ."

"No!" I cried. "It can't be!"

"His lordship passed away an hour since, after much suffering,"
said the secretary. "The doctor was with him at the end. I have
not dared yet to inform Mr. Giles of the so tragic death of one of
his houseguests. He will be most upset, though not acquainted
with Lord Peter."

I stared at the lean, catlike face before me, with its yellowish eyes. Listened to the unbelievable things he was saying, the smooth platitudes he was using to mask the hideous tragedy that had taken place during the past few hours since Peter Chalmers had been a living and breathing male animal whom I had personally detested.

"But how?" I whispered. "*How* did he die, Mr. Obadiah? He was perfectly well last evening. All he did was to prick his finger on that hateful goblet!" I heard my voice rising shrilly.

The yellowish eyes slid furtively sidelong, avoiding mine.

"I have no news of that, miss," he said. "The doctor has not seen fit to confide in me on the matter, though no doubt we shall all soon learn the cause of his lordship's demise. For the present, the doctor has insisted that the police be called in."

"The police!" I exclaimed. "Is there, then, some question of foul play?"

For an instant I thought that the secretary was going to faint clean away; he clung to the wall as if for support and stared at me, a line of sweat forming across his pale brow.

"Heaven forbid that it should be so, miss," he said hoarsely. "I do not know how I could possibly break such news to Mr. Giles, I really don't. Foul play! It doesn't bear thinking about."

The man was quite impossible. Mindful of my obligations to Esmeralda, I asked him to keep me informed of any developments, and went back into the bedroom. Esmeralda was awake and sitting up. As ever, apart from a slight and becoming tousling of the hair and a pinkness on one cheek from lying on it, she looked as fresh and beautiful as ever.

"Who was that, Meg?" she asked. "Was that a message from Peter? How is he?"

"Esmeralda, I . . ."

"Well, how is he? Why are you staring at me like that?"

I said quietly, "Esmeralda, you must brace yourself for a shock. He—he's dead. Peter's dead."

"Dead?" she repeated. "But he can't be dead. What are you trying to tell me? He's my fiancé. We're to be married later in the year. And then I shall be Lady Peter Chalmers. Later, much later, when his father has passed away, I shall be the Marchioness of Lochspiel. Marchioness of Lochspiel . . ."

Her voice trailed away, and I saw by the glazed expression in her eye that she was not living in a world of reality, but that her mind was half-gone in sleep. It was then I realized, with thankfulness, that the little Venetian doctor's prescriptions had not been so ineffectual after all.

She lay back with a sigh. I hastened to cover her shoulders with the silk sheet.

"Sleep, my dear," I told her.

"Yes," she whispered docilely, like a child, the way she had been all those years before, on her good days, in the nursery. "Yes, I am very tired, Meg."

"I'll wake you later."

"Yes. Meg . . ."

"What is it?"

"Did you say something about Peter—just now?"

"It will wait till morning," I said.

"Till morning. Yes." She closed her eyes.

I went out into the corridor and shut the door quietly behind me. There was a balcony at the far end, with a view out across the canal. I went out there, welcoming the cool morning air after the heat and humidity of Esmeralda's airless bedroom. I breathed in the sea air, relishing the faint tinge of ozone and the unmistakable tang of shellfish and seaweed. Leaning my head back against the silvery woodwork of the balcony, I closed my eyes and let my mind wander over the events of the previous night, and the hideous aftermath.

Peter Chalmers was dead . . .

My enemy, my tormentor, was no more. The man who had threatened my very existence was no longer a living and breathing thing, but lay somewhere in the great house, sleeping the first hour of his long, last sleep.

And the police were coming.

The little doctor's prescriptions remained effective throughout that morning. Esmeralda woke at midday, and I had the ordeal of breaking the news to her for a second time. Strangely, she took it very well, and I only suppose that some part of her mind had already been made aware of the news that I had given her in her half-sleeping state, and that, by the strange ways that nature has, she had been able to absorb some of the shock during her drugged sleep.

She cried a little. Once more she bewailed that she would never be a marchioness now. And she was able to take a little nourishment when I sent down for a luncheon tray.

Afterward came a tap on the door. It was Obadiah again. He had shaved and tidied himself, but looked as shifty as ever.

"The Chief of Police would like to see you, miss," he whispered.

"Me?" I said, alarmed.

"In the dining room, miss. He has already spoken with several of the guests and the servants."

"Does he want to see Miss Demaury also?" I asked.

"As I understand it, miss—no. Not yet. Not till he has seen you, miss."

Without saying a word about it to Esmeralda, I went straight down to the dining room, descending a wide staircase that led to the patio where I had spoken with Peter Chalmers alone for the last time. The honeysuckle's night scent was gone, and it all looked very different. Glancing over the edge of the balustrade, I saw the burly figure of a gardener tending the vines that surrounded the nymph-and-dolphin fountain on the ground floor of the patio. He must have heard my footsteps, for he looked up and doffed his broad-brimmed straw hat in a greeting. Dark and handsome in the Italianate manner, he had a look of easy familiarity that gave me a pang of curious unease. I noticed, too, that he was barefoot . . .

I tapped upon the door of the dining room, and a voice bade me enter.

I gave a start of alarm. Nothing had changed since the previous night. The shutters had not been drawn, the chandeliers still glittered on high, and the remaining candelabra blazed upon the ruined table-setting. The wine-stained white tablecloth, half pulled to the floor, where Peter Chalmers' clutching hands had taken it, was just as it had been, and the scattered glassware and dishes also. Even his chair still lay overturned.

A man in black occupied the place at the far end of the table from where I stood: the place that Bertrand Demaury had occupied during dinner. He rose at my entry, bowed, addressed me in a deep voice, in clear and unaccented English.

"Miss Margaret Gaunt, is it not? Ma'am, my name is Giolitti-Crispi. At your service. Please be seated. Sergeant—" he gestured, and a tall figure in cocked bicorne and brass-buttoned uniform frock coat stepped from out of the shadows behind me and drew back a chair for me to sit upon. The very chair, at the very place, where I had sat the night before. Looking down, I saw that my name was written on a card which lay there.

The man at the end of the table then addressed the sergeant in rapid and, to me, incomprehensible Italian, and the latter saluted and went out of the room.

"A glass of wine, ma'am?" asked the police chief.

"Thank you, no."

"A cup of coffee, perhaps? No? Well, I think I will myself partake." He got up and walked across to the sideboard, where stood a coffee jug, from which he poured a steaming brew into a tiny Sevres cup. I had the opportunity to study him. He was tall, and handsome as men are reckoned to be handsome. Aged, I guessed, in his late thirties. His thick thatch of hair was black with steely blue lights, like a raven's wing—save for a sprinkling of gray above the ears. He wore black: black frock coat, waistcoat, pantaloons. A frilled white shirt, and a black stock with a black jet pin. His slender middle was swagged by a gold "Albert" watch chain hung with a seal. And he wore a gold ring upon his signet finger. As he took the coffee cup and returned to the table, I was able to see his easy, loping gait: the walk of an athlete, or a soldier.

"A most unpleasant business, Miss Gaunt," he said. "Most distressing for you all. Tell me, how is Miss Esmeralda Demaury taking the tragic news of her fiancé's death?"

"As well as can be expected," I told him.

He nodded. "You English have great fortitude in these matters," he said. "Which is no doubt the reason why you own half the world. Do you think Miss Esmeralda will be sufficiently composed to see me? Not now, but later, after I have spoken with you."

"I think so," I replied. Then I gestured about me, at the ruined table. "But I would suggest not here—not in this room, with its memories of what happened last night."

"Quite so," he said. "I entirely agree. Indeed, I apologize for having brought you in here, ma'am—as indeed I have apologized to the other guests. But I have my reasons, as you will discover."

The long-cased clock in the corner of the candlelit room solemnly chimed the hour of two. The police chief drained his coffee cup and laid it on the table before him.

"You have a question to ask me, I think, Miss Gaunt," he said quietly.

I gave a start. "Why—yes," I faltered.

"Then ask it, pray."

"About Lord Peter's death, of course. How did he die?"

"He was poisoned."

"Poisoned? But—how?"

"With—*this!*"

There was a napkin covering it, and I had not noticed. He snatched away the square of linen, and there it stood, the Gorgon's head staring down the table at me, the snakish locks entwined into two handles.

"The Borgia goblet!" I cried.

"The very same."

"But you said—you said that he was poisoned. Lord Peter never drank from that goblet."

"There is more than one way to administer poison, ma'am," he said, taking up the cup gingerly in both hands. "No death-dealing wine is needed in this fiendish contrivance. It carries its own deadly sting within itself. Like the fangs of the serpent, or the dart of the scorpion."

"I—I still don't understand."

"Then I will demonstrate. It is really quite simple, like all truly ingenious contrivances. The secret is in the handle, you see—this one, the one that I am holding in my right hand. By exerting an upward pressure on this handle—do you notice that it moved to my touch?—I am able to compress a powerful spring within it.

The mechanism—if you are of a mechanical turn of mind, Miss Gaunt—is really no more than an adaptation of the lock of a flintlock pistol. Which, as a matter of historical interest, dates the goblet at least a century and a half after the Borgias, so this is one infernal device which cannot be laid at the door of that much-maligned family. There, I have compressed the spring. The contrivance is now cocked."

"Cocked?" I repeated.

"Cocked, Miss Gaunt, to kill! Watch the handle in my right hand, and watch closely. I now take up the goblet once more, in both hands, just as Lord Peter did last night. Only, I take care to hold it at the lower part, well away from the top of the handle, where one's thumb would naturally rest. In holding the goblet, which is quite heavy, I am obliged, of course, to exert some slight pressure upon the handles. Listen, Miss Gaunt. Listen—and watch . . ."

I could not have dragged my gaze away for a year of extra life. A few moments of silence crawled past, and still I stared at the goblet: at the convoluted strands of snakish locks just above his hand.

Then I heard a barely audible click, as when a key turns in a lock.

In the same instant, a tiny sliver of brightness flickered out of the handle and immediately withdrew from sight again.

"Did you see it, Miss Gaunt?" he said. "The serpent's fang. The sting in the goblet! That is what wrought the death of Lord Peter Chalmers."

"A poisoned needle!" I breathed.

"Tipped, without a doubt, by some such poison as is used by savage tribes of South America for their blowpipe darts," said my companion. "Swift acting. Irreversible. Utterly fatal."

"But how could such a thing be lying around in the palazzo for so long without harming anyone before?" I said. "At least, I assume that no one else has been harmed—?" I looked at him questioningly. He shook his head.

"To my knowledge, ma'am, Lord Peter was its first and only victim," he said. "And you miss the point entirely if you suppose that someone might *accidentally* have fallen victim to the so-called Borgia goblet."

I distinctly felt my flesh creep all over, describing to me the whole shape of my body.

"I—I don't follow your meaning," I said.

"The needle cannot come into operation till the device is cocked," he said. "And, once having delivered its poison, it is perfectly safe till it has been recocked."

Again I felt the prickling of fear creep over my body.

"You mean that—?"

"I mean, Miss Gaunt, that someone at this dinner table last night had the knowledge to compress the spring within the handle. And that same person handed it to Lord Peter, with the intent of causing his death. Now, cast your mind back, ma'am. Tell me, if you can, who passed the Borgia goblet to Lord Peter?"

I had seen the question coming, and had no way to avoid answering it, for the truth lay in other mouths than mine, and prevarication would help me not at all.

"I—I gave it to him," I said falteringly.

Later that afternoon, I was permitted to take a few minutes' rest from the interrogation. Giolitti-Crispi was waiting for me when I reentered the dining room, and rose to his feet, as before, bowing me to my seat.

"Shall we retrace our steps once more, Miss Gaunt?" he said quietly. "How did the subject of the Borgia goblet arise last night?"

"I've told you I don't know," I said. "I was talking to Lord Peter at the time."

"Might I inquire as to the topic of your conversation with Lord Peter?"

This was a new question, right out of the blue. I gave a sudden intake of breath that he could not have missed, nor could he have overlooked the color that I could feel burning in my cheeks.

"We were discussing a—personal matter," I said weakly.

"A personal matter. I see. And while you were discussing this—personal matter—the Borgia goblet became a topic of general conversation elsewhere around the table?"

"Yes."

His eyes were very deeply set and a steely gray.

"And then the goblet was brought to the table. At whose request?"

"Mr. Bertrand Demaury."

"And from Mr. Bertrand's hand it passed—to whom?"

"I suppose to his daughter, who sat on his left. She showed a great interest in the story of the goblet."

"And from there?" The disconcerting gray eyes fixed me unwaveringly.

"I don't know!" I cried. "I've told you time and time again, I don't know. I can't remember how it reached me!"

"You have no recollection of whose hand passed you the goblet? Was it not Herr von Wuppertal, who sat there on your right?" And he pointed to the seat next to me.

"Perhaps. I can't remember."

"I should tell you, Miss Gaunt, that according to Herr von Wuppertal, the goblet did not pass his way. Indeed, he never had it in his hand."

"I've told you I couldn't remember."

The long-cased clock chimed the half hour. Half past four in the afternoon. He had been interrogating me for two and a half hours, less a short break. Yet he had managed to see several of the other guests of the Palazzo Demaury, and the servants, in the course of a single morning.

He said, "How well did you know Lord Peter Chalmers?"

Once more, it could not have escaped those watchful gray eyes that the question unnerved me.

"He—he was the fiancé of my cousin and companion," I murmured.

"Quite so. That, however, is not an answer to my question. I am aware of your relationships. I seek to know the degree of familiarity that existed between yourself and the deceased."

"There was no familiarity," I said. "I invariably addressed him formally, as Lord Peter."

"And he—how did he address you, Miss Gaunt?"

I looked down at my hands.

"Mostly as Meg," I breathed.

"I am sorry, but I did not hear that, ma'am."

"Meg," I said. "He insisted on calling me Meg."

"Insisted?" One eyebrow went up quizzically. "Do you imply that he adopted the familiar name against your wishes, Miss Gaunt?"

"I—offered him no encouragement so to do," I replied.

"I see." The eyebrow returned to its place. I felt the thin edge of relief; perhaps I was out of the wood. And then he said casually, "And yet, with this man whom you insisted on formally addressing by his title, and who addressed you against your wishes by your familiar name, you had a conversation at the dinner table on what you describe as a 'personal matter.' Do I have it correctly?"

"Yes." I was not out of the wood. Far from it. This strangely disturbing man was leading me to the very thickest part of the wood, and I could see no escape.

"Personal, and also—*private*?"

"Yes," I said. I would not willingly take one step further toward the trap into which I was being led. If he wanted to know what Peter Chalmers and I had been talking about, he would have to drag it out of me.

He seemed to have no inclination to do any such thing. Instead, he sat back in his chair, crossed his legs, flicked a speck of dust from his immaculate waistcoat, and gazed evenly across at me.

He said, "I should inform you, Miss Gaunt, that I am well aware of the deceased man's reputation."

"Indeed?" I murmured, uneasily.

"Indeed so, Miss Gaunt," he said. "Lord Peter was no stranger to Venice, having visited here many times for cultural, and other, pursuits. As a police officer, I naturally take a lively interest in such of our visitors whose behavior tends toward the—shall I say, extravagant? Do I make myself clear, Miss Gaunt?"

"Yes," I replied, as calmly as I was able.

"And, bearing that in mind, there is nothing you would wish to confide in me? Nothing concerning the relationship between yourself and Lord Peter that might throw some light upon this case?"

I shook my head. "Nothing!"

"And you still cannot remember whose hand it was that passed you the Borgia goblet?"

"No!" I could detect a note of hysteria in my voice. "I've told you a dozen times. No!"

"But you did pass it on to Lord Peter."

"Yes, I passed it to him!" I cried. "But I didn't know how the horrible thing worked. I'd never seen nor heard of it before in my life. I didn't kill him!"

The searching gray eyes never faltered at my outburst.

"You have not been accused of killing Lord Peter, ma'am," he said calmly.

He allowed me to go after that. By then, Esmeralda had risen and attired herself, with the aid of a lady's maid who had been deputed to look after her. Dressed befittingly, and becomingly, in black from head to foot, and trailing a black chiffon handkerchief with which she occasionally dabbed her lustrous eyes, she received the Chief of Police in the sitting room of her apartments on the second floor of the palazzo. I was not present at the interview, but heard an account of it from Esmeralda afterward. It seemed that Giolitti-Crispi had been all consideration toward her feelings, and, touching upon the tragic events at the dinner table, had only inquired if she had handled the Borgia goblet—which, as I knew, she had not.

Not a word, it seemed, of his sharply barbed insinuations concerning myself and the dead man. Nor had he given Esmeralda any cause to think that my being the person who had handed the cup to her fiancé was a matter of any significance. Indeed, Esmeralda appeared to have been given the impression that Peter Chalmers had met his death by accident, simply by tampering with a dangerous toy. And if that was what Giolitti-Crispi wanted her to think, who was I to persuade her otherwise?

I joined Esmeralda for a light supper in her sitting room. We sat for a little while, till the setting sun sent long shadows down the Grand Canal, then, pleading tiredness, I took my leave and went up to my room on the floor above. But there was little sleep for me that night, and though I had firmly locked and bolted my door against my barefoot intruder, I could not rid myself of a sense of dreadful vulnerability. I lay wakeful, listening to the small sounds of the advancing night: the splash of oars in the canal below my window, the distant murmur of folks talking in passing boats, an occasional burst of song. An early dawn set cockerels crowing all over Venice, and that mingled with the shrieks of seabirds as they swooped down upon floating rubbish. Before the sun was properly up, I drifted off into an uneasy doze from which I woke in bright sunlight at midmorning.

I felt refreshed and somewhat less troubled, which says much for the recuperative qualities of the human frame. I put on a good gray blouse and a dark skirt. As a mark of mourning, I pinned a black ribbon round my neck with a cameo brooch. Then, after doing the best I could with my untidy hair, I ventured downstairs.

On my way down, I came upon Axel von Wuppertal. He was clad in a Norfolk jacket and knickerbockers, and carried a deer-stalker hat and cane.

"Meg," he said. "I looked for you everywhere yesterday. How did you get on with that stupid policeman?"

"Between looking after poor Esmeralda and being questioned by the policeman, I was kept busy most of the day," I said. "And I'm surprised you should have thought him stupid. I must say he struck me as being extraordinarily shrewd."

"Oh, I think not, Meg," he said. "Oh, surely not. The fellow has the look of a dilettante. But enough of him. I have secured the services of the palazzo's private gondola and am setting out to reacquaint myself with Venice, which I have not seen since I was eighteen. I had it in my mind to invite you to accompany me, and lo!—here you are. What do you say?"

"I shall be delighted, Axel," I told him. "But first I have to make sure that Esmeralda doesn't need me."

I went to my cousin's room and found her still asleep, with the look of someone who would remain so till noon. I scribbled a brief note and left it by her bedside; then, after fetching a straw boater and an umbrella for protection against sun and rain, I rejoined Axel.

The private gondola of the Palazzo Demaury, like every other gondola in Venice, was painted an austere black and was shorn of all but the most rudimentary decoration. However, it possessed exceedingly comfortable armchairs and fringed black cushions. Our gondolier was none other than the burly gardener whom I had seen tending the vines in the patio the previous day. He raised his hat to me. He was barefoot, as before.

"What I have in mind," said Axel, "is a short trip as far as St. Mark's Square, which is the heart and center of Venice. There we will sip coffee and watch the world stroll past for a short while, before taking to the waters again and making a tour of the canals. At the conclusion of our tour I will take you to luncheon at a restaurant which, if it has not greatly deteriorated in these last twelve years or so, will be a memorable gastronomic experience. How does that itinerary strike you, Meg?"

"Most enthralling," I said.

"Then let us be off," said Axel. "Give way, Giuseppe."

"*Si, signor*," said our gondolier, with a grin.

As he bent his back to the oar, and we swept out into the middle of the canal, I looked back over my shoulder at the dark bulk of the palazzo, which was in shadow from the morning sun. The windows were still shuttered—all save one on the upper floor, and it was in this window that I saw a face looking down at us. A wrinkled face surmounted by a domed pate. It was there for only a brief moment and then it was gone.

The recluse of the Palazzo Demaury was aware of our departure. The thought was curiously disquieting.

There was an orchestra playing outside one of the cafes of the square. They played Verdi and Wagner with tremendous attention to the dramatic qualities. Their conductor was a little man with a great deal of flowing white hair, who ruled them imperiously with his baton and his expressive fingers, and could command a cymbal clash with a mere flash of his dark eyes.

The cafe was called Florians, and we sat at a table under the shade of a cool colonnade that ran round three sides of the huge square. The fourth side was occupied by the facade of St. Mark's Cathedral, with its cluster of golden domes, where innumerable pigeons circled and swooped. Crowds strolled slowly in and out of the sunshine and the shade: all Venice with wife and children, and a great deal of the rest of the world, surely.

Presently, the orchestra ended its final piece with a blare of brass and a thunder of timpani. When the polite applause had died away, Axel and I smiled across the coffee cups at each other.

"Now we are able to chat," he said.

"What do we chat about?" I countered.

"Meg, I am worried for you," he said. "It is, of course, the talk of the palazzo that you were questioned for almost the whole of yesterday afternoon, and I had cause to be aware of the likely reason." His pale blue eyes met mine, questioningly.

"Because you were sitting next to me," I said. "And because you saw me hand the goblet to Lord Peter. Now, I wonder if you think that I did it with deliberate intent? The Chief of Police thinks so," I added bitterly.

"Oh, Meg, surely not," he exclaimed. "My dear, what possible reason does he think you could have for wishing to do such a thing? Why, the very idea is insupportable."

His face: so honest and uncomplicated in its expression, so earnest and concerned. I warmed to him as a friend, and resolved to test his friendship by bringing him into my confidence.

"Axel," I said, and chose the words ahead very carefully: "Giolitti-Crispi has a shrewd suspicion that I might have had good cause to harm Lord Peter. And I have to tell you that his suspicion is not entirely unfounded."

He gave a sharp intake of breath. "Meg, Meg, what are you trying to tell me?" he said. "How can this be? The idea that you would wish to harm anyone—why, it doesn't stand a moment's examination."

"You are very kind, Axel," I said. "I think you are the sort of person who would never see evil in anyone, even in the worst of us. Even in a man like Lord Chalmers."

"Not to speak ill of the dead," said Axel, "but I have to admit that I did not much like Chalmers on a short acquaintance. I found him arrogant. Overbearing. A typical aristocrat. I should explain, Meg, that my political sentiments incline toward the radical. But tell me, what was the evil in Chalmers that I did not detect?"

I said, "It was his wish that I should become his—mistress."

"But he was affianced to Esmeralda!" exclaimed Axel. "They were to have been married this year."

"A consideration like that scarcely entered into Peter Chalmers' plans," I replied. "As you will understand when I tell you that the last words he addressed to me—only minutes before he picked up that goblet—were to suggest that he would use his future wife's money to set me up in a villa. As his mistress."

"But surely, even one so arrogant, so vile, must have realized that you would never agree to such a thing," said Axel.

"He quickly realized that I would never willingly agree to his wishes," I said. "But he came to believe that I could be forced."

"Forced?" echoed Axel. "But—how?"

"I am nobody," I said. "And I have nothing. Only Esmeralda's grace and favor saves me from the gutter, where my lack of attainments would speedily land me. His last threat was that he would induce Esmeralda to send me packing. And I think he would have done it if he had lived."

Some disturbance in the passing crowds alarmed the pigeons who had settled on the flagstones in front of St. Mark's. They rose in a gray cloud, to a frenzy of whirring sound.

Axel drove one fist into the palm of his other hand. And again. His face was pinched with fury.

"By heaven!" he exclaimed. "That swine deserved . . ."

He paused.

"Deserved to die?" I prompted him. "I think, Axel, that the Chief of Police believes I shared that sentiment. He knows what manner of man Peter Chalmers was. Dilettante he may be, but he has made the shrewd guess that I am concealing the truth about Peter Chalmers' sentiments toward me and mine toward him. And I believe that somehow he will trap me into revealing the truth as I have revealed it to you. And I'm afraid, Axel. Terribly afraid of the consequences that will follow, because I am defenseless."

The pigeons had not come back, and a bank of cloud had moved across the sun, causing a sudden chill. The people in the great square moved more quickly. A waiter in a very long apron scooped up our empty coffee cups and cast an interested eye at the woman in the straw boater, and the blond man who had suddenly reached across the table to take her hands in his.

"You are not defenseless any longer, Meg," said Axel. "For you have me as your friend and champion. If this accusation is ever made against you, we will fight it together. But believe me, my dear, I do not believe it will ever come to pass. In your distress— your very natural distress—you have imagined danger where no danger exists. There is nothing that can be proved against you, for you are innocent. If Chalmers did not die by an accident . . ."

"It was no accident," I said. "Giolitti-Crispi explained to me, most carefully, that someone around that table must deliberately have planned it to happen."

Axel shook his head; bewildered, concerned.

The early bright promise of our expedition was never fulfilled. Try as he might—and he tried very hard—my companion was not able to recapture it. We returned to the steps where our gondolier was waiting, and were borne down the length of the Grand Canal, while Axel pointed out the important buildings along the way and was a mine of diverting information about their history and the famous and infamous people connected with them. We alighted at the Rialto bridge, and he took me to a delightful restaurant that smelled deliciously of newly baked bread and spices. He fussed over the menu; recommended that I try a delicately flavored vegetable soup, followed by tender slices of veal grilled in Marsala wine. I toyed with the beautiful soup, and I pushed the veal around my plate in the hope that it would dwindle and go away. Axel knew it was no use; we both knew it was no use. The terrors of the long and sleepless night had returned to haunt the golden day.

"Don't bother to try to eat any more," said Axel. "Drink up your wine, which is mild and gentle and will do you no harm, and I will take you back to the palazzo. One day, perhaps, we will come here again, and in happier circumstances."

"I'm sorry, Axel," I told him.

He squeezed my hand. "An early night for you, Meg," he said. "And tomorrow you will feel better. Come." He settled the bill and we left.

Mr. Obadiah put in an appearance so smartly upon our alighting from the gondola at the steps of the palazzo that it was clear that he must have been lying in wait for our return. It was to my companion that he addressed his first remarks.

"Herr von Wuppertal," he said fussily. "Herr von Wuppertal, I have sent messengers all over Venice to find you. I have been at my wits' end, sir. I really have."

"What is it—what is the matter?" asked Axel.

"Why, sir, it's Mr. Giles calling for you, that's the matter, sir," replied the secretary. "Mr. Giles wishes to see you as soon as you are able. He awaits you in his apartment with much impatience, sir. Much impatience." Mr. Obadiah was clearly in a state of nerves: he continuously licked his dry lips and fussed with his hands. I realized I had been wrong to liken him to a cat; cats never display their emotions so obviously.

"Meg, I must leave you," said Axel. His face had become suddenly more alive. With a tiny stab of something like disappointment, I again became aware that my friend was also a Demaury. And at this juncture, moreover, a Demaury in full scent of a fortune.

I murmured, quietly, so that Mr. Obadiah should not hear it, and taking Axel by the hand and kissing him upon the cheek, "Good luck. And thank you for being so understanding."

"Thank you, Meg," he said. Then he was gone, with Mr. Obadiah trotting at his heels.

The latter had not passed through the doorway before he remembered something that he had forgotten in the excitement of the moment. Pausing, he turned and regarded me.

"Miss Gaunt, ma'am," said the secretary. "You also have received a summons."

"A summons, Mr. Obadiah?" I repeated.

He pointed—to the edge of the steps, beyond the place where Axel and I had alighted from the gondola. My heart gave a lurch, as I saw there a long, low craft—not a gondola, but a boat of ordinary build, with four oarsmen and a man in a cocked hat seated in the stern—which I had not noticed upon our arrival. The man in the stern rose to his feet and gave me a salute. I recognized the police sergeant.

"They have been here since midday," said Obadiah. "The

Chief of Police requires you, ma'am, to attend him." The secretary's shifty eyes slid away from meeting my gaze.

A sharp order from the police sergeant brought the boat neatly to my side. Four oars were tossed in unison; the sergeant leapt ashore and handed me aboard.

"Is honor to greet *signorina* again," he said in fractured English. He was in his mid-forties, with a soup-strainer mustache and a considerable paunch, and smelled strongly of garlic. "Please to be seated."

I took my place in the stern, and the sergeant did likewise. He rasped an order, and the oarsmen smartly lowered their oars and set the craft in swift motion.

We soon left the Grand Canal: slid into a shadowed side canal that passed under innumerable small, humpbacked bridges, with the dark waterway getting ever narrower, till the men's oars all but touched the green-streaked stonework at either side. I saw a rat, black as a mole, emerge from a drain and, taking fright at the sight of our oncoming boat, strike out to swim ahead of us, its small, frantic eyes glancing back from time to time as it sliced through the water, trailing a long herringbone wake behind it, till it found another bolt hole and disappeared.

There was no sign of life or habitation in the tall buildings about us; no sound of voices, nor even the barking of a dog. Everything was silent, secret, shut-in, and still. A part of Venice, it seemed to me, that had died and been forgotten. I fell to wondering where they were taking me. To prison? If such a place existed in the city, the neighborhood through which we were passing would accommodate it admirably well. I cast a sidelong glance at my companion, the sergeant, but he was staring steadfastly ahead. The men at the oars seemed deliberately to avoid me with their eyes.

We came at last to the end of the narrow canal, and debouched into a curved sweep of water that put me in mind of the moat at Murchester Hall. Indeed, it appeared entirely to surround a hotchpotch of black-walled buildings: a domed church, or chapel, with a heavy forbidding portico; and alongside it a many-storied palazzo with shuttered windows and a dark archway, over which was set a coat of arms carved in stone.

An order from the sergeant brought the boat to a gentle halt just within the archway, where the water lapped at the foot of a flight of steps leading upward into a patch of sunlight.

We had arrived. But—where? Was this prison, or was it merely a place of inquisition?

"*Signorina.*" I was roused from my uneasy reverie by the sergeant, who was reaching out his hand to help me ashore, a duty that he performed unsmilingly. "Please to follow me, *signorina.*"

The steps brought us to a patio not unlike that at the Palazzo Demaury, with the four interior walls of the building stretching up to the edge of red-pantiled roofs that framed a square of intense blue sky. The statuary was darker and heavier than that of the Demaury residence, and the foliage grew in wild and unkempt abandon.

We crossed the patio, the sound of our footsteps greatly magnified in the enclosing stillness, and the sergeant led me through an archway and into a long and uncarpeted corridor, at the end of which were double doors of oak and bronze, upon which he tapped and entered.

I waited. He had a murmured conversation with someone beyond, at the termination of which he drew aside the door for me to enter, bowing as I went past him.

The door closed behind me. I was immediately facing a window through which the sunlight was pouring with such intensity as to throw all else into relative darkness. Only after some moments, when my eyes grew more accustomed to the glare, was I able to pick out the shapes of furnishings: a table, chairs, the rectangles of pictures on the walls, a chandelier hanging from the ceiling and reflecting pinpoints of sunlight.

And the figure of a woman seated close by the window.

"You are the young English lady of whom my son spoke. Come over here, child. Let me look at you."

She was dressed in black, with a cap set with widow's weeds, like that worn by our own Queen Victoria. The hand that was extended to me was pale and unlined, and cool to the touch. The eyes that made a swift appraisal of my face, my figure, my clothes, even of my fingernails, were steely gray. I took her to be in her sixties, and marvelously well preserved, though her hair, which was drawn back into a severe chignon, was as white as bleached bone.

"I am Princess Giolitti-Crispi, mother of Prince Lorenzo," she said. "My son had expected you earlier and has unfortunately been called away. However, this has given me the opportunity to meet you, and presently we will have some tea. The English habit of taking afternoon tea has translated itself to Venice since the eighteenth century, and I have my own consignment of blends, both Indian and Chinese, dispatched from London thrice yearly. Will you take a seat."

"Thank you, er—"

"Address me as Princess, my dear, My son has been called away to investigate a robbery. It is not a form of activity of which I greatly approve, as you may well imagine."

"Quite," I replied, puzzled as to whether she disapproved of robbery, police work, or both. I was soon enlightened.

"I would have wished my son to have been content with the elegance of idleness," she said blandly. "But he is forever active, and has been since childhood. Commerce was out of the question, of course, for a Giolitti-Crispi. Venice was founded on commerce, and it is an activity which is perfectly acceptable in many Venetian families of title, whose fortunes have been founded on trade. The Giolitti-Crispis, however, predate even Venice herself and have never dabbled in commerce. Do you follow?"

"Yes," I said hastily. "Yes, I do, Princess."

"The only permissible activity for a Giolitti-Crispi," she said, "is the service of the State. And it is in this capacity that my son finds an outlet for his tremendous energy. Do you see?"

"Yes, Princess," I said.

"It goes without saying, of course, that he performs this service entirely without remuneration. No Giolitti-Crispi would seek financial reward for performing a service to the State."

"Naturally," I said.

The promptness and brevity of my responses won me a small smile of approval from that astonishing lady.

"Are your parents living, my dear?" she inquired.

"Both died soon after I was born," I replied. "I was brought up by the Demaurys."

"The Demaurys—ha!" She meditated on the Demaurys for a few moments, then went on: "I have no doubt that you have turned out to be a credit to your foster parents, and will in time make a suitable marriage."

"I trust so," was my reply, while quenching a sudden impulse to laugh out loud.

"A modest marriage, naturally enough in your case. But suitable."

"Of course."

"There is no profit in unsuitable marriages," she declared with considerable firmness, striking the arm of her chair with the palm of her hand, so that a thin cloud of dust arose from the material, each particle shimmering in the sunlight from the window. "Be warned by me, my dear. I have seen it in my own experience. An unsuitable marriage, a *mésalliance*, whether in respect of disparity in rank, religion or race—but most particularly in respect of rank—is greatly to be deplored."

"I'm sure you are right, Princess," I responded.

Now she was becoming quite agitated, showing a spot of bright color on each smooth cheekbone. And her breathing quickened.

"Standards of conduct are being eroded all about us," she said. "Much of it I blame upon the deleterious influence of modern dancing, which promotes an unhealthy sense of freedom from responsibility. Most particularly, I blame the waltz." She leaned forward and tapped my arm. "In this respect, your present sovereign must be apportioned her share of the blame, for was it not she and the late Prince Consort who did so much to popularize the waltz throughout Europe?"

I was assembling some sort of reply to that astonishing observation, when there came a tap upon the door and a young woman entered.

She began to say something in Italian, but paused when she saw me.

"Come in, Giovanna," responded the Princess in English. "I shall not require to be read to this afternoon. This lady is from England. My dear, I did not quite catch your name, this is my daughter, Princess Giovanna."

"Meg Gaunt," I said, extending my hand. "How do you do, Princess Giovanna."

"How do you do," she replied unsmilingly. She had the same

gray eyes as her mother and brother, and her hair was the same jet black as his, and as her mother's had undoubtedly been. But whereas mother and son both shared a vitality of manner and expression, Giovanna's eyes lacked sparkle, and her exquisitely modeled lips turned down at the corners in a sulky way that immediately put me in mind of Bertrand Demaury's daughter. She was older than I, perhaps by five years or so. Glancing at her left hand, I saw that she wore no wedding ring—nor, indeed, ring of any kind.

"What have you been doing since luncheon, Giovanna?" demanded her mother.

"I helped Angelina in the kitchen," was the reply.

"Quite unnecessary!" snapped her mother. "I will not have you doing servants' work, Giovanna."

Princess Giovanna drew a deep breath, and replied in the wearied tones of someone who is repeating an oft-told truth.

"Mama, it is necessary that I help Angelina in the kitchen," she said. "As you very well know, Angelina is over seventy, and is quite incapable of lifting heavy dishes and carrying buckets of water."

"There is Paolo!" said her mother shrilly. "Let him lift and carry."

"Paolo is half-crippled with rheumatism, Mama," said Giovanna.

This response angered the older woman even further, and she retorted in Italian, not one word of which I could pick out; but the manner of delivery was such that the general drift was quite clear. Giovanna, after a swift glance in my direction, answered her mother back in the same tongue, and with equal vehemence. I sat uneasily watching them, helpless to intervene, lacking the assurance to go away and leave them to quarrel in decent privacy.

In the end, Giovanna turned on her heel and ran out of the room, slamming the door behind her. Her mother leaned back in her chair, breathing heavily.

Presently, she said, "You see what a pass things have come to, even here, in the Palazzo Giolitti-Crispi. This modern world. What is to become of us? Would you care for some tea now, my dear? Then be so kind as to pull that bell cord, will you?"

In the fullness of time, the summons brought an old woman hobbling in with a silver tray laid with a teapot and water jug, also of silver, and teacups and saucers of near-transparent china. Having placed these on the table, she stiffly curtsied and shuffled out.

The tea was weak and lukewarm, but my hostess drank five cups with every appearance of relish, talking all the time. And when we had finished, Prince Lorenzo, the Venetian Chief of Police, made his entrance.

"How are things at the Palazzo Demaury—how is Miss Esmeralda bearing up?"

"Esmeralda was asleep when I went out," I replied. "And I haven't been back there all day."

"You were accompanied by Herr von Wuppertal," he said.

"Yes."

"Mmmm."

He looked away and narrowed his eyes against the sun, and gave me the opportunity to study his profile closely.

We were on a terrace overlooking the canal, a place of cool greenness, overhung with vines, where he had taken me after greeting his mother with a kiss on the forehead and a murmured inquiry as to her well-being. There were a pair of wicker armchairs set upon the terrace. He had motioned me to one seat and himself taken the other.

His ears were very neat and close to his head. His hair had a way of curling over the edge of his collar. I was near enough to see the trace of a slight, old scar that ran along the angle of his jaw: a relic of some boyhood scrape?

Suddenly I realized that he was speaking to me.

"I—I'm sorry?" I stammered.

"I said, there are two things I wanted to discuss with you. And I much preferred to do so in private, away from the Palazzo Demaury. The reason for that will become apparent when you have heard what I have to say."

I met the straight glance of those disconcerting eyes.

"Yes," I said. "Please go on."

"First, concerning the matter upon which I pressed you closely yesterday," he said. "The matter of your relationship with the dead man. No—please don't say anything now. Nothing, till I have finished.

"Miss Gaunt, Lord Peter Chalmers was of the same social class as myself. And you must understand that to be a member of the European aristocracy is rather like being a member of a small and exclusive club. We all know each other. As children, we are reared by the same small army of British nannies, educated at the same schools and universities, frequently intermarry, attend the same social functions, listen to the same gossip. Quite apart from being a policeman, I am uniquely qualified to be well aware of the deceased man's reputation. Armed with that knowledge, Miss Gaunt, I went for a little fishing expedition with you yesterday.

"Knowing what I know of Chalmers, a certain possibility occurred to me, as a result of which I threw a couple of questions at you and saw them strike their mark. You will never make a successful criminal, do you know that, Miss Gaunt? Not even a dissembler of the most innocent kind, for your honesty is truly of the sort which earns itself the name 'transparent.'"

"He pursued me and made my life a misery," I admitted. "I think I might have been driven to killing him. But I did not."

"I believe you," he said. "And there is no need to say more, Miss Gaunt. As I am about to explain, what passed between you and Lord Peter has scarcely any bearing on the case."

One thing else had to be said, and I said it: "I never yielded to him. Because of that, he threatened to have me turned out, so that I would go to him in sheer desperation. I think if it had really come to that, I might have wanted to kill him."

"What you have told me exactly fits the reputation that Chalmers gained for himself in Society," was his reply. "However, as I said, it no longer has any import in the case."

"Why is that?" I asked.

He said, "Last evening, I finished questioning everyone who was present at that dinner party, and examined the results. You would scarcely believe the disparity in the evidence that I received, in even such simple observations as who requested the Borgia goblet to be brought to the table, and in what order was it passed from hand to hand. Nothing unusual about that: as a policeman, one is well aware that the evidence of people's eyes is simply not to be trusted. However, by balancing one disparity against another, I was able to piece together the most likely sequence in which the goblet was circulated. Except for one particular."

"And what was that?" I asked.

"No one, not a single person around that table, was able to recall who passed the goblet to you," he said quietly.

In the silence that followed, I let my gaze slip from his face to his hands, which were folded in repose upon his knee. They were long-fingered, sun-bronzed, capable hands, the backs crisscrossed with fine black hairs.

"I—I wonder why no one saw who it was?" I ventured.

"That question occupied me throughout a long and excessively wakeful night," he said. "And the answer is inescapable: the person who passed it to you—the person who had cocked the mechanism and turned the Borgia goblet into a killing machine—took advantage of some slight diversion, some momentary shift in the attentions of all parties around the table, to place the goblet in such a position that you would presently pick it up."

I distinctly felt the hairs of my scalp stiffen and stir.

"But—that means . . ." I began.

"It probably means, Miss Gaunt," said Prince Lorenzo, "that it was you, and not Lord Peter, who was the intended victim of the Borgia goblet!"

He gave me his polite and stilted assurances that the Venetian Police would offer me every protection against my unknown enemy, and would bend every effort to apprehend and punish that person.

The sun having descended below the line of roofs at the far side of the canal, and the vine-hung terrace being in deep shadow, we had repaired to a pleasant paneled room that was marked with the stamp of his masculinity: with sporting guns and pictures of the chase, a large painting of himself at the wheel of a racing yacht, another of him as a young boy in a sailor suit holding the hand of his mother—and she looking the image of his sister Giovanna, but without the discontented mouth. There he offered me a glass of sherry—and his consolations.

"But why?" I asked for the umpteenth time. "Why should anyone want to kill *me*? I've no fortune, nor any prospect of a fortune."

"Now you are angry," he said. "And that surprises me, Miss Gaunt, for I had placed you in mind as a lady of placid temperament."

"My grandfather," I said, "always claimed that I had the shortest temper of anyone he knew. And, though I am terrified by what you have told me, I am also angry. Angry that anyone should wish to have—" Suddenly shocked to see that my hands were trembling, I broke off, and immediately dissolved into uncontrollable tears.

When next I was able to see, his hand was held out to me, and in it was a white silk handkerchief.

"It has been a terrible experience for you, Miss Gaunt," he said. "And I fear that my own action in subjecting you to such protracted and searching questioning has served to increase the burden that has been laid upon you."

I took the handkerchief and dabbed my eyes. "You had your duty to perform, Prince Lorenzo," I said.

"You are free to leave Venice," he said. "No suspicion now rests upon you. You could go tonight. Back to England, Miss Gaunt, where you would be safe."

"Safe? From whoever tried to kill me, you mean?" I shook my head. "The idea is tempting, for I tell you, I'm not a very brave person. But all else besides, I can't abandon my cousin Esmeralda. Not now. Not after what's happened. Peter Chalmers may not have been what he ought, but I'm certain she loved him in her own way. And, in her own way, she needs me. Always has, I suppose. And the more so now."

The gray eyes regarded me. "Your sentiments do you credit, Miss Gaunt," he said. "But if you must stay, I caution you to be on your guard always. If possible, take your meals alone and not in company with the others. Do you have a servant you can trust —a lady's maid, perhaps?"

"There's a girl named Assunta," I said.

"If you think you can trust Assunta, have her bring your meals from the kitchen," he said. "That will rid you of a considerable hazard. As for the rest—whenever you leave the Palazzo Demaury, you will be discreetly watched over by my plainclothes officers. In the palazzo, keep your door locked always."

"I have kept it locked since the first," I said. And then I went on to tell him about my barefoot intruder, an incident which now appeared all the more sinister in the light of what had happened.

Prince Lorenzo looked grave. He strode up and down the room with his hands clasped behind his back, deep in thought.

Presently, he said, "I have decided that I must place an officer on duty in the Palazzo Demaury, day and night, till this case is settled. I will attend to it at once. In the meantime, Miss Gaunt, my sergeant will accompany you home in the boat."

I rose and gave him my hand. "Thank you for being frank with me," I said. "I much prefer to know the worst, rather than live in a fool's paradise. And at least I have the consolation of knowing that I am no longer a suspected murderess."

"You were never that," he said simply. "That I promise you."

He escorted me to the bottom of the steps, where the police boat bobbed in the shadows. We shook hands once more.

"Give my farewells to your mother and sister," I said. "And please thank the princess for my tea."

"If that tea was of the usual standard served in the Palazzo Giolitti-Crispi," he said with a smile, "it must have been quite awful. Good evening, Miss Gaunt."

I was handed into the boat. The sergeant gave an order, and we swept out into the canal.

My return journey was curiously unlike the gloomy outward voyage. The late afternoon sun was shining directly down the narrow canal, turning its water to dancing patterns of light. I had been mistaken in supposing that the area was deserted; I heard the laughter of children and the sound of a woman's voice raised in song. One high wall was overtopped by a profusion of flame-headed flowers and cool greenery that told of a secret garden. And the police sergeant actually smiled at me and asked in his broken English if I was quite comfortably seated. The oarsmen also met my eyes and smiled companionably.

I thought back to what had taken place between Prince Lorenzo and me, and was puzzled at the way in which—so completely at variance with my earlier resolution—I had readily admitted to what had really taken place between Peter Chalmers and me. And why, I asked myself, had it also seemed important to let him know that I had never yielded to the dead man's importunities? It was really very odd.

Now I walked in danger of my life, yet in a way that was better than being under suspicion of murder. And had not Prince Lorenzo promised to protect me? That was curiously comforting.

A splash of white silk protruding from the opening of my reticule revealed that I had forgotten to return his handkerchief after using it to dry my eyes. It would have been the easiest thing in the world to hand it to the sergeant and ask him to return it to his chief. Why, then, did I stuff it firmly out of sight in my reticule?

So he was a nobleman? And presumably rich, for, though sparsely furnished, the Palazzo Giolitti-Crispi bore the unmistakable signs of inherited wealth, as I had learned to recognize them from my connection with the Demaury clan: the faded softness of Persian rugs; dark paintings in ornate gilded frames; beautiful china; the touch and feel of effortless luxury. Yet for all that, his sister, Princess Giovanna, was obliged to help the old woman in the kitchen. Why were they unable to obtain younger and more energetic servants?

And Giovanna herself—she was surely thirty or more. Why, with her beauty and her background, had she never wed; never, in her mother's phrase, "made a suitable marriage"? Was mature spinsterhood the cause of the bitter set of her mouth, the lackluster eyes?

At that point in my conjectures, our craft swept out into the Grand Canal, and I saw the Palazzo Demaury rising above the bustle of the evening boat traffic passing to and fro on the wide waterway. The sight of it made me aware of the danger in which I stood and drove all other considerations from my mind. It was with reluctance that I parted company from the police sergeant and his men, watched them row away and leave me standing there.

I was greeted by Mr. Obadiah. The secretary was in a fine state: wild-eyed and fussing, and his relief at seeing me was something to behold.

"Oh, Miss Gaunt, Miss Gaunt!" he exclaimed. "Thank heaven you've returned. It's Herr von Wuppertal, I don't know what to do with him, I really don't."

"Don't know what to *do* with him, Mr. Obadiah?" I repeated. "Whatever do you mean?"

The secretary looked sidelong, both ways, as if to assure himself that we were not being overheard. I am fairly tall and I had to incline my head to catch his whispered words.

"Herr von Wuppertal has been at the bottle, miss," he said.

"At the bottle—you mean he's been drinking?"

"Right after he came down from Mr. Giles's apartments, miss," said the secretary. "Went straight into the white drawing room, where is kept a tray of whiskies and brandies and such. Now he's in a fine state, miss, and I fear what will happen if he appears for dinner with the other guests. I can't persuade him to go up to his rooms and take a rest."

"I will go and see him and try to talk him into having a quiet lie-down, Mr. Obadiah," I told him. "The white drawing room, you said?"

Relief washed over Obadiah's face like the sun coming out from behind a cloud. "This way, follow me, miss," he said.

The white drawing room was at the rear of the palazzo, on the second floor. It was a large apartment with a painted ceiling, paneled in white and gold, and set with exquisite eighteenth-century chairs and sofas, and it was in one of the latter that my new friend and confidant was lolled with his head back and a large glass of spirits spilling from his hand onto his lap. He was singing to himself in his native language: something slow in tempo and with a great deal of sentimentality.

"I will leave you to deal with the gentleman, miss," whispered Obadiah, and made himself scarce, shutting the door behind him.

"Meg! Meg *liebchen!*" Axel opened one eye and regarded me. "Have a cognac, dear Meg, and—as your national poet has it—'let us sit upon the ground and tell sad stories of the death of kings.'" A lock of his butter-blond hair had fallen over his forehead. He looked pale and sickly, like a little boy who has gorged himself in a forbidden apple orchard and has come to regret it. The smell of spirits hung about him.

"Poor Axel, you have had a very great disappointment," I said.

"Poor Axel," he echoed. "Oh, Meg, with what shrewdness you search me out. Yes, I have seen Giles and learned my fate. He is quite pleased with Demaury's of Berlin, and my brothers and I are to be given a two percent increase on the profits."

"You are a very lucky young man," I said evenly.

"Lucky? Yes, I am lucky, Meg. I shall be able to move to a smarter townhouse and buy myself a small estate in East Prussia, perhaps aspire to a yacht—a yacht of modest proportions—on the Baltic coast. I may even aspire to marriage. Not to a *junkerin*, you understand; as I am a man with radical opinions, she must be solidly bourgeois. How do you fancy the position, Meg? Would you care to be married to a man who will go through the rest of his life with the thought that he narrowly missed being one of the richest men in the world?"

"Axel, please . . ." I began.

To my horror, he was crying now, the tears streaming unashamedly down his smooth cheeks. Angry tears. Angrily, like a small boy in a tantrum, he began to beat his bunched fist against the striped silk upholstery of the priceless eighteenth-century sofa, and through his sobs he repeated over and over again the burden of his misery.

"Two others stand between me and the inheritance. That's what he told me, that vile old man. Two! Two lives separating me from—all that!"

And to my mind again came Miss Harriet's words: *There is more than one Demaury . . . who would murder for it!*

CHAPTER FOUR

NEXT DAY, the menfolk of the Palazzo Demaury (all the menfolk, that is, save the recluse on the top floor) followed Lord Peter Chalmers' funeral gondola in procession across the Grand Canal to the Anglican church for the last rites.

It had rained all night, and the skies were still leaden and dripping, the surface of the canal pitted with splashlets, the cross at the top of the dome, opposite, all but hidden in drifting grayness. I stood at my window and watched them set off in six gondolas, the floating hearse in the lead, with the black-draped coffin under a crystal canopy set with nodding black plumes. The men of the Demaury clan wore top hats heavily draped with black crepe. I recognized Bertrand from his bulk, Philippe from his birdlike tallness and leanness. Axel was there: pale from his excesses of the previous evening, and now contrite. I had managed to persuade him to go to bed, and in the end he had departed shamefacedly, like a little boy, pleading my forgiveness for the scene he had made. I falsely framed the words of forgiveness, and later that night found it in my heart to forgive him in fact. Who was I, I asked myself, to judge a man who has had the glittering prize of limitless wealth snatched from under his nose?

The somber procession slid out of my gaze and I closed the shutters against the chill grayness and the slanting rain. Esmeralda was lying down, having succumbed to a blinding headache. She could not abide the very thought of funerals and the mortality and dissolution that they implied. On that, the third day since Peter Chalmers' passing, she was dry-eyed, and had not alluded to her dead fiancé since they had informed her of the arrangements for his obsequies.

I had asked Assunta to come and see me in my quarters, to give her instructions about bringing my meals from the kitchen; and when a knock came upon the door shortly after the funeral party's departure, I went to unlock it—to find not she, but secretary Obadiah. And with an unbelievable message to impart.

"Mr. Giles bids you to attend him in his apartment, Miss Gaunt," he said in awed tones.

"*Me?*" I stared at him unbelievingly.

It was true. I left him standing out in the corridor while I flew to make what reparations I could to my appearance. The chignon I had made on rising had fallen like an unsuccessful loaf of bread and only resumed a reasonable shape again with the support of a battery of hairpins. My nose looked red at the tip, my cheeks too healthy by half. There was a grease spot on the collar of my blouse, which I hastily covered by pinning my jet brooch over the top of it. I looked dreadfully nervous, and if someone had offered me an immediate passage back to England, I would have taken it.

Another tap on the door: it was Obadiah reminding me that time was passing and his master was not to be kept waiting. I took a deep breath, summoned up my courage as best I could, and went out.

Obadiah led me up a narrow back staircase that went directly to the upper floor without connecting with the intermediate stories: Giles's private staircase, I supposed, though he could scarcely have used it since he had been confined to a Bath chair. On reaching the top, the secretary tapped upon a heavy oaken door, and, opening it, motioned me to enter. He closed the door behind me, leaving me alone in a dark-paneled room, at one end of which a log fire burned sullenly in an open grate. It was a stuffy, airless chamber, and smelled of ancient mold.

I was alone. There was an armchair by the fire, and close by it was set a small table, upon which stood a crystal flask containing what looked like water, and a tall drinking glass.

I had the immediate sensation of being watched, and was filled with resentment on this account. If I had been summoned for no other reason than to be spied upon like some animal in a zoo, then the hidden watcher—supposing that I was right in my instinct—would not have the pleasure of seeing me overawed or frightened. I crossed to the exceedingly comfortable looking chair and sat down, disposing my skirts and smoothing the fullness of my sleeves unconcernedly. In a like attitude of assumed casualness, I sat and cooled my heels for ten minutes by my watch, till at length the sound of creaking wheels announced the approach of the recluse of the Palazzo Demaury. The door through which I had entered was opened by a blank-faced lackey. Another followed, pushing the Bath chair.

"Set me before the fire," said the old man. "Do not trouble to get up on my account, Margaret Gaunt."

Since I had pointedly made not the slightest attempt to rise upon his appearance, I supposed the remark to be intended as irony; but the ageless, wrinkled face told me nothing, and his eyes were half closed and hidden from me.

"I hope you are well, Mr. Demaury," I said.

He made no answer, but waved the lackeys to leave us, which they did, bowing deeply and closing the door quietly behind them. A splattering of rain descended the chimney, hissing into clouds of steam among the smoldering logs. Giles Demaury reached out his gloved hands toward the fire, rubbing them together.

"They are burying Esmeralda's late intended, I am informed," he said.

"The party left a little while since," I replied.

"Does Giolitti-Crispi think you killed him?"

Taken aback by the brutal directness of the question, I was thrown off my guard, and cast a shocked glance at my inquisitor. The vivid blue eyes were upon me, and glittering with amusement.

"No, he does not," I replied.

"He's no fool, young Prince Lorenzo," said Giles. "I knew his father, and he was no fool either, for all that he never did aught but drift from one to another of Europe's watering places and fill the interminable hours between sunrise and sunset by gambling, or by simply sitting and watching the world go by. They tell me you are entirely without fortune, child."

I nodded. "That is so," I replied.

He pointed to my fob watch. "But that bauble is worth a pretty penny. Why do you not sell it?"

My hand flew to the watch, and I replied with some heat, "It belonged to my mother. If I were starving, I wouldn't part with it."

The wrinkled, gashlike mouth broadened in a grin, and the brilliant eyes sparkled with sudden amusement. Embarrassed, I let my gaze fall to his feet: those tiny feet in their slippers of black jet.

"Sentiment is a poor substitute for independence," he said. "Any pawnshop would give you fifty guineas for that watch. With fifty guineas, what could you not do? Why, child, you could snap your fingers at that minx Esmeralda and be independent for a year—many young working women exist on far less—till you had found yourself a better position. Oh, fifty guineas at least you would get for it. I paid thirty for it over twenty-five years ago, and the value of a good gold watch is greatly enhanced in these times."

"It was you who gave it to my mother as a wedding present?" I asked him, surprised.

"Indeed it was," he replied. "It was a modest token of the wistful regard I held for your parents. I did not know them well; indeed I only met them on one occasion; but one could not fail to be aware of the almost tactile aura of understanding that existed between them."

Tears prickled my eyes. "Mother only survived my father by a few months," I said. "They told me—those who knew them—that the life went out of her when he had gone, and that nothing—not even her small child—could quicken her again. They said that she withered and passed away before their eyes, and no one could give her any help, any consolation."

"I observed them together," said Giles Demaury. "I do not exaggerate when I say that the outward and visible signs of the great love they bore for each other was for me a quite unforgettable experience."

I gazed at him wonderingly. The simple sincerity in his voice prompted me to essay a subject which I had never dreamed of broaching with the recluse.

"But surely, Mr. Demaury," I said, "you yourself are uniquely able to speak of great love. Yours has been described as one of the great love affairs of the century."

The fire hissed. He did not reply. I thought of the gray waters of the canal flowing past the walls below, and of the mist-shrouded lagoon beyond. And I would have given much to have been able to recall my hasty and ill-advised remark. Here was a man so old that he was almost beyond the reach of life. What right had I to intrude upon the memories that must teem behind that wrinkled forehead?

"Please forgive me . . ." I began.

"The love of Giles Demaury and Estelle Amor," he said, "was of a very different order from that which existed between your parents, my child. In the latter case it was a complementing of two similar hearts and minds, a sweetness and a gentleness that spilled over and blessed the lives—however briefly—of all who came within the orbit of their love.

"We were—fire and air. The passion of one was fed by the fury of the other, and we were indivisible, since our roles constantly shifted: at one moment, Estelle was the searing flame; next, she was burned alive by her lover. We also had the most appallingly vulgar rows."

I saw his gloved hand reach out to take hold of the water flask, and forestalled him by leaping up and pouring the water and handing him the glass. He took it with a nod of thanks and sipped. His hand was trembling.

"It must tire and upset you to speak of the past, Mr. Demaury," I said. "Would you like me to leave you?"

He waved me to be seated again—fussily, the way old folks do. I watched him slowly drain the glass and set it back upon the table.

"Water," he said, "bottled water from Vichy—since the water of Venice is fit only for vermin to drink—is almost my only sustenance. That and a little fruit and an occasional dish of pasta. Oh, when I think of the gargantuan repasts of my youth! The banquets that have taken place in this palazzo. My wife, you know, my Estelle, now she had a most incredible appetite for one of her sex. Yet, would you believe it?—she never showed the slightest sign, but remained as slender as any sylph. But she was very cruel. Very cruel . . ."

His voice died away. The questing, lively eyes clouded, and the hands fell limply to his lap. I watched him with bated breath—and was greatly relieved to detect, from the slight rise and fall of his shoulders, that he was still breathing. Hastily, I assembled my thoughts for something to say, to change the subject.

I said, "Yesterday I went to the Palazzo Giolitti-Crispi and met Prince Lorenzo's mother and sister. They . . ."

"Not cruel, I hasten to add, in a deliberate and premeditated manner," said Giles Demaury, interrupting me. "Not the sort of cruelty that is exercised by persons who are driven by envy, hatred, jealousy, and such. Estelle envied no one—for how could she? She was incapable of hate. Her jealousy was of an order that sparked and died on the instant, as when a flint is struck against metal. I understood that, I understood it perfectly. What I did not understand, what I was unable to come to terms with, was her—casual cruelty."

His voice—that high, clear voice—began to waver, and I had a premonition that he was on the verge of breaking down under the stress of his emotions.

"Mr. Demaury," I said, "you mustn't upset yourself—"

"Casual cruelty that was really no more than an expression of boredom," he said. "When bored, and merely to amuse herself, she would be most appallingly cruel to some poor creature. A maidservant, perhaps. Not out of common envy, as I have explained, not because the girl was too pretty for her taste; indeed, she seemed to take a special delight in wounding the ugly, the weak, the inept. She would wound—and wound deeply. And immediately regret her action. Immediately. The victim would perhaps fly from the room in tears. Estelle would rush after, weeping with contrition. Would shower her victim with kisses, with promises, with presents. Yes, I know how she suffered for her casual cruelty, and what agonies of remorse it cost her."

He shifted in his chair and pulled the cloak more closely about his shoulders, as if with cold, though it was stifling in the airless room.

I said, "I think I see the point you are making, Mr. Demaury. Your wife, I would guess, suffered more from her own actions than those against whom her—casual cruelties, as you call them, were directed. And, surely, that was virtuous."

The shrewd blue eyes flickered over me, seemingly making a new appraisal. He grunted and nodded.

"True enough," he commented. "And I understood that perfectly. But, as I have said before, I was never able to come to terms with that flaw in her character. Nor, indeed, was Estelle always able to wash away her casual cruelties with acts of contrition. Sometimes her cruelty was—*irreversible*."

Something in the inflection of his voice when he uttered the last word made a chill in my heart, and, despite the closeness of the room, I shuddered.

The silence that followed was broken by the chimes of a church bell striking the hour, a sound that was repeated by another, and another, from all of Venice.

"I should like you to come and see me again, child," said Giles Demaury. "I have enjoyed our discourse. You will remember, won't you, what I told you about that watch you are wearing? Do not place too high a premium on sentiment while at the same time bewailing your lack of independence. The selling of that bauble could provide the first step to your freedom. Bear it in mind."

There was no point in further disagreeing with the old man on the subject of my mother's watch, so I muttered something noncommittal and got up to go.

"I look forward to our next meeting, Mr. Demaury," I said.

He took my hand. His touch was cool and dry.

"You greatly resemble your father," he said. "I would say, from my recollection, that you have his eyes and his nose. I have also heard it said that he was a very brave man. Are you brave, Margaret Gaunt?"

"Not very," I admitted.

"You are in no danger here, you know," he said. "Be assured of that. The menace is not directed at you. Did Giolitti-Crispi say that it was? If he did, I am exceedingly disappointed in that young man, whose career I have followed—though at a considerable remove, of course—with a lively interest. No, you need have no fears. No one is trying to kill you."

I was so astonished by his declaration that I could summon up

no answer to it, but merely stared at him and let my hand fall
limply from his grasp.

By some means of communication that evaded my notice, the
two lackeys were made aware that the interview was concluded.
They entered the room and escorted their master to some other
part of his domain, one leading, the other pushing the chair. The
strange trio passed down a shadowy corridor and out of sight, the
wheels of the Bath chair squeaking all the way.

A movement at my elbow made me turn with a start, to see the
ubiquitous Obadiah waiting to lead me downstairs.

Two days passed uneventfully at the Palazzo Demaury, in
which time it never ceased to rain, and I was told that the level of
the lagoon came to within two steps of flooding St. Mark's Square
—an occurrence which had never taken place within living
memory.

With the connivance of the girl Assunta, I took meals in my
room, and no one made any bones about it. I supposed that none
of the Demaury clan so much as noticed my absence from the
dining room. Esmeralda also shunned the company of her relations, and frequently sent down for a luncheon tray. Her mourning attire greatly flattered her delicate fairness, and she had taken
on a most becoming pallor. This I attributed to the fact that she
seldom left her suite, but sat cooped up with all the windows shut
—waiting. Waiting for the summons from above.

She was consumed with curiosity and resentment about my visit
to the top floor of the palazzo, and questioned me closely. I answered her sparingly, but gave her to understand that the idea of
my inheriting a penny piece from her Great-uncle Giles was really
quite preposterous. I almost went so far as to tell her about the
irony of Giles Demaury's seriously advising me to sell my mother's
watch and win myself freedom with the proceeds—but prudently
abstained from doing so. Esmeralda's resentment faded when she
realized that I was not dissembling in any way about my interview
with the recluse of the Palazzo Demaury. But she remained
curious.

"Why, then, did he send for you?" she asked again and again, when we were together in her stuffy sitting room. "You, of all people, Meg."

"I gathered that he rather liked my parents," I said.

"Hmmm."

"Talking of parents, have you heard from Peter's people?" I asked her.

"Not a line," she responded coldly.

Someone—one of the more important of the Demaury menfolk, Bertrand or Philippe, I supposed—had taken the step of telegraphing the Marquess and Marchioness of Lochspiel to inform them of their son's sudden demise and of the funeral arrangements. It was, of course, out of the question for the bereaved parents to travel from Scotland to Venice in time for the obsequies, but one might have expected a reply to the effect that the noble couple were on their way to pay respects at the grave of their departed son. No such message came.

In the long, empty hours of rain, when I was not sitting with Esmeralda (who slept a lot, so I had a lot of empty time to kill), I played chess with Axel in the white drawing room. I am not a good player, for I can never see more than a couple of moves ahead nor concentrate on the careers of more than three pieces at a time, at most. Oddly, though Axel was manifestly a better player than I, I occasionally beat him quite soundly. It did not require a great voyage of the imagination to reason why.

"Four of us," he said, on the second day of the rain. "Since we've been here, Meg, four of us have had the summons."

"Check," I said. "Your King's in check."

"First it was me," said Axel. "Then you, Meg. Yesterday he sent for that silly daughter of Bertrand's, and then her husband, that walking tailor's dummy. Why? I ask myself. Why?"

"I don't think Helena Brayne's at all silly," I told him. "I wouldn't know about her husband, but I think she looks rather nice when she's not looking sulky. And I'm sorry—moving the Knight doesn't help. You're still in check."

He said something in German which did not sound very polite, and then: "But consider, Meg. Since we have been here, he has personally interviewed only four. And of that four—there is no point in beating about the bush—only I had any real expectations of the inheritance. What of the others, I ask? What of Bertrand, who must surely be the strongest contender? What of Philippe?"

I thought for a moment about that, then I said, "Well, Philippe doesn't have any children, but Bertrand has Helena and her husband to succeed him. It's possible that, before entrusting the inheritance to Bertrand, Giles Demaury wanted to assure himself that Bertrand's heiress and her husband are suitable."

"Oh, do you think so?" said Axel, who did not seem to like my reading of the situation.

"It's a possible explanation," I said, adding unhelpfully, "Can you think of a better?"

He shook his head and glumly moved his Queen's Bishop.

"No, I cannot," he said.

"Well, don't despair," I told him. "There may be a dozen other perfectly reasonable explanations." I gently took his Queen's Bishop from the board. "And that's checkmate. Do you want to play again?"

We played one more game, in which I was confidently harrying poor Axel, who was clearly too absorbed in speculations about the legacy to care much about chess.

Having got him into an uncomfortable fix, I relaxed and said, "Surely, after Peter Chalmers' death, Bertrand Demaury isn't going ahead with the proposed party on his yacht for the Feast of the Redentore—that's been canceled, of course."

"That it has not," replied Axel. "There was a family powwow this morning. Esmeralda tactfully wasn't invited; and the question was put to the vote of everyone else present. It was decided to carry on with the arrangements. There will be a party aboard the *Semiramis* throughout the night of Saturday and Sunday, with a sumptuous buffet, and a splendid view of the fireworks and the lantern-lit boats."

"I wonder if Esmeralda will attend?" I mused. "You know, Axel, I shouldn't be a bit surprised if she does. Mourning and all. Do I sound cynical?"

"And you—shall you be going with her?"

"I haven't been asked."

"Your friend the aristocratic policeman has been invited," said

Axel. "He declined Bertrand's last shipboard junket, but he's accepted for this one."

"Has he?" I said with a shrug.

"Yes," said Axel. "Now, why did you just go and make an idiotic move like that, Meg? That's cost you your Queen. And you've put yourself in check!"

I was right about Esmeralda: she made a great play of struggling with her conscience and finally decided that, in mourning or not for her late fiancé, it was her duty to the family to go to the party aboard the *Semiramis* on the night of the Redentore; and she had a dressmaker brought to the palazzo to measure her for an evening gown—in black, of course—for the occasion. And she made it clear that I should also be required to attend, as her companion.

The following day I had two encounters that set me thinking. The first occurred in the palazzo . . .

The sheer size of the building; the fact that, quite apart from the abundance of salons and drawing rooms, all the guests—even one so insignificant as myself—possessed spacious private apartments; and the circumstance that I avoided eating with the others: all these reasons contributed to the result that, in the time that I had been there, I had scarcely had the opportunity to get acquainted with any of the Demaurys save Axel. Next morning I extended my knowledge of the clan by one person. It came about this way: Esmeralda had risen early with a bad temper and the conviction that the dressmaker (who had stayed for over three hours the previous evening, measuring and remeasuring, receiving one immediately countermanded instruction after another, till the poor woman was half out of her wits) had almost certainly forgotten that she, Esmeralda, had finally decided against a train (because of the difficulty in managing it on shipboard) and had emphasized that the cap sleeves must be exaggeratedly tiny, in the current Paris mode. Would I go immediately to the dressmaker's establishment and reiterate the instructions about the train, and take with me one of Esmeralda's new Paris gowns with the correct Paris-style sleeves for the woman to copy?

I agreed with a good grace, looking forward to the expedition, for the rain had abated overnight, and the canal and lagoon glittered in diamonds of reflected sunlight as far as San Giorgio Maggiore. I was provided with a lackey, to carry the Paris gown in a dressbox. We were to travel in the palazzo's gondola, but there was some delay in its return from a trip to the *Semiramis*. Would the *signorina* kindly wait in the morning room?

The morning room was on the ground floor, with windows looking out over the canal to one side and back into the shaded patio on the other. Like most rooms in the palazzo, it was large and gloomy, with overpowering ceiling paintings and heavy furniture. I did not at first notice Helena Brayne standing by the window. She turned from gazing out across the canal when I entered.

"Rupert, I—oh, it's you, Miss Gaunt," she said.

"Good morning, Mrs. Brayne," I replied.

"My husband," she said. "My husband is over in the yacht. I—I'm waiting for his return. He is taking me out to luncheon." She made the closing observation with a note of pride.

"It's a beautiful day," I ventured.

"Yes," she replied. "And after luncheon, we are going to the Isle of Murano. That's where they make the Venetian glass, you know, that's famous all over the world. In my guidebook it says that in bygone days the Venetians considered the secrets of their glassmaking so important to the prosperity of the city that any glassblower who went abroad was automatically condemned to death in his absence. Now, what do you think of that?"

"That's very interesting," I said.

She was no longer attending to me; her eyes had strayed back to the window, to the Dogana, behind which the *Semiramis* lay at anchor.

"What can be keeping him?" she murmured.

"I suppose you must be full of preparations for the party on the yacht?" I asked her, by way of making conversation.

She turned to look at me, almost as if she had just noticed my presence. Her eyes were limpid blue: Demaury eyes. They gazed at me in puzzlement.

"What did you say?" she asked.

"The party," I said. "The arrangements for Saturday's party must keep you and your family busy."

"The servants do all that," she said flatly, and looked back toward the window.

I studied her, there being nothing else to do or say. Helena Brayne possessed a most splendid figure, which was enhanced by a tailor-made costume in royal blue with white facings trimmed with gold braid, high shoulders, and a slight fullness at the back of the skirt. It was not an ensemble that everyone could have worn with success; the beautiful American carried it in the manner of a queen. A queen with a mouth that I had first thought to be petulant—but which, on closer acquaintance, I now saw to be the mouth of a desperately unhappy woman.

Suddenly, she said, "Here comes my husband!" And the blue eyes danced for joy, and the lips softened in a glad smile. I saw in that moment, as clearly as if I had seen into her heart, that Helena loved her polo-playing husband, who had picked her out because of the price label that her father had attached to her.

"I hope you enjoy your luncheon," I said, "and your visit to the isle where they make the glass."

She had no eyes or ears for me, but continued to gaze down till the craft that was carrying her husband finally deposited him at the palazzo steps. She then turned to look at the door through which he might enter—and I saw the full and unashamed glory of her love.

The door opened.

"Rupert, I'm ready when you are—oh, but you've changed."

Rupert Brayne was wearing an excellently cut riding coat and breeches. His high boots were polished to a mirror finish. He eyed his wife across the long room, ignoring me completely.

"I went across to the yacht to change," he said. "I didn't bring all my stuff over with me, you see."

"But—why?"

"Why?" he repeated testily. "Because I'm going for a ride across at the Lido, that's why. I met a feller last night who has stables over there."

"But, Rupert," she said, "you won't have time to get back here for luncheon."

"Who cares?" he replied. "I'll snatch something to eat over at the Lido."

I would have left then, but he was barring the way through the door, and I did not have the assurance either to brush past him or ask his leave to pass. In the event, I stood there and was witness to Helena Brayne's agony.

I saw the hurt pass over her face, cloud her perfect eyes. She drew breath as if to protest: to question him as to why, and how, he could have forgotten what had presumably been a promise made to her idly, absently. Or did he hold her in such low regard that he would deliberately make a promise and then break it knowingly, callously?

The words trembled on her lips—and died there.

Instead, she said, brightly, "Well, have a good time, darling. Don't fall off or anything silly, will you."

He grunted some sort of reply and walked out, closing the door behind him.

She turned to me, her eyes already swimming with the tears that she would have given the world to hide from me.

"I guess—I guess he must have forgotten," she said in a false, bright voice.

The second of my two encounters took place in the bustling city.

After a short voyage by gondola to St. Mark's, the lackey acting as guide took me to the dressmaker's, which was in a narrow alleyway behind the great church. There I was amused—and not entirely surprised—to learn that Esmeralda's worst fears were unfounded; the woman had very clearly remembered that her erratic customer had finally plumped for no train and the very tiny cap sleeves in the Paris manner. Nor did she require the help of any Paris dressmaker's work, she added coldly, eyeing the gown that we had brought. My journey had been wasted.

Yet not wholly wasted. I dismissed the lackey, telling him that I would hire a gondola to take me back to the palazzo. And I went for a walk in the sunshine and the cool shadows.

The narrow streets were crowded, presumably because of the proximity of the Festival of the Redentore, which yearly attracts visitors from near and far. Though it was scarcely ten in the morning, there was an atmosphere of unbridled gaiety in the crowds that passed to and fro all about me. Most of the people were in holiday attire, and the local folk wore wide-brimmed straw hats adorned with ribbons. There was a lot of singing and, from the bucolic appearance of many faces, not a little drinking.

Wandering at will, guided mostly by the movement of the people about me, I drifted in a river of humanity till I came to a pleasant tree-lined square with a fine church at one end and a row of shaded cafes facing it. Feeling the need for midmorning refreshment, I took a seat at a table under one of the cafe awnings and ordered a coffee from a passing waiter.

It was then, and only then, that I looked between the shoulders of two persons sitting nearest to me and saw—her.

Princess Giovanna Giolitti-Crispi was at the next table but one, and so positioned that her profile was turned to me. Her dark hair was drawn up in a becoming chignon under a boater, and she wore a striped blouse with a white lace collar. She was quite unaware of my presence, for she was talking with great animation to a young man seated opposite her. He was about her own age—thirtyish—and Italian by his looks, with a heavy mustache and the air of a working man out for a day's enjoyment, in a shiny blue serge suit, and with a choker knotted about his neck. His hands—large, brown, and work-worn—were clasping those of Princess Giovanna. They had eyes for no one but each other.

The waiter soon brought my coffee, and I sipped at it, taking as much refuge as I could behind the sizable cup. I reckoned that my approach and sitting-down had passed unnoticed by the princess, but must almost certainly have been observed by her companion. My next thought was that I must get away, and speedily, before she turned and saw me.

It was obvious—the merest child would have known—that they were lovers. One had only to see the expression on both their faces, the way in which they looked into each other's eyes, the unyielding clasp of their hands.

And my thoughts went back to the words of Princess Giolitti-Crispi, her mother: her observations on marriages suitable and unsuitable. One did not need to be told—in view of all that—that the mother would certainly regard her daughter's holding hands with a workman in a public place as something approaching a *mésalliance*.

Though public, it was clearly a secret meeting: secret from her mother, and presumably from the rest of her family.

And what—I asked myself, nearly choking on my coffee with sudden alarm—if, turning to see me sitting there, and instantly recognizing me, she formed the opinion that I had been spying on the two of them?

Escape—and immediately. No time to finish the coffee. I lowered the cup, gathered up my reticule, slid quietly out of my seat, and tiptoed silently away, grateful when I was able to turn my back on the princess and her lover. She would certainly never recognize me from the back view, even if she looked round at me.

I had not gone more than a half dozen paces, when:

"*Signorina*—hey!"

The waiter! In my haste to escape, I had forgotten to leave money for the coffee!

I heard his approaching footsteps. Without turning, I fumbled in my reticule, praying silently that my fingers would speedily light upon a large enough coin to settle the score. I opened my purse, tried to take out a handful of money, overturned the purse in my haste. A shower of coins fell to my feet and rolled everywhere.

I closed my eyes in agony; opened them a few moments later to see a smiling mustached face—*his* face—beaming amiably down on me. He was holding a pile of coins in his hand. Beyond, over his shoulder, I met the suddenly shocked and resentful eyes of Princess Giovanna.

On Saturday morning, the day of the festival, I was awakened early by the sounds in the canal below my window. Leaping out of bed and throwing my peignoir about my shoulders, I ran to the window and opened the shutters part way to look out.

I gasped to see that the waterway below was almost entirely hidden by throngs of jostling boats: gondolas large and small, rowboats, sailboats, steamboats, canoes, barges, all of them moving one way: toward the Dogana and the lagoon beyond. The noise was clamorous, with voices raised in song, with the jangle of guitars and mandolins, the staccato notes of a concertina. The sound of an entire band drew louder and closer, taking over from the lesser sounds, till the ensemble from St. Mark's Square was carried below my window in a barge, the white-haired conductor drawing forth their music with his baton, his fingertips, his restless eyes. So early in the day, and the festival had already begun!

Esmeralda was in one of her most demanding moods that morning. I went to see her immediately after I had had my breakfast of coffee and new-baked rolls (brought up by Assunta; despite Giles Demaury's assurances of my safety, I had adhered to Prince Lorenzo's advice—just as he had continued to station a police officer, day and night, in the ground floor of the palazzo). She was fussing about her evening gown, which had just been delivered. It stood on a dressmaker's dummy in the center of her magnificent bedroom. The dressmaker and her assistants must have worked day and night to complete it, and the effect was quite stunning. I hastened to assure her that she would look quite perfect, and bethought me how I should compare with her—I in my one and only dinner gown that scarcely merits a description.

The junketing on the canal continued all day. As evening approached, the lights of countless Chinese lanterns made the surface of the water sparkle like fire. It was dark when the gondolas came to take the Demaury clan—myself included—over to the *Semiramis*, where we should enjoy a grandstand view of the climax of the night's proceedings: the discharge of fireworks. I traveled with Esmeralda, Helena Brayne, and her husband. Esmeralda had livened up her somber ensemble by the addition of a magnificent parure of diamonds—tiara, necklace, bracelet, and ring, all set in platinum—that had belonged to her mother. She glittered in the night.

Helena Brayne's mouth had resumed the petulant, downward-turning look that I had first noticed. Her husband was a bored, handsome face above a starched white shirt front. And thus we came to the yacht: a lean shape lying close by the Dogana, blazing all over with fairy lights, with white-clad sailors lining her rails to welcome us with cheers.

"I must say the old man's doing us damned proud," drawled Rupert Brayne.

Bertrand Demaury was there with his wife to greet each and every one of his guests—myself included—when we had been handed up the accommodation ladder, by earnest sailors, to the scrubbed white quarterdeck. I offered him my hand, and his bright, astute eyes swept over me.

"Good evening, my dear," he said. "How did you find Giles when he summoned you?"

"I found him most agreeable," I replied.

"That was exactly the experience of my daughter and son-in-law," he said. "I've always been convinced that the old devil's bark is worse than his bite, and that one has only to get him on his own and he is quite human. Ah, good evening to you, Philippe. And how are you, Countess?" He murmured in my ear, "Go and get yourself a glass of champagne and a bite to eat, my dear."

I turned and saw Prince Lorenzo standing by a buffet table that glittered with silver and glassware under the fairy lights. He bowed to me. A blue watered-silk sash spanned his shirt front, and the star of an order was attached to the left breast of his evening tailcoat.

I gave him my hand. He bowed over it, and I felt the light brush of his lips through my glove.

"All is well?" he asked quietly. "You have experienced nothing else to arouse your fears?"

"Nothing," I told him. "In fact I have received assurances from none other than Giles Demaury that I am in no danger."

"Have you now?" One dark eyebrow was raised, and the unwavering glance searched me. "Did he so?"

"He put it rather oddly," I said. "He told me—how did he phrase it?—that the menace is not directed at me. He added, also, that he was disappointed in you for alarming me."

A smile flittered across his lips and was instantly gone.

"Never straying a step from the top floor of the Palazzo Demaury," he said wryly, "Mr. Demaury is singularly ill-placed to criticize the police. Or perhaps he is not. We shall see. Are you taking champagne, Miss Gaunt? Permit me. Waiter, a glass here."

"Is Princess Giolitti-Crispi here tonight?" I asked him.

"No," he replied. "My mother does not attend social functions any longer."

"And your sister?"

"My sister." For the first time ever, I thought I detected a wavering—no more than a slight shifting, as when a breeze ruffles the surface of a lake—in those resolute gray eyes. "My sister, also, does not mix in Society."

Did he know, I wondered, that his sister was a very ardent mixer in society of her own choosing? I thought back to the silent fury in Princess Giovanna's face when, despite all, I had seemed to have betrayed myself as an eavesdropper; how she had immediately turned her back and refused to acknowledge our acquaintanceship.

"But you are here," I said. "And are you here in a social capacity, or on duty?"

"A little of both, Miss Gaunt," he said.

An orchestra struck up the lively "Barcarolle" from *The Tales of Hoffmann*, and I saw Bertrand Demaury had hired the ensemble from St. Mark's Square for the occasion: they were grouped behind the buffet table, every man with a fully charged glass by his feet.

"Miss Esmeralda looks very fine in her mourning," said Prince Lorenzo. "Grief becomes her mightily."

I followed his glance. Indeed, Esmeralda was at her ravishing best, and charming the wits out of one of Bertrand's entourage, an exceedingly handsome young man with red hair.

"Poor Peter Chalmers," I said. "I'm afraid there were few tears shed for him. Even his parents, you know, never so much as acknowledged the telegram informing them of his death."

"I would have been very surprised if they had," he replied.

"Why do you say that?" I asked.

"Don't you know?" he countered, looking at me with one eyebrow raised. "Surely Miss Esmeralda must have told you. The Lochspiels have not spoken to their son for years. He was forbidden to set foot over the threshold of the family castle till his father's death. The old man would have barred him from succeeding to the marquisate if it had been possible."

I stared at him, bemused.

"Esmeralda never knew that," I said. "She was to have visited her prospective in-laws this summer."

He shook his head. "If Chalmers told her that, he was lying," he said. "The Lochspiels would never have received her, or him."

"But—why? Why?" I asked.

The searching gray eyes searched me out.

"You knew the quality of the man," he said. "None better."

"Yes," I faltered.

"There was more," he said. "Much more. A married woman killed herself for him. There was also an American heiress—but it would be indelicate to go into that. He was also heavily in debt. Did Miss Esmeralda know that?"

"I'm sure she had no idea," I said.

"And it was worse even than that," he said. "Chalmers had committed fraud. Issued worthless checks at his club. Forged his father's name to obtain loans. I doubt if he could have survived the year without writs being issued against him."

"Before the end of the year," I said, "if he had lived, he would have married Esmeralda. Then his financial problems would have been at an end."

Prince Lorenzo nodded. "Particularly if she had succeeded to the control of the Demaury fortunes," he said. And then, in a lighter, bantering tone of voice: "Tell me, Miss Gaunt, do you have any expectations in that direction?"

"None at all," I told him.

"A pity," he said. "I have a philosophy about wealth—inherited wealth. If I had it in my power to bequeath a very large fortune to whom I chose, I think I would go out in the highways and byways of this earth and find someone—a total stranger to me, without doubt—who possessed that elusive and ineffable quality that should go with effortless, inherited wealth."

"And what is that quality?" I asked him.

"Style is the name of the quality," he replied. "And style is what *you* have, Miss Gaunt."

I suppose my mouth must have sagged open and I must have looked very foolish. The orchestra stopped playing the "Barcarolle" and I think a galaxy of rockets burst into many-colored fragments high over the lagoon. I think I may have spilled some champagne down my skirt. I only know that at that moment I would not have changed places with Esmeralda Demaury for all her parure of diamonds.

"*Mon cher Prince!*"

It was Philippe Demaury's French countess. Prepared only to acknowledge the presence of a fellow aristocrat of title, she swept past me without a glance and held out her white-gloved hand to Prince Lorenzo, who took it and brushed a kiss upon her fingertips. She immediately engaged him in rapid French, to which he replied in the same language. I was totally excluded, for it was obviously not her intention that I should play any part in the conversation. I turned away, and saw Miss Harriet approaching me, a glass of champagne in one hand and a leg of cold roast chicken in the other. She was wearing her white tulle gown covered in rhinestones—now perceptibly grubbier, even under flattering fairy lights. But her raddled, painted face showed a heartwarming pleasure to see me.

"My dear Meg," she said. "Oh, I am so happy for you. Come over here, do. Let us sit down and have a little chat."

Puzzled and amused at her manner of addressing me, I did as I was bidden. We took seats side by side near the ship's rail. Miss Harriet gnawed a large piece of meat from her chicken leg and masticated it with rapid movements of her jaw. The hush following the orchestral piece was taken up by a buzz of conversation all round us. From near at hand, I heard Philippe Demaury's countess saying: "*Mon cher Prince, je suis désolée . . .*"

"Why, Miss Harriet, are you happy for me?" I asked.

"Mmmm—mmmm." She indicated by pointing to her mouth that speech was out of the question. I composed myself to wait with amused patience. Meanwhile, it was curiously pleasant to sit here and gaze about me; to enjoy a quite remarkable new feeling that had seemed to begin a very short while ago: a feeling that I could not put a name to, nor find a reason for; something just out of reach of my memory, but one that would come back to me, I knew, in a moment of tranquility.

A feeling of—what?

Joy? Yes, there was joy; but joy was waking on a summer's morning and hearing the pigeons calling in the far copses, the scent of new-cut hay, children's laughter, bare feet in a running stream. The new joy was not of a piece with all those things. What, then . . . ?

"You have made a good choice, my gel," declared Miss Harriet presently.

"Indeed, Miss Harriet?" I replied. "And what choice is that?"

She seemed not to hear me, but went on: "Not a penny piece in hard cash to bless themselves with, of course. Everything's entailed: pictures, furniture, silver, the lot. Don't like the old woman. Never have. Stuck-up old baggage. But the father was a fine fellow, and a fine figure of a man, I can tell you. Heh! I remember him well." She chuckled to herself.

"Miss Harriet," I said cheerfully. "Before you take another bite of your chicken, please be so kind as to enlighten me. What *are* you talking about, Miss Harriet?"

"Why, him, of course," she said, pointing with the leg of chicken to where Lorenzo Giolitti-Crispi was listening with an air of patient and attentive boredom to the countess. "Bless me, gel, you don't have to play the innocent with me. It's written all over you. Saw it as soon as I clapped eyes on you together.

"You're head over heels in love with the feller. Look at you now: eyes shining like stars, and blushing like a rose."

I am in love—in love . . . I tried it silently, at first. Then in a whisper, to accustom myself to the strangeness of the phrasing, the unaccustomed conjunction of the "I" with a fairly commonplace sentiment: the fact of being in love, of loving another person. Of loving a man.

Miss Harriet had been right, of course. She had seen the bud burst into flower in my mind at the moment when he—Lorenzo (that was another thing, I should have to get used to calling him Lorenzo, in my mind)—had offered me the graceful compliment of possessing style. He had smiled when saying it. A galaxy of colored rockets had chosen to burst overhead. And Margaret Gaunt, spinster of the parish of Hardbook in the County of Cambridge, had fallen in love.

"Oh, the sound of those awful fireworks is going through and through my brain. Meg, shut that silly round window, do!" wailed Esmeralda.

"I think it's called a porthole," I said indulgently, obeying.

Esmeralda had been taken with one of her "heads." Its coming on had blessedly saved me from further embarrassing probings from Miss Harriet, and I had accompanied Esmeralda down below deck, to a comfortable cabin decorated with red plush and gold. I had loosened her corset and she was lying back on the satin bedcover with a handkerchief sprinkled with eau de cologne over her face.

"I think a little nap would do me good," said Esmeralda.

"I'm sure it would, dear," I agreed. "Would you like me to go away and leave you?"

"Yes. No—stay and talk to me for a while."

This was Esmeralda from nursery days, when she had never wanted to be left in the dark, when I had so often sat and read her to sleep.

"What do you want to talk about?" I asked her.

Silence, and then: "Meg, how long do you think I should stay in mourning for Peter?"

"I've really no idea," I replied. "I've always been a little vague about the etiquette connected with mourning."

"A year—six months?"

"Well," I said. "Since you were only engaged, and not married to Peter, I should think six months would be ample."

"Less than six months, do you think? Three months, perhaps?"

I considered, and said, "More than three months, I think, and less than six months."

"Four months?"

"That sounds about right to me, Esmeralda."

"Mmmm. I think I should like you to turn out the main light and leave me to have a nap now, Meg."

I turned off the big overhead chandelier, and went for the door.

"Meg," came the voice from under the cologne-sprinkled handkerchief.

"Yes?"

"Don't you think auburn hair is tremendously attractive in men?"

"I've never really thought about it," I said. "Why do you ask?"

"Oh, no reason. Meg . . ."

"Yes?"

"I think three months would be quite sufficient time for mourning," she said. "After all, as you point out, I wasn't actually *married* to poor Peter."

"If you feel happy about three months, let it be three months," I told her.

No reply. I went out and quietly shut the door. So that was it. A very familiar pattern. Off with the old and on with the new. Esmeralda had fallen under the spell of the good-looking redheaded man in Bertrand's entourage; or, to put it more accurately, she had fallen for the delight of weaving a spell about that unfortunate young man. But even Esmeralda, at her most outrageous, could not openly flirt in full mourning—and in front of her assembled clan at that. And Esmeralda, faced with a dilemma of that sort, simply had one of her "heads." It had been the same since childhood: let Esmeralda be denied anything (not that she had ever been denied much), and she developed a headache. Or tantrums.

I smiled to myself and shook my head. Poor Esmeralda and her doings seemed very trivial and unimportant now.

I hastened my steps along the corridor leading from the cabin where I had left Esmeralda. Somewhere up above my head, *he* was standing, free now, perhaps, of the enveloping countess. Free, perhaps, to talk to me . . .

"*Damn you, is it true?*"

"*Damn you, what if it is?*"

Angry voices. Coming from an open cabin door ahead of me. And I recognized them immediately: the first voice carried Bertrand's harsh, nasal accents; the reply was delivered in the French-inflected tones of his cousin Philippe.

"By all that's holy, I could kill you with my own hands! You infernal—"

The tableau, frozen in midmotion, was presented to my horrified gaze as I drew abreast of the door: the two men posed in the middle of the floor; Bertrand, the shorter and stockier, with one hand reached out to grasp his cousin's lapel, the other fist raised to strike; Philippe, tall and willowy, recoiling from the other's grasp. And both men turning their heads to stare at me, wide-eyed.

I averted my gaze and hurried on.

There was no sign of Lorenzo on the upper deck. I made discreet and oblique inquiries (the subterfuges one gets up to when one is in love—how soon I was to learn!), and discovered that he had been summoned on urgent police business and had just left the yacht.

Venice under the stars.

I stood at the rail with Axel, who pointed out the details of the glorious panorama of light and darkness that stretched before us. The *Semiramis*, lying at her anchor off the Dogana point, commanded a view of the long island called La Giudecca, upon which stands the Church of the Redentore, built as a thanks offering to commemorate the end of a plague that had raged in Venice in the sixteenth century, and it was this church that gave the festival its name.

The broad canal separating the city from La Giudecca was a mass of boats of every kind. Every craft that bobbed and dipped upon the dark waters was decorated with branches and Chinese lanterns: countless pinpoints of light stretching across the wide sweep of the canal, from end to end. Everyone would spend the whole night on the water, explained Axel, and they would feast upon mulberries, the traditional repast of the festival. Later, most would cross the lagoon to the Lido, there to wait the coming of dawn.

Someone shuddered at my elbow. I turned to see the raddled face of Miss Harriet, white as a clown's in the lamplight.

"I'm cold," she said peevishly. "Will someone fetch me a cognac?"

A cascade of rockets spluttered in the sky above La Giudecca, illuminating the buildings beneath it, and the serried lines of boats before them, in an intense light, so that one could count every window and every column, every upturned face. Glancing sidelong at my fellow guests, I saw Helena Brayne, beautiful and tragic-eyed in a gown of white silk, like a new bride. Her husband was not with her.

The rockets died in the sky. All Venice gave a murmur of appreciation, quite clearly, from out of the darkness about us.

"Do you know, Meg," said Axel, "this nautical life has made me feel quite hungry. How about you?"

I was wryly amused to discover that the revelation of my love for Lorenzo Giolitti-Crispi had not banished my own grosser appetites. The sight of the buffet table looked distinctly tempting. I allowed my escort to lead me over there.

Bertrand Demaury's chef stood proud sentinel over the finest fare that Venice could provide from the markets of the Rialto, as Axel explained to me. There were the fruits of the sea: crab, lobster, oysters, and mussels in wine; shrimp and octopus, scampi and John Dories. And cheeses: gorgonzola and parmesan, cream cheeses of suavely tempting consistency. And freshly cooked pastas: tagliatelli, spaghetti, vermicelli, taglierini, fanti—Axel reeled off all the names, while the chef beamed and nodded. I remembered Bertrand Demaury's furious face as I had seen it through the open cabin door earlier on.

Axel and I ate spaghetti with a subtle cheese sauce at a table for two near the orchestra, who were playing a Viennese waltz with a very great deal of vibrato.

"Would you say that Bertrand and his cousin Philippe are very friendly to each other?" I asked him.

"No one member of the Demaury clan is friendly to any other member of the clan," declared Axel. "That is the first proposition. Secondly, I would say that, of all the clan, Uncle Bertrand and Uncle Philippe are demonstrably most at odds. I will rephrase that—they detest the sight of each other."

"Why?" I asked.

"Two reasons spring to mind," said Axel. "First, they are the principal contenders for Giles's controlling stake in the Demaury empire. And if that were not enough to set two Demaurys at each other's throats, there's the matter of the Panama scandal."

"Panama scandal," I repeated. "Yes, I remember the two of them arguing about Panama when first I saw them together at the palazzo."

"You may or may not have followed the affair in the newspapers," said Axel. "Briefly, what happened was this: when Fer-

dinand de Lesseps was appointed president of the company set up
to build a canal across the Isthmus of Panama, everyone flocked
to invest their money in the enterprise, on the premise that what
De Lesseps could do in Suez, he could also do in Panama. In fact,
as is now perfectly apparent, no one will *ever* devise a means to
build a Panama canal. Mismanagement and corruption brought
the company to bankruptcy. A lot of people lost a very great deal
of money. One of them was Uncle Bertrand."

"And how does that concern Philippe?" I asked.

Axel wound up a long string of spaghetti on the end of his fork
with deft expertise, and said, "Philippe it was who gave Bertrand
the tip, very early on in the enterprise, to buy shares in the Panama Company. Bertrand lost more than he could afford."

"Oh!" I exclaimed.

"Oh, indeed," said Axel. "And the fact that Philippe also got
his fingers burnt was no consolation to Bertrand. He will never
forgive him. Never."

I toyed with the notion of telling Axel of the incident below
deck of which I had been the unwilling witness—but rejected it.
What business was it of mine? What business, indeed, when another, and infinitely delightful, field of speculation lay open to
me?

Axel was continuing his answer to my question: particularizing
about Philippe, Bertrand, and their quarrels over the Panama
affair. I listened with my eyes, nodded and smiled, frowned at all
the right places. (The art of seeming to be an enrapt listener
while one's mind is roaming in distant and more entrancing pas-
tures is an accomplishment that I had picked up during my life
with Esmeralda. I suppose that impoverished companions of rich
ladies are all adept at it.) And I thought about Lorenzo.

Only half accustomed to the notion of being in love, I could
not bring myself to consider what his feelings might be toward
me. He had said that I possessed "style." Well, some furniture has
style. Also some garden statuary. I have always thought that the
Princess of Wales has tremendous style; likewise Mr. Oscar
Wilde, the dramatist. What quality of style did Lorenzo see in
me? I wondered. He had called it—what was his phrase?—an elusive and ineffable quality that should go with effortless, inherited

wealth. Well he should know, for though Miss Harriet had said that the Giolitti-Crispis were short of hard cash (was that why they could not afford to keep servants other than the old man and woman?), if the evidence of his palazzo was anything to go by, he had been brought up in the very lap of inherited wealth. But how could he possibly detect such a quality in me, who had only lived as a poor relation, by grace and favor, in the shadow of great wealth? It was very puzzling.

Axel was still talking, and I directed my attention toward him sufficiently to deduce that he was still explaining the details of the Panama scandal.

He was interrupted—all conversation, everything on the lamplit deck of the *Semiramis* was interrupted—by a terrible cry. Halfway between a scream and a shout; hoarse, penetrating, commanding all attention; the sound of a human being in mortal terror.

It was almost immediately followed by a shout from farther along the deck: "MAN OVERBOARD!"

"Great heaven!" exclaimed Alex, leaping to his feet and rushing to the rail. "Who can have gone over?"

I joined him there, with the others. We peered down and out, into the swirling black waters below us. There was no light down there; the illuminated boats were massed some distance away, in the center of the canal, and the fairy lights strung across the decks of the yacht did not reach to the deep shadows at her waterline.

"There he is! There!" Somebody shouted and pointed.

I saw a head bobbing past below, close by the white-painted hull; saw lean hands scrabble and try to take hold of the smooth side as the current pulled them away. The man—it was a man—was choking and screaming for help.

"Call a boat!" I heard Axel cry out.

Someone was shouting to the boats out in the middle of the canal to come and help. I saw a life belt splash into the water, but the victim had been swept far from where it fell. He was almost at the yacht's stern, and would be lost in the darkness beyond in a matter of seconds.

"Here goes!"

I looked up to see Axel climbing the rails. He had thrown off his coat and shoes. He clung there for an instant, as if steeling himself. A woman's voice called to him to stop.

He jumped, and landed with a splash below us, disappeared from sight, came back into view some distance toward the stern, and with powerful strokes of his shirt-sleeved arms, set off in the direction in which his quarry had gone.

A ship's boat must have already been lowered and waiting by the companionway, for it swept into sight round the sharp bowsprit within moments, and sliced past below, the oarsmen going at full stretch. With the chorus of shouts and pointing fingers—in which I joined—to guide them, they were so obviously in close and accurate pursuit that there was a perceptible relaxing of tension on the upper deck. We looked at each other and gave sighs of relief.

"He'll be all right," drawled Rupert Brayne, lighting a cigarette. "The German feller will catch him and the boat will catch 'em both."

"Who was it fell overboard, hey?" demanded Miss Harriet, peering round the assembled company with her kohl-streaked eyes narrowed shortsightedly. "Who's missing, hey?"

Everyone looked to his neighbor.

"Maybe it was one of the crew."

"I don't see Bertrand!" essayed another.

A shout from out of the darkness sent us rushing to the rail once again. The white-painted boat reappeared. One of the *Semiramis*'s officers, standing at the poop, called out to it.

"What news? Have you got them?"

"Yes! Both!"

"Both safe?"

"One of 'em's unconscious. Best get a doctor!"

Unconscious! We hung with bated breath over the rails, to see the boat pass by below. They had lit a lantern in its stern, by the light of which I could see, with a sudden stab of relief, that Axel was crouched on one of the stern seats. He looked up, saw me, waved and shouted something. The same thin rays of the lantern illuminated the pale face of the man who lay on the planking by Axel's feet.

It was Philippe Demaury.

A scream made me turn with a start of shock. The countess was close by me, her heavily beringed hands pressed to her cheeks, her eyes staring down toward her husband. She was still standing in the same posture, staring, unmoved to any other reaction, when sailors carried Philippe Demaury's limp form up into the lamplight and laid him down on the deck.

I rushed to greet Axel, who looked exhausted, He grinned weakly at me.

"That was very brave of you, Axel," I told him. "You could have been drowned."

"It was a close thing," he said. "He grabbed at me in his panic and it was like the grip of a madman. We could both have gone down together."

"But you saved him."

Axel shook his head, looked sidelong at the tragic figure of the countess gazing in unbelieving horror at her husband, who was being ministered to by three sailors, one pushing down sharply upon the unconscious man's chest, the others chafing his hands and feet.

"He was already under water when I came upon him," he murmured in my ear. "It was only by his clutching hand that I found him, and it's likely that he had just gone down for the last time."

"Oh, no!" I breathed. "You mean . . . ?"

"The grip he put on me could have been his death throes," murmured Axel. "I never was so held by any living man!"

The sailors' attentions having no visible effect upon the victim, some of the frantic onlookers shouted wild and drastic-sounding remedies of which they had heard. One averred with considerable force of argument that the nozzle of a common pair of bellows, placed into the victim's nose, and the bellows being violently pumped, will set the lungs functioning again; another declared that warm bricks under the armpits had a similar effect. Neither expedient being possible with the means to hand aboard a yacht, it was left to the sailors to continue their less dramatic ministrations. This they did till the arrival of a doctor—the small man in the large hat who had attended the dying Peter Chalmers—put an end to their efforts.

Kneeling by the victim, the little doctor won himself an audience of breathless silence as he sounded the heart with his stethoscope and felt the pulse. He then informed us quietly that it was useless to continue with the attempts at resuscitation: life was extinct.

The countess cried out in a loud and terrible voice:

"*Assassin! Murderer!*"

Vehement, eyes flaring, she pointed across the circle of shocked faces surrounding her drowned husband. All eyes—mine included—followed her finger: to the rotund countenance of Bertrand Demaury, which was suddenly washed of everything but terror.

CHAPTER FIVE

SO FAR as the Demaury clan was concerned, it was the end of the Festival of the Redentore. The fireworks displays lasted far into the night; as dawn showed its first light in the east, the masses of boats moved over to the distant, low-lying strip of the Lido; later that morning, a long procession crossed over a bridge of boats connecting St. Mark's with the Church of the Redentore on La Giudecca; priests and acolytes leading, with censers swinging and chants rising to the high blue sky. I saw the procession from a porthole of a cabin that I had been allocated aboard the *Semiramis*. Esmeralda not having wakened, I elected to remain aboard with her instead of joining most of the shocked and silent remainder, who had preferred to return to the palazzo.

The countess had been the first to leave: borne off by one of her dead husband's entourage. After the single accusing outburst, she had collapsed in a paroxysm of weeping, and had wept, still, when the gondola bore her into the night.

I never saw what arrangements were made for the drowned man: the body was discreetly carried away. Bertrand simply disappeared after the countess's denunciation.

I told Esmeralda the terrible news upon her waking. Her baby-blue eyes widened with shock. I then noticed a slyness creep into them. Was she calculating that the passing of Philippe meant one less strong contender between her and the inheritance? The Demaury streak again!

"And you say that the countess accused Bertrand?" she asked. "Why ever would she do a thing like that?"

"Apart from the matter of the inheritance," I said, "they had had some quarrel over the business of the Panama canal scheme. Axel was telling me." I saw no point in confiding in her about the quarrel to which I had been witness so short a time before the tragedy.

"But—what did she mean about Bertrand *killing* Philippe?" persisted Esmeralda. "Did she mean that he pushed him overboard?"

"I suppose so," I said. "Perhaps Philippe couldn't swim. The brief glimpse I had of him in the water gave me the impression of someone who couldn't swim." I shuddered at the memory of that white, frightened face; the long fingers scrabbling for a hold against the smooth side and finding none.

There came a tap on the cabin door.

"Who is it?" I called.

"Chief steward, ma'am. Prince Lorenzo conveys his compliments to Miss Gaunt, and will she please attend him in the saloon at her convenience?"

Lorenzo was back aboard the *Semiramis!*

"I'll be there in a few moments," I answered.

"Very well, ma'am."

Esmeralda sat up and reached for her looking glass from the bedside table.

"I expect he'll want to see me afterward," she said. "He's really quite attractive, don't you think? And from one of the oldest noble families in Venice, you know. Oh, dear me, I look such a fright. Why did you let me go to bed in my clothes? And I've simply nothing to change into."

With an unworthy twinge of jealous resentment, I noted that, despite everything, Esmeralda looked as fresh as if she had just stepped out of a bandbox. Even her skirt and bodice, though she had lain in them all night on top of the counterpane, were smooth and uncreased; and the slightest touch was enough to tame her sleek blond hair to acquiescence. I, who had slept—and slept badly, haunted by visions of drowning—in my underwear, looked as if I had been dragged through a hedge backward.

With a sigh, I patted my unruly chignon into some sort of order, and smoothed my skirt, which seemed to have taken on a shape that had not been intended by the little dressmaker in Cambridge who had made it for me.

"I'd better get along to the saloon," I said.

"Come straight back and tell me how you got on," demanded Esmeralda.

The *Semiramis*'s saloon—its principal cabin—was a large and splendidly appointed apartment that occupied all below the poop deck at the rear of the vessel. It was extremely light and airy by reason of wide windows that let out onto a stern gallery where one could sit out and enjoy the views.

It was in the stern gallery that he—Lorenzo—was awaiting me. He rose from a deck chair on my arrival, and my heart gave a lurch when he smiled gravely, bowed, and took my offered hand.

"Good morning, Miss Gaunt," he said. "Yet another tragedy has struck this gathering, then. I hope you have recovered from the worst of the shock."

"I have to admit that I slept badly," I told him.

"Shall we be seated?" He indicated a pair of deck chairs.

I sat down, eyeing him covertly as soon as his gaze was elsewhere. He was dressed in black, as ever, but less formally than before: in a braid-trimmed suit of a more casual cut, and he wore a silk bow instead of the severe black stock. My attention drifted to his hands; I was fascinated by the latent power in their stillness as they lay upon his lap. Then I gave a start, seeing that he was looking at me again.

"Do not be alarmed," he said. "This is not to be another interrogation. I have interrogated everyone still aboard. Everyone save Miss Esmeralda—who was not on deck last night—and Mr. Bertrand Demaury, who is indisposed. What I have to say to you, Miss Gaunt, is something quite different from an interrogation. I am asking for your help."

"I—help you?" I replied. "Indeed, I should be most delighted. But—how in the world?"

A black gondola swept past below us, the man at the oar leaning far forward with every stroke, his bare feet precariously balanced upon the narrow piece of deck upon which they were placed. Looking up, he saw my companion, and, recognizing him, lifted a hand from his oar and saluted. Lorenzo acknowledged with a wave. The canal was still crowded with boats, and the bridge of boats bore a constant procession to the Church of the

Redentore opposite us. Their chanting reached us quite clearly across the water.

"Miss Gaunt, I have formed a very favorable opinion of your intelligence," said Lorenzo. "Your immediate grasp of a situation, your acute powers of observing detail, impress me greatly."

"Thank you, Prince Lorenzo," I said in a small voice. It was a cold pebble to be handed by the man to whom one had so recently given one's heart: to be told that one is intelligent, quick-witted, observant. Though no raving beauty, I have nice hands, and my teeth and complexion have been commented upon favorably. Why not mention *that*? I screamed to him silently.

"I recall, for example, the question of who passed you the Borgia goblet on the night of that memorable dinner party," he said. "And how you were swift to appreciate the significance of the fact that no one, yourself included, was able to name that person."

"Mmmm," I responded. And if my hair *is* nondescript and unmanageable, I told him in my mind, my green eyes have not gone unnoticed. So why don't *you* notice them?

"In view of this, Miss Gaunt, I have decided to ask for your help," he said. "Indeed, I have hopes that you will be my—collaborator—in the solving of this case. For there is a case, I assure you. As Lord Peter was, in my view, deliberately poisoned by the Borgia goblet, so was Philippe Demaury deliberately pushed from the deck of this yacht."

I was absorbing the sudden delight of his proposal: that I should be his collaborator, that I should actually *work* with him, when his comment on the cause of Philippe's death—soberly delivered, and the more impressive for that—shocked me out of such frivolity.

"Pushed?" I echoed. "But, from where? The ship's rails are quite high. How could anyone push a grown man over waist-high rails, and in full view of anyone who happened to glance in that direction, without being observed?"

"A good question, Miss Gaunt." The gray eyes were upon me, approvingly. I retreated before them; looked hastily down at my hands. "A good question. However, our murderer—and I am more and more convinced that the Palazzo Demaury harbors a murderer among its guests—was able to take advantage of the chance circumstance that, a short time prior to the tragedy, the sailors had taken aboard a further supply of champagne and other liquors to supplement the buffet. In doing so, they had removed a short section of the ship's rails—they are easily detached by means of screws—in order to lift the crates, by means of ropes, from the boats below."

"So the murderer . . ." I interposed.

"So the murderer, Miss Gaunt," he said, "observing the gap in the rails—which was some distance from the poop deck of the yacht, where the party was assembled, and in a relatively dark place under the bridge—the murderer had only to entice Philippe Demaury, on some pretext, to the vicinity of the gap in the rails, which the sailors had delayed in replacing, and he—or she—almost literally had a murder weapon in his—or her—hands."

He was so clever, so devastatingly overbearing. Half of me melted to those gray eyes; the other half of me resented that he thought of me only as being intelligent, quick-witted, observant. Well, let him have the benefit of those qualities . . .

"Or Philippe Demaury may simply have wandered along the deck," I said, "paused by the gap in the rails, failing to notice it—and fallen through."

The gray eyes flickered. I thought I had him checkmated; not so.

"It was not all *that* dark by the gap," he said. "Demaury must have seen it. Moreover—as I am informed—he was acutely aware that he could not swim a stroke. Add to that, he had an intense dislike of the water. No, Miss Gaunt, you will not easily persuade me that, given all those conditions, a man would accidentally drown himself. No, it simply will not do."

"Then who pushed him?" I countered.

Lorenzo spread his hands. "Who indeed?" he asked. "Let us examine the question, Miss Gaunt. First, let us for a while put aside the temptation to pursue the countess's hysterical accusation. Let us instead address ourselves to the question: Who could *not* have pushed him? Who—from the evidence of your eyes?"

"Not I, for a start," I said.

"Naturally not. And who else?"

"Axel. Axel von Wuppertal. He was sitting and talking to me when we heard the cry."

I detected a frown flicker across his brow, but it disappeared almost immediately.

"You are quite sure of that? Von Wuppertal did not leave you for an instant at any time immediately preceding the cry?"

"I am quite sure," I said. "I remember that he was talking to me about the Panama scandal." And I was thinking about you, I added to myself.

"The Panama scandal. Ha!" His gray eyes narrowed. "And what was Von Wuppertal saying about the affair?"

"I—" I faltered. There was so much of what Axel had said that —for reasons I could not possibly divulge to my companion, my "collaborator"—I had not registered in my mind.

"Surely, Miss Gaunt, you recall some of his remarks?" he persisted.

"He was telling me how Philippe and Bertrand Demaury had quarreled over the Panama business," I said. "Apparently it was Philippe who persuaded Bertrand to buy shares in the enterprise. They both lost a lot of money, and Bertrand never forgave him. And what's more . . ."

"Yes?"

I took a deep breath. "What's more, I heard and saw them quarreling last night."

Lorenzo leaned forward, an expression of great interest on his finely chiseled face.

"And what was said—and done?" he asked.

I thought back. "I heard Bertrand saying something like: 'Confound you, is it true?' and Philippe replied, 'What if it is?' Only, they both used a swear word."

"I will not ask you to repeat that word, Miss Gaunt," said Lorenzo gravely. "And what else?"

"I was walking past the cabin in which they were standing," I explained. "As I drew abreast of the open door, I heard Bertrand say that he could kill Philippe with his own hands. And I saw him holding his cousin by the coat collar and making as if to strike him."

"Did either of the two men see you?" asked Lorenzo.

"Both of them saw me," I answered.

"Ah!"

"I suppose," I said uneasily, "that what I have told you puts Bertrand Demaury under very grave suspicion?"

"It is possible," he said. "Taken in conjunction with the countess's accusation, what you have told me is certainly very significant. Tell me, was Bertrand among those you saw on deck immediately prior to the cry?"

We were back with my poor recollection of that time and place, when I had been so absorbed with my own thoughts.

"I really don't remember," I told him. "I was with Axel, and the other guests were simply a chattering crowd in the background."

"Herr von Wuppertal's conversation must have been most stimulating, to have engaged your attention so completely," he said.

"I suppose so," I said feebly.

"And yet you were extremely hesitant when I asked you to recall the burden of his conversation," he said sharply.

"Now you're *interrogating* me!" I snapped.

"Miss Gaunt, I am sorry," he said gently. "A policeman, it is to be regretted, can seldom forget that he *is* a policeman. Am I forgiven—collaborator?"

"Of course," I said. "You are quite right to have pointed to the discrepancy in my story. I can only explain it by saying that I was only listening to Axel with half an ear—having another, personal matter on my mind at the time." And wouldn't you be surprised to know what *that* was? I added to myself.

He nodded. Then, rising to his feet, he walked to the rail of the balcony and looked out over the canal, to the bridge of boats. He stood for a while, tapping on the edge of the rail with the signet ring that he wore, his profile set and pensive, gray eyes shadowed by his brows. My heartbeat quickened as I watched him.

"What are you thinking, collaborator?" I ventured at length.

"I have returned to your speculation about Philippe Demaury's fall being an accident," he replied. "Since it opens up another possibility."

"I don't follow you," I said.

"It is possible that the man may indeed have fallen accidentally," he said, "but subsequently was murdered by drowning."

"By whom?" I asked, amazed.

"Can you not guess, Miss Gaunt?"

"You mean—?"

"Axel von Wuppertal dived in after the man in the water," said Lorenzo. "All present, yourself included, naturally assumed that he was going to his rescue. But there is another construction that can be put upon his action: *he could have taken the opportunity that presented itself to ensure that Philippe Demaury did not survive!*"

"But why?" I demanded. "For what reason?" And then I thought I understood. "Oh! Axel was told by Giles Demaury that two others stood between him and the inheritance. It's likely that Philippe may have been one of them. But—no, somehow I can't see Axel murdering for financial gain. No, not even though he was bitterly angry and disappointed—and I was witness to how he reacted after he received the news."

Lorenzo nodded gravely. "I respect your judgment, Miss Gaunt," he said. "And I think your summation of von Wuppertal's character is likely correct. However, it is not on the matter of the inheritance that I base my theory—and it is merely a theory—of his murdering Philippe Demaury."

"Then—why?" I asked. "Why else would he do it?"

"I know a little of the Panama scandal," he said. "Not a great deal—but I shall speedily set inquiries afoot to learn all there is to know. You say that Bertrand Demaury lost a lot of money through taking his French cousin's advice to buy shares in the venture. I will tell you of another party who also suffered greatly when the Panama Company collapsed in bankruptcy last year. That person was Von Wuppertal's father.

"Axel von Wuppertal Senior shot himself!"

Lorenzo left the *Semiramis* soon after. He departed with a handclasp and a grave smile that left me breathless. I was flattered, also, that he made no attempt to secure my assurances that what had been discussed between us, as "collaborators," was entirely confidential and not to be revealed to anyone else—an unspoken condition that I naturally accepted without question.

I watched him descend the accommodation ladder and step into the waiting police boat. My friend the sergeant unbent even further than on the previous occasion and threw me a broad smile that was only half hidden by his enormous soup-strainer mustache. I stood by the rail as the oarsman swept them away, and my heart went with the man I loved.

Esmeralda was piqued that she had not also been required for an interview. I said nothing to her of my new-found collaboration with Venice's Chief of Police, merely pointing out that, since she had not been on deck during the previous night's tragedy, there was nothing that she could have contributed in the way of evidence. Esmeralda accepted the explanation but continued to pout, and I realized that Lorenzo had been dragooned into the great regiment of eligible and attractive men upon whom her baby-blue eyes had directed their predatory glance.

The two of us returned to the Palazzo Demaury by gondola soon after. There I found a message waiting for me, from Miss Harriet. Would I attend her in her apartments as soon as convenient upon my return? Mr. Obadiah, who gave me the message, conducted me to the old lady's sitting room, which had a line of windows commanding a view across the city and the islands in the lagoon beyond.

Miss Harriet was in high good humor, and had dressed herself that day in a tea gown of magenta velvet that would have been entirely suitable for a woman in her twenties during the early 1880s, since it had frills and furbelows galore and—of all things—a bustle. Not a word about what one would have supposed to be the subject uppermost in her mind: the shocking death of one of her relations. She plunged straight into the cause of her high spirits.

"I have been summoned, my dear," she informed me. And, pointing upward to the ceiling: "Up to see—*him!*"

"Congratulations, Miss Harriet," I said, for want of anything better.

The haggard countenance, thick with powder, creased into a smile of pure pleasure.

"Thank you, my dear," she said, squeezing my arm. "I know

that the sentiment, coming from you, is perfectly genuine. Of all the people here, you are my true friend. I know it well."

"Indeed, I hope so, Miss Harriet," I assured her.

"Yes, I have been summoned," she said. "I am to go up there this afternoon at four thirty o'clock. Not that I have any expectations, I hasten to add. There are many with prior claims to the fortune. I am only a despised old female relation. Furthermore, Giles has never liked me. Even when I was a child, he could not bear to have me about him, and could never understand why Estelle made such a fuss of me." The old eyes went suddenly cunning; slid from side to side, narrowly, as if to ensure that we were not being overheard. "But I have my aspirations, dear," she whispered in my ear. "Oh, yes, even the humblest aspirant is entitled to dream. What a triumph, if Giles confounded everyone by settling his fortune on old Aunt Harriet, eh? Heh, that would be one in the eye for Esmeralda, would it not? Can't you see the minx trying to ingratiate herself with me? What lengths would she not go to, with 'darling Aunt this' and 'darling Aunt that.' Can you see her, eh, Meg?"

I smiled and nodded. Knowing Esmeralda as I did, I could picture her antics all too clearly in the unlikely event of Miss Harriet's succeeding to the coveted inheritance.

The old lady gave me a playful prod in the ribs and chuckled. "Ah, but all this talk is of no interest to you, I know that full well, my gel. There's none so old that can't remember what it is to be young and in love. How is he, eh? Have you seen him again since last night?"

There was no point in dissembling before the shrewd gaze of Miss Harriet. Had she not espied my secret almost before I had stumbled upon it myself?

"I had a long conversation with him this morning," I admitted.

"Has he declared himself yet?" she demanded.

"Declared himself?" I countered, puzzled.

"Bless the gel, being in love has stolen her wits!" cried Miss Harriet. "Has he asked for your hand, or at least begged for leave to court you?"

I stared at her in amazement, and then I said, "Miss Harriet, you are greatly mistaken. Yes, I have fallen in love with Prince

Lorenzo. I suppose, all unknowing, I loved him from the first moment I set eyes on him. The way my feelings persuade me now, I think I shall love him all my life. On the other hand, I may get over it. And, in many ways, that may well be for the best," I concluded miserably.

"For the best?" echoed Miss Harriet. "What is the gel blethering about? All for the *best?*"

I gazed at her earnestly. With no one else to turn to, no one else in whom I could repose my confidences, I found myself suddenly glad to pour out my secret misery to a sympathetic ear.

"Miss Harriet, you don't understand," I said. "Though I love Prince Lorenzo, I am nothing to him. He treats me with courtesy and consideration—just the way he treats everyone else, because he is a gentleman and an aristocrat. Aside from that, I am no more to him than a piece of furniture. A stylish piece of furniture. He thinks I have style—he told me so." I felt tears prickling my eyes when I recalled it.

"My dear gel," said Miss Harriet, placing a thin arm about my shoulders. "Don't take on so. My apologies for leaping to conclusions. When I saw the two of you together, I had the notion that the affair had already progressed to the exchange of endearments. Nothing of a very advanced nature, of course, but I had thought to hear that wedding bells were in the air quite soon. Oh, dear me, now you are really upset. What's to be done? What can I say?"

"Don't worry, Miss Harriet," I told her, dabbing my eyes. "I shall get over it, just as I shall probably get over my love for Lorenzo."

"It may not be necessary," she said. "As my father used to say—and he was a man of the horsey persuasion, who lost his patrimony, and much besides, on the racecourses of England and Ireland—there's many a winner that's slow off at the starting post. Your handsome prince may show no signs of returning your affections, but it's early days yet. Don't despair. Be like me and the Demaury inheritance—feel free to hope and dream."

"Miss Harriet, Miss Harriet," I murmured. "What use to hope and dream? What chance have I with a man like Prince Lorenzo Giolitti-Crispi? You've no idea of the family pride those people have. His mother made it quite clear what she thought about *me*. She condescended to hope that I would in time make a suitable marriage. A suitably modest marriage—as befits my station in life. Can you imagine *her* countenancing *me* as Princess Lorenzo Giolitti-Crispi?"

"And why not?" demanded Miss Harriet. "Your father was a Commander, Royal Navy, an officer and a gentleman, and a finer and more upright man never drew breath. That woman's a snobbish old baggage. I've never liked her. But the son takes after the father, unless I'm much mistaken. When he decides to marry a gel, be she ever so humble in birth or fortune, marry he will, take my word for it."

I relished the thought for a little while, wondering at the glory of it. Then I came down to earth.

"Enough of my problems, Miss Harriet," I said briskly. "So you have been summoned by Giles Demaury. And yet you say he never liked you. Surely you must be mistaken."

"Never liked me," she insisted. "Never. It was jealousy, you know. In the insane jealousy he felt for Estelle, he could not abide the thought that she had affection even for a young child. She was very affectionate, was Estelle."

A recollection prompted me to put a question to the old lady:

"Yet Giles Demaury told me that his wife was capable of cruelty," I said. "Did you find her so?"

The reply was unhesitating. "Yes, I knew of her cruelty."

"The term he used was 'casual cruelty,'" I said. "She was cruel only occasionally, and out of boredom and to amuse herself. And always she was remorseful."

"I remember well," said Miss Harriet. "She had this monkey. An ugly little creature that she bought, purely on a caprice, from a street market in Tangier. Brought it to London, carried it around with her everywhere. Dressed the thing in the most exquisite small clothes: satins, silks, embroidered stuff, sewn with diamonds and brilliants, hats to match, and a walking stick with a gold knob. How well I remember it.

"She and Giles gave a reception at their suite in the hotel where they were staying, in Trafalgar Square. I went with my parents. Wore my first long frock and had my hair up. She and Giles

had one of their notorious quarrels over supper. Estelle brooded
for the rest of the evening. It was a hot night. During the dancing
—in which she refused to take part—she sat out on the balcony,
fanning herself and looking bored and sulky, with the monkey
squatting by her side on its lead. And then—would you believe it?
—she threw aside her fan and picked up the monkey . . ."

"Miss Harriet!" I interposed. "Please don't go on. I don't think
I want to hear—"

"Picked up the monkey," continued Miss Harriet, seeming not
to hear my interruption, "and, giving a laugh, she threw it over
the balcony, to the courtyard far below. Now, what do you think
of that?"

The principal rooms of the Palazzo Demaury contained ample
evidence of the source from which the family fortunes had been
derived. My own particular favorite was a smallish chamber adjoining the great drawing room in which, on that first memorable
occasion, Giles Demaury had welcomed his assembled relations—
if the word "welcomed" adequately fits. I suppose it had been an
annex or retiring room for ladies of bygone days, who, tiring of
the heat and the noise in the drawing room during crowded recep-
tions, retreated with their lady's maids, had their stays unfastened,
and were fanned and cosseted till they felt themselves again. The
chairs and sofas there were of an especial and beguiling softness,
the decoration and furnishings of pastel, feminine colors: pale
pink, powder blue, muted gold. And the paintings—an interna-
tionally famous part of the Demaury family collection—were all
of the eighteenth-century rococo style, from both the Venetian
and French schools. My particular pet was a large confection by
the great Venetian painter, Giovanni Batista Tiepolo. It depicted
a nude lady of svelte and languid appearance reclining upon an
exceedingly comfortable-looking cloud amidst a bevy of well-
nourished cherubs who were plying her with assorted comestibles,
such as grapes, pomegranates, peaches and so forth, as well as
wines both white and red. I am not a connoisseur of painting, but
it did not require a great deal of artistic knowledge to see that
Signor Tiepolo's composition, by the breathtaking handling of the
paint—like liquid light—and the authority of the drawing, far

transcended the banality, not to say the absurdity, of the subject matter. I grew to love the slender Venus with her cherubs and her convenient and accommodating cloud.

That same afternoon, at about the time that Miss Harriet must have been ascending the stairs for her meeting with the recluse of the Palazzo Demaury, I was taking my ease in the little retiring room (in fact, I was working upon a piece of petit point: the cushion cover bearing the Demaury coat of arms that I had ambitions to finish for Esmeralda's birthday present), when a light tread caused me to look up. The door opened—and in walked Helena Brayne.

"Oh!" she exclaimed. "I'm sorry to disturb you."

She was wearing an afternoon gown in a pretty flowered print. Her hair was unbound. Her eyes were red and swollen with crying.

"Don't go," I said, getting to my feet, as I saw that she was about to retreat, averting her face from me so that I should not observe her condition. "Stay here. I was just leaving."

She paused. "You are very kind, Miss Gaunt," she murmured. "I—I was looking for someplace quiet where I could be alone for a while."

"You could not have chosen better, Mrs. Brayne," I told her. "No one ever comes in here but I. It's my favorite room in the palazzo."

"And now I am driving you away," she said.

I took a deep breath and said, "Mrs. Brayne, tell me to mind my own business if you will, but—well—is there anything I can do to help you?"

"Help me?" Her pretty, sad mouth twisted in a bitter small smile. "I doubt very much if you can, Miss Gaunt, though it's good of you to ask. My father, you see . . ."

"Yes?"

She overcame her hesitancy with the air of someone who has decided to unburden herself regardless of the consequences.

"You were there, on the yacht last night," she said. "At that terrible scene when the doctor declared that Uncle Philippe was dead. You saw that woman, that insufferable wife of his, accuse my father."

I nodded. "Yes."

"It affected him greatly," she said. "He is an ill man, Miss Gaunt. More ill than he will ever admit. As for my mother"—here she made a dismissive gesture of contempt—"my mother cannot bring herself to accept the fact of his illness, so she simply pretends it does not exist, in the hope, perhaps, that it will go away. Last night, in his cabin on the *Semiramis*, Papa had another of his heart attacks."

"Oh, I'm so sorry," I exclaimed. "I had no idea. I heard he was indisposed, but never dreamed it was anything serious. Is he—is he recovered?"

"We sent for the doctor again," she said. "My mother was hopeless, as ever. I sat with him throughout the night. He is well enough today to have been brought over to the palazzo."

"I'm glad to hear that," I said.

"Thank you." She seemed about to say more, then bit her lip and turned away. I watched her as she walked to the end of the small chamber, her head bowed, her hands clasped together. When she turned to face me again, I saw, with a stab of compassion, that she was in a state of uncontrollable tears.

"Mrs. Brayne!" I exclaimed, moving swiftly toward her. "Helena, what's the matter? Is it your father? Surely, if he's better, you've no cause for concern."

She drew a shuddering breath, wiped a tear from her cheek. "I've got to confide in someone," she said brokenly. "I must, or I think I shall go out of my mind. I don't have any real fortitude, you see. I'm not one of the strong ones. I'm a weak person. A spoiled brat who's never had to stand on her own two feet. And it's too late to start now, because my feet are made of clay anyhow."

"Confide in me if it will help," I told her.

"I can't tell my mother," she said. "For, as I've explained, she is quite hopeless. She's like me: no fortitude, nothing. And then there's Rupert, my husband. He's, well, not tremendously understanding about some things. But he loves me."

"Of course he does," I said.

"Sometimes he doesn't show it," she said. "Like the other day, when he forgot that he had promised to take me to Murano. But he loves me. People—people who don't understand—whisper behind my back that he married me for Papa's money, but it's not true."

"Of course not," I said reassuringly, with my heart going out to her in her misery.

"So, having no one to confide in, and since I shall go mad with worry unless I do tell someone, I must tell you. You called me by my first name just now. May I call you by yours?"

"Call me Meg," I said.

A pretty French clock of blue porcelain and gilt tinkled the half hour over the marble chimneypiece. Helena Brayne took a folded piece of paper from her corsage.

"The countess hurled an accusation at my father last night," she said. "At the time, I thought she was insane. Now—I no longer know. Last night, Meg, while I was watching over Papa, I found this lying among the things we took from his pockets, my maid and I, when we undressed him and put him to bed."

She handed me the paper, unfolded. It bore no superscription save the previous day's date. No address. No signature. Just the message in anonymous script:

18th July, 1891

You are of the belief that your cousin, Philippe Demaury, advised you to purchase shares in the Panama Canal Company in all good faith, as a fellow investor, with no other personal interest in the company. This is not the truth of the matter.

Financial control of the company was exercised by Baron de Reinach, Cornelius Herz and others—among whom was numbered Philippe Demaury.

Your cousin lied when he told you that he had lost a fortune like yourself. He was party to a fraud that cheated thousands of investors, you included.

I read it through a second time, then looked up to meet her eyes.

"It was delivered aboard the *Semiramis* last evening," she breathed. "I inquired of my father's valet. A gondolier handed in the envelope addressed to Papa at the companionway soon after the party began. He read it and afterward went down to his cabin, where he sent for Uncle Philippe."

"I see," was my response. I saw all too well now the cause of the violent quarrel to which I had been witness. "But who could have sent such a thing—and why?"

"Does it matter?" she cried. "All that matters is that it provided a reason, a motive, for my father to—"

"Helena, you mustn't say that!" I exclaimed. "You mustn't even think it. Not of your own father. No one saw Philippe Demaury fall into the water. The likelihood is that he fell accidentally. You must tell yourself that, and believe nothing else, nothing!" I took her by the hands and gazed earnestly into her frightened eyes.

She nodded. "Yes, you're right, Meg," she said at length. "That's what I must do, I see it clearly now. How lucky I am to have found someone strong like you to advise me. Pretend it hasn't happened, thrust it out of sight—that's what I'll do. I shall find that quite easy, just as my Mama would find it easy. I'm very like her, you know."

"You're stronger than you think," I told her. "Everyone is stronger than they think."

"But what about the note, Meg?" she asked. "What do I do with it—burn it?"

I weighed the alternatives in my mind, conscious of my own unwritten allegiance to Lorenzo, in the role of collaborator. I arrived at a compromise.

"Keep it safe," I advised her. "Say nothing to anyone about it for the time being. And—I'll say nothing to anyone."

I had no encounters with any of the Demaury clan that day or the next, but from bits of gossip gleaned from servants, augmented by a short conversation with Esmeralda, I learned that the embalmed body of Philippe Demaury was to be laid to rest on the following evening, Tuesday, in the crypt of the palazzo, there to lie along with the great G. F. Demaury, founder of the family fortune, and others of the clan who had died in Venice.

I also learned that Philippe's countess had suffered a complete nervous collapse and had been taken to the Carmelite Hospital, and that Bertrand Demaury was up and about.

All this, however—even the affecting conversation I had had with poor Helena in the retiring room—was forgotten in the heady thrill of receiving, on the Monday morning, by hand of a private gondolier, an invitation from the Palazzo Giolitti-Crispi, written by the princess herself, mother of my secret love; requesting the pleasure of Miss Gaunt's company at dinner that same evening; reply, please, by way of the messenger.

I replied with joy, penning a brief and formal note of acceptance. This done, I summoned up my nerve and, bursting in upon Esmeralda's pre-luncheon nap, I asked and received—and with surprisingly little resistance, so astonished was she by my unique request—the loan of one of her evening gowns. Nor did Esmeralda question me closely as to the reason for the request. I told her I had been invited out to a dinner party, but not by whom, or where. She did not ask.

The gown I chose was of a color and style that never in my wildest dreams would I have associated with myself, it being of pink and white striped silk, with red silk roses at the shoulders and the waist. It was Esmeralda through and through, and it must have been a midsummer madness that guided my hand to it. Yet that evening, when I had bathed and scented myself, and when Assunta had put up my hair with a red rose that was companion to the roses on the dress, and when I had donned the gown and gazed into the mirror, I knew that my midsummer madness had been of the inspired sort.

It was—me.

"*Signorina* is beautiful like a rose," said Assunta.

My heart sang. "Thank you, Assunta."

"*Il Principe* will be wild with passion," she declared.

I laughed. Was it so obvious, even to this child, that I was in love with Lorenzo? Who else had noticed? At that moment, in the triumph and surprise of my transformation, I was beyond caring.

The police boat called for me at seven. The sergeant and his men were in full-dress uniform of bicorne hats, cutaway coats, white bandoliers and brass buttons. My friend the sergeant bowed low and presented me with a nosegay of flowers before handing me into the stern of the boat, to a silk-cushioned seat.

The journey through the narrow waterways was a delight heightened by anticipation of joy to come. How I had ever seen the approach to the Palazzo Giolitti-Crispi as grim and alien was beyond explaining. At night it was gently lamplit, and the heady scent of honeysuckle lay heavily in the air. The policeman in the prow of the boat laid aside his cap, and leaving the sculling to his fellows, he uncased a mandolin and commenced to sing in a very commendable tenor voice. And so we came to the palazzo.

Lorenzo was there to greet me: a tall, dark-clad figure at the head of the steps under the entrance arch. He handed me out of the boat, stooped, and brushed my fingertips with his lips, murmuring a formal compliment about my appearance.

"My mother awaits us in the Titian salon," he said.

The chamber into which he led me was half again the size of the great hall at Murchester, and entirely lined with large panel paintings in the grand manner of the Renaissance; likewise the ceiling. I am not an authority, but I have an eye for comparison, and it was clear to me that the pictures had all been painted by the hand of a single artist. Since Lorenzo had referred to the chamber as the Titian salon, it followed that I was entirely surrounded by the works of the preeminent genius of the Venetian school of painting.

"Good evening, Miss Gaunt. So nice of you to come."

Princess Giolitti-Crispi was seated upon a chaise longue at the far end of the room, and approaching her down its vast length was how I had always imagined it must be to walk into the presence of a queen in her throne room. As I reached her, she extended her hand. I took it and dropped her a curtsy, for the circumstances seemed to call for it. My action appeared to please her. She tapped the space beside her, indicating that I should sit down.

"Has Giovanna arrived home yet, Mother?" asked Lorenzo, consulting his pocket watch.

"Giovanna has not returned," said his mother in a voice of sepulchral coldness. "Not to my knowledge. Indeed, I have not seen her since shortly after luncheon, at which time I informed her that we had a guest for dinner. It is very remiss of her not to be present already. If she is late I shall be most vexed." She turned to me. "My heart went out to your Queen Victoria when I heard the latest scandal concerning her dreadful son."

"I think my mother is referring to the recent affair in which His Royal Highness the Prince of Wales was present at a game of baccarat in which one of the players cheated," said Lorenzo.

I nodded.

"Only a mother," intoned the princess, "only a mother who has suffered at the hands of her offspring, can truly appreciate the agony that your sovereign must have suffered from the scandalous conduct of that erring boy."

"That particular erring boy," murmured Lorenzo drily, "is fifty years of age and the father of five."

His mother appeared not to hear. "It is truly said that to have children is to give hostages to fortune," she declared. "How well I can attest to that. How well!"

"Oh, come, Mother," said Lorenzo good-humoredly. "You have little of which to complain, though it's true that I have distressed you by becoming a policeman. Perhaps you would have been happier if I had devoted my life to amiable idleness, like Papa."

"Idleness is the natural state of the aristocrat," responded his mother. "For an aristocrat to indulge in any form of overt activity is to invite comparison between himself and persons of the lower classes—and with disastrous results. The French nobility committed the folly of sitting in parliament with their lower orders. The result—the French Revolution."

"Mother dear, you are quite incorrigible," said Lorenzo, smiling fondly at her.

At that moment the double doors at the far end of the long room opened to disclose the astonishing figure of a very old man dressed in the attire of the previous century. His wrinkled, monkeylike face peered out shortsightedly from under a powdered wig, and his bandy shanks were encased in silk knee breeches and stockings. In a loud but quavering voice, he announced what I with my imperfect command of the Italian tongue took to be: "Dinner is served, Princess." And such proved to be the case.

"And Giovanna still not returned," said Princess Giolitti-Crispi, rising. "I really am vexed."

"Ladies, your arms," said Lorenzo. "It is not often that I have the opportunity to escort two ladies in to dinner."

The dining room, which lay immediately beyond the Titian salon, was scarcely less impressive than the latter. Instead of paintings, it was hung with tapestries of astonishing size, all depicting scenes from the history of Venice. A long table was set down the center of the room, and places were laid for four, one at each end and the others facing in the middle. The vast distance between the settings was marked by an expanse of polished oak, set with a mass of silverware and sparkling glass.

The princess took her place at the nearest end of the table and gestured to me. "Be seated on my right, Miss Gaunt," she said. "My daughter—if and when she arrives—will be opposite you."

It was a long walk to the center of the long table, and a longer walk still for Lorenzo, who was placed at the far end. When we sat down, I could see only his head and shoulders above the serried ranks of glassware, sauce boats, *épergnes*, candelabra.

The old servant, who had fussily seen the princess to her place, bowed and withdrew. He was shortly to return, followed by an old woman—the same who had served tea on my first visit to the palazzo—bearing a tureen. She having placed herself on the princess's left, the old man ladled soup from the tureen into his mistress's plate. They then moved with shuffling steps to me, and repeated the process. It was a clear soup, with a few thin strands of vermicelli floating forlornly in its pellucid shallows, and it did not look to be very hot.

The old couple's slow progress to the far end of the table, and their protracted serving of Lorenzo, gave me time to examine at leisure the tapestries that were hung on the walls immediately opposite me. One depicted what I knew to be the scene of the ancient, annual ceremony of the "Wedding of the Sea," when the Doge of Venice took ship aboard his massive, gilded ceremonial barge *Bucentaur* and cast a wedding ring into the Adriatic, as symbol of Venice's maritime greatness. I was puzzling over the subject matter of the adjacent tapestry—a sea battle—when the *clink-clink* of spoon on plate announced that Princess Giolitti-Crispi was leading the attack upon the soup course. I took my first mouthful: as appearance had predicted, it was lukewarm.

"Regarding the conversation we had aboard the *Semiramis*, Miss Gaunt . . ." Lorenzo's voice, surprisingly clear and close at hand in the vast, echoing space of that great room, made me start and almost drop my soupspoon.

"Er—yes?" I stammered.

"I have dispatched inquiries to Rome for further and better information upon the Panama affair," he said. "I have already received some quite significant telegraphed replies."

"I hope," said the princess, "that we are not going to discuss *police matters* over the dinner table."

"I beg your indulgence for a few moments only, Mother," replied Lorenzo. "This is of interest and quite important."

"Humph!" was his mother's comment.

"The whole Panama affair," said Lorenzo, "is a sorry tale of mismanagement and corruption. It centers in France and must surely end in the trial and imprisonment of the principal figures— including, perhaps, the builder of the Suez Canal, Ferdinand de Lesseps himself. Names so far mentioned include one Baron Jacques Reinach, a financier, and two adventurers named Leopold Arton and Cornelius Herz. There are other names: names of people acting only as sleeping partners to the enterprise, but who are equally guilty of mismanagement and corruption. One of these names will surprise you greatly, Miss Gaunt. Can you guess it?"

I looked at him down the long and confused mass of silverware and glass that separated us, and my heart melted for love within me as I uttered the lie: "I really have no idea, Prince Lorenzo."

"Philippe Demaury!" he exclaimed, with the air of a man declaiming a paradox. "Now—confess, Miss Gaunt—you are surprised?"

"I am amazed," I replied. "Who would have thought it?"

The slow shuffle of the old couple announced the removal of our soup plates and imposed a pause in Lorenzo's revelations. I thought of the confidence I had received from Helena Brayne and felt relieved, On one aspect of those revelations, at least, I no longer stood in hazard of betraying the trust of my "collaborator," for he already knew of the secret contained in the anonymous note that had been so mysteriously delivered to Bertrand Demaury on the night of the tragedy. What else had he learned from Rome?

This I was not to discover—not on that occasion.

A rapid *click-click* of heels, a *frou-frou* of skirts, and Princess Giovanna swept into the dining room.

"Good evening, Mama. Good evening, Lorenzo." Her steely gray eyes (so like his) swept over me and totally dismissed me. "Am I late for dinner?"

"You have missed the soup," responded her mother, "which was excellent. Giovanna, I am very vexed with you."

"You are frequently—I may say constantly—vexed with me, Mother dear," replied the other.

Lorenzo had risen to his feet.

"Giovanna," he said in a chill voice, "I think you have not greeted our guest, who is Miss Margaret Gaunt, from England."

Her eyes met mine at last: I saw contempt and hatred there.

"Miss Gaunt and I have met before," she said. "In fact, we have met on two occasions. Is that not so, Miss Gaunt?"

"Yes," I murmured.

"And how are you keeping, Miss Gaunt?" she asked, seating herself and shaking out her napkin.

"Well enough, thank you, Princess Giovanna," I replied. "And yourself?"

She made no reply, and the awkward silence that followed was terminated only by the reappearance of the two old servants. The woman was bearing a covered dish which, upon being presented to Princess Giolitti-Crispi, proved to contain spaghetti.

The ritual of serving the four of us with the spaghetti, its accompanying sauce, and grated parmesan cheese—all at the slow, shuffling pace of the old couple—was a protracted business. Her mother having started, Princess Giovanna stabbed a small coil of the spaghetti, tasted it, and threw down her fork.

"This is quite disgusting!" she declared. "The meanest workman's family in Venice would not countenance the cooking that we put up with in this place."

"I find it quite tolerable," said her mother, nibbling reflectively. "A trifle overcooked for some tastes, perhaps. But I have to admit that I have little or no interest in food. Never have had."

Another long silence.

"Did you have a pleasant evening, Giovanna?" asked Lorenzo at length.

"Quite pleasant," responded his sister flatly. "Thank you," she added.

"Where did you go, Giovanna?" queried her mother.

"Walking, Mama," was the reply. Giovanna's eyes were fixed upon her plate. The fingers that were toying with the stem of her wineglass were quite perceptibly trembling.

"Walking?" exclaimed the older woman. "Did you not take the gondola to—wherever it was that you went?"

"I had the fancy to walk, Mama," replied Giovanna.

"Not unaccompanied, surely?" breathed her mother, horrified.

Giovanna's fingers having increased their trembling so that the wine was in danger of being spilled, her hand was swiftly withdrawn from sight upon her lap.

"Not all the time, Mama," came her reply.

"Ah, you encountered a friend," said her mother, with a note of relief. "Really, my dear, you gave me quite a turn. The thought of your walking the streets alone, and in the early evening, when the riffraff of the city is parading about. Who was your friend? Was it Violetta Carillo-Lodi? Which reminds me that I really must have her mother, the contessa, to tea before very long."

"No, it was not Violetta," said the daughter.

"Then it was Maria di Balbo, perhaps?"

"Not Maria."

"The Rinaldo girl, perhaps? I forget her name."

"No," responded Giovanna in scarcely more than a whisper.

"*Mother!*" Lorenzo's voice from the end of the table—loud and peremptory—made me start and almost upset my wineglass. "Mother, this present topic of conversation is becoming tedious."

Princess Giolitti-Crispi responded by throwing back her head and regarding her son with narrowed, gray-eyed defiance.

"I will pursue the present topic for as long as it suits me, Lorenzo," she replied. "And you will not wish to interrupt!"

"We have a guest, Mother," said Lorenzo evenly.

It was then that Giovanna's chair scraped on the marble-tiled floor, and she was halfway to her feet when her mother's imperious command halted her.

"*Sit down, Giovanna!*"

The younger woman obeyed, her eyes averted, face pale, mouth turned down at the corners.

"Yes, Mama," she said expressionlessly.

"Giovanna," said Princess Giolitti-Crispi, "who was the lady whom you met while out walking in the street this evening?"

"It was not a lady," came the reply—scarcely audible, since Giovanna's head was bowed almost to her bosom.

"Ah, not a *lady*. Then it was a female of the lower orders, perhaps?"

"It was—a man."

"Ah, a *gentleman!*"

Giovanna's head flicked up on the instant. Her eyes, glazed with sudden tears, flashed defiance at her mother.

"No, Mama!" she rasped bitterly. "Not a gentleman but a man. An ordinary man. What you would describe as a male person of the lower orders!"

Princess Giolitti-Crispi's face was a picture of baffled affront. Her lips worked upon articulating, but the words were some time in coming.

"A man of the lower orders?" she breathed in strangulated tones. "Are you telling me, Giovanna, that you—a daughter of one of the oldest, if not *the* oldest, noble houses in Venice, in all Italy—are acquainted with—have encountered in the street and have walked in company with—a male person of the lower orders? Who is this person, Giovanna? Answer me!"

The wild, tear-blinded eyes flashed in my direction. Her trembling finger was pointed straight at me.

"Why do you not ask *her?*" she cried. "Ask the spy—the snooper!"

The clatter of a falling chair announced that Lorenzo had leapt to his feet. I glanced down the table. His face was quite impassive as he addressed his sister, his tone even and controlled.

"That was quite unnecessary, Giovanna," he said. "You should not let your own troubles blind you to the normal civilities. Miss Gaunt is our guest."

Princess Giolitti-Crispi interrupted with a loud despairing cry. "Oh, I had known, I had guessed, Giovanna, that you had formed a liaison with a person of the opposite sex. I had deduced, by discreet questioning of my friends among Society, that you were not being courted by one of the more eligible bachelors. I had thought that, perhaps, you had formed an attachment with a scion of one of the *newer* noble families—one connected with trade or commerce, perhaps. I could have learned to accept that, I think. It would have been difficult, but a mother's love can lead to the accomplishing of many distasteful things. But the thought that you have been meeting—have made a liaison with—a male person of the lower orders . . ." Her voice trailed away.

"And why not?" Giovanna's voice rose almost to a scream. "Why shouldn't I accept the love of a good man, whatever his estate? Look at me, Mama. I'm a woman of thirty-two. I've spent my whole adult life dancing attendance upon you in this dreary palazzo. Your eligible bachelors, Mama—they look upon me as an old maid. The women you mentioned just now, the friends of my girlhood: Maria, Violetta, Juilietta—they are all married and with children, all of them. I thought love had passed me by, Mama—but I was wrong." Her tear-glazed eyes blazed with a triumphant light. "I am loved, Mama. And I love in return!"

"But—a common person," wailed her mother. "That a Giolitti-Crispi could bring herself to—to even contemplate a liaison with a man of the common sort!"

"A Giolitti-Crispi!" exclaimed Giovanna. Her gaze flashed to meet mine. "I will tell you, Miss Gaunt, a little of the life and times of the noble, the highborn Giolitti-Crispis. Do you see that tapestry over there? It is quite priceless. So are all the rest. The Titians in the salon next door have been bid for by your relations the Demaurys at a sum that would feed all the poor of Venice for a lifetime. We live here, surrounded by the splendor of the ages, but it is useless to us—useless! The pride of the Giolitti-Crispis, the conditions of our inheritance, prevent us by law from selling so much as a single crested teaspoon. So my brother, over there"— she pointed to Lorenzo, who had resumed his seat and was gazing at her impassively—"my brother is obliged to defy a thousand-year-old tradition and take employment. He is a policeman, and a very good policeman, Miss Gaunt. One of the best in Italy, did you know that?"

"But his services to the State are performed without remuneration," exclaimed her mother. "No Giolitti-Crispi would dream of . . ."

"Why do you continue to deceive yourself, Mama?" cried Giovanna. "Lorenzo is paid, just like all the others. How else could we eat, do you imagine?"

"I will hear no more!" declared Princess Giolitti-Crispi. "This is a tissue of lies, Giovanna, to obscure the issue of your most regrettable liaison . . ."

Giovanna silenced her mother with a peremptory gesture of her hand; addressed herself to me again. "Do you know how I spent my morning, Miss Gaunt—and I a Giolitti-Crispi? I spent my morning in scrubbing the floor of this dining room, because we have no servants save Angelina and Paolo, and they are both incapable of getting down on their knees."

"Angelina and Paolo are excellent servants!" said her mother shrilly. "I have no time for your modern servants, who are forever demanding what they call their rights. Why, the Contessa Toscano-Salvatorelli was telling me only the other day that her butler was actually demanding a whole day's holiday every month, which I think is appalling."

"Mama, we endure Angelina and Paolo because we cannot afford to pay anyone else," said her daughter wearily. "And they in their turn are grateful to work for their food and a roof over their heads, as an alternative to the poorhouse."

"Lies, all lies!" cried Princess Giolitti-Crispi. "You are dissembling, Giovanna. You are deliberately vexing me, in order to avoid having to explain your disgraceful conduct. I demand that you finish this charade and answer a question: What are your intentions toward this—this man of the lower orders?"

Gazing covertly at Giovanna, I saw her draw breath as if in preparation for a declaration of some great moment. She looked down at her hands; clasped them together as if to control their trembling.

Presently, she said, "I will tell you my intentions, Mama. I hope that this man—whom I love with all my heart—will ask me to marry him. He may not. He might decide that the fact of my being a Giolitti-Crispi is a barrier that even our mutual love cannot scale. The decision will be his; I shall not seek to influence him.

"But if he chooses aright, Mama, if he decides to ask me, I shall accept him. And then I shall leave this place forever and forget that I ever was a Giolitti-Crispi, for that is the only way our marriage could endure. But, believe me, I shall think of you often and with regret, the two of you, living here together. Surrounded by the relics of the past, strangled by family pride, in horrified contemplation of your future.

"And now I bid you goodnight."

With great dignity, Princess Giovanna rose and walked to the door, went out, and closed it behind her.

Yet another long silence.

And then Princess Giolitti-Crispi said, "Lorenzo, I find the weather rather inclement. Do you think that a short stay in Monte Carlo or Menton will suit me?"

"I should think either would suit you admirably, Mother," responded Lorenzo.

"Ah, but your dear papa always complained that the summer's heat of the Riviera was scarcely an improvement on Venice," said his mother. "Perhaps, after all, I will remain here. And perhaps go to Monte Carlo or Menton in the winter."

"As you wish, Mother," said Lorenzo blandly. "Do just as you choose."

At ten o'clock, the disastrous meal over, Princess Giolitti-Crispi announced that she would retire. She offered a parchment cheek for her son to kiss and gave me her hand. No mention of what had taken place at the dinner table, no word of regret or apology. She seemed to have put the matter entirely from her mind and become again her calm and unflurried self, a bastion of aristocratic aloofness, safe within the enclosing walls of a thousand years of privilege.

I was alone in the Titian salon with Lorenzo. He poured coffee, set my cup upon an occasional table at my elbow, crossed over and sat at an armchair opposite.

He said, "I am sorry for what happened, Miss Gaunt. You must think us a very odd family."

"Please don't be sorry on my account," I said. "My sympathies are entirely with your mother and sister. I just wish that it hadn't happened in front of a stranger."

"I promise you that my mother suffered not the slightest embarrassment on that score," he said. "As for Giovanna . . ."

"Her embarrassment was considerable," I replied. "As a woman, I can assure you of that."

He frowned with a sudden recollection. I thought I knew what was coming next, and I was correct.

"Giovanna attacked you," he said. "Accused you of being a spy. A snooper. That was most offensive. Offensive—and curious. She also said that you had met on two occasions, whereas I had thought that you had met her only once, here."

"We have indeed seen each other on two occasions," I said, and then told him of my embarrassing encounter with his sister and her lover in the cafe.

"You formed an opinion of the man in question, I don't doubt," said Lorenzo when I had finished my tale.

I felt a prickling of resentment at his question. What right had he to probe for my opinions of the man to whom his sister had given her heart? I decided to be noncommittal.

"I scarcely noticed him," I said. "He seemed—very respectable."

"His name is Alfredo Zucchi," said Lorenzo shortly. "I am somewhat ashamed to admit that I have taken advantage of my official position by having a watch kept upon my sister's comings and goings. He is, as you say, respectable. Unmarried. Aged thirty-three. And a carpenter by trade."

"Is he—a good carpenter?" I asked.

Lorenzo's right eyebrow went up quizzically.

"Quite probably," he said. "But it scarcely affects the issue."

"You would not approve of your sister marrying a man who worked with his hands—even if he did it well, with skill and honesty?"

"You are aware of my mother's views upon the matter?" he countered.

"Of course. And you share her views?"

He did not reply immediately, but rose to his feet and walked over to the fireplace: a vast edifice of carved and gilded marble surmounted by a great oval mirror supported by bronze cherubs. He gazed into the mirror for several moments.

"In the matter of marriage," he said, "it is my opinion that the perfect union—of the kind that is made in Heaven, as the saying goes—is a very rare occurrence. The remaining marriages survive, or founder miserably, in direct consequence of the compatibility of the partners concerned. All things being equal—given two people of similar or complementary natures, of like race, religion, social standing—there is no reason why a marriage should not be perfectly successful. But let there be any disparity between the two parties and—in my opinion—the marriage will be at a risk that is in direct proportion to the extent of the disparity.

"In the case of my sister and Alfredo Zucchi, I would say that the disparity is so immense—she an aristocrat to her fingertips (and believe me, Miss Gaunt, for all Giovanna's protestations, she also is strangled by family pride and will not shake off her ties with a simple act of pious endeavor), and he a humble workman, who no doubt loves her very sincerely—that there can only be one outcome: disaster.

"Do I make myself clear, Miss Gaunt?"

He made himself abundantly clear, all too agonizingly and bitterly clear. Any thin gleam of hope that I had managed to keep alive, despite everything, was brutally extinguished by his words.

I now knew where my prospects stood with Prince Lorenzo Giolitti-Crispi, the Venetian Chief of Police—nowhere!

I left the palazzo soon after, and he did not offer to escort me but handed me over to the charge of his sergeant. I am ashamed to say that I cried all the way through the dark canals, and was grateful that most of the lamps had been put out along our route so that the sergeant and his men were not able to see my tears.

There was little sleep for me that night. The restless catnaps I endured in the early hours of the morning were haunted by Princess Giovanna's agonized countenance and by Lorenzo's implacable denunciation of marriages between the haves and the have-nots, the nobility and the nobodies. I woke from my uneasy dozing in the thin, gray hour of dawn and wondered if by any chance he had penetrated my facade and realized that I was in love with him. That would account for the careful precision with which he had delivered his views on what his mother referred to as *mésalliance*. The very idea was so hurtful, so bitterly humiliating, that I flung myself out of bed and, throwing my peignoir over my shoulders, went to the window and, pulling back the shutters, looked out over the waking scene below.

There was no escape. The breathtaking beauty of the most enchanting city on earth was no diversion for my anguished heart, and the waters of the Grand Canal served no purpose but to be a receptacle for the tears that I spilled into them, to be borne out on the current that scours the lagoon twice daily and bears the flotsam and jetsam of the teeming city and its attendant islets into the Adriatic and beyond.

Yes, he must have discovered my secret. Somehow—by a word, a glance—I had betrayed myself. How embarrassed he must have been to discover that a plain little nobody from England had— what was the expression?—set her cap for him. And he already in the embarrassing position of trying to prevent his only sister from marrying yet another nobody.

The longer I reflected, the clearer everything became. The invitation to dine at the Palazzo Giolitti-Crispi, seen in the light of my theory, took on a new and humiliating aspect. No longer a gesture toward someone with whom he had established a rapport, it became an opportunity for him to make quite clear to me that it was out of the question for me to entertain any hopes that my love would ever be returned, or consummated by marriage. So he had asked his mother to invite me to dinner. Chance—his sister's outburst—had provided him with a pretext for declaring his views on unsuitable marriages. Deftly, cleanly—as with the surgeon's scalpel—my hopes, my dreams, my sole desires, had been slashed away into nothingness. Small wonder that I wept into the dawn.

Later, dressed, and with a bold face on, I sought company—any company. Esmeralda was not awake, so I went down to see who else was about. Guided by the aroma of freshly made coffee, I ventured into a room that I had never entered before: a ground-floor apartment with windows that looked out across the busy Grand

Canal. There, seated alone in a sea of gleaming silver and sheer white napery, and tucking into a heaped plateful of saffron-colored kedgeree with every appearance of delight, was Axel von Wuppertal.

"Meg, good morning. How delightful you look." He rose and, taking me by the hand, led me over to a side table where stood rows of covered dishes upon hot plates. "Come, what do you fancy? Shall it be deviled kidneys? I can vouch for the kedgeree, which is most excellent. A little bacon perhaps? No?"

"Just coffee, please, Axel," I told him.

"No appetite?"

"No."

"You look sad, my dear," he said. "A trifle *triste*. Is something the matter? Something about which I can help?"

I shook my head. "You are very kind, Axel," I said. "But, no, there is nothing you or anyone can do. I shall have a cup of coffee and talk to you—and then I shall feel better."

"Then I will bring your cup over here and you will sit beside me," he said, suiting the action to the words. "And what would you like to talk about?"

"Anything you choose," I said.

He looked serious. "There is something I must tell you," he said. "Our mutual friend the aristocratic police chief sent for me yesterday. Oh, you have spilled coffee all down your dress. Here—take my napkin."

I set my coffee cup down, and was uncomfortably aware that my hand was perceptibly unsteady. If so much as hearing Lorenzo mentioned was going to have such an effect upon me, I was doomed to a lifetime of small disasters. I mopped up the mess and tried to compose myself.

"Really, and what did he want with you?" I asked him at length.

"It concerned the Panama affair," he said gravely. "If you will remember, that night on the yacht I was explaining to you why Philippe and Bertrand were on such bad terms, and had not finished my story when we heard the cry of 'man overboard.' What I did not have time to tell you is that my father was also in-

volved. He lost a very great deal of money, as a result of which he
—committed suicide."

"Axel, I really am most sorry," I murmured, reaching out and
laying my hand on his.

He shook his head. "We were not very close, my father and I,"
he said. "Indeed, he made it quite clear, right from the days of my
early childhood, that he cordially detested me. My mother, you
see, was a Demaury, and I take after her. Father worked for the
Demaurys but always resented the fact. It was the ambition of his
life to make a great fortune by his own efforts. Hence his heavy involvement in the Panama Canal Company. When it failed, he
was personally ruined. For a man with Father's temperament, it
was a blow from which there was no recovery and only one avenue
of escape—death. However, in the eyes of our highborn policeman
friend, taking one circumstance with the other, I am now a
murder suspect."

"Because of Philippe's involvement in the fraud," I said.

He glanced at me sharply. "You know about that?" he asked.

"Prince Lorenzo told me," I said.

Axel nodded. "And me also," he said. "In addition he implied—
quite gently but nonetheless directly—that my father's suicide
could have provided me with a motive for ensuring that Philippe
was drowned by the time the rescue boat reached us."

"And did you do that?" I asked him. "Did you drown him?"

His clear blue eyes never wavered. "No, Meg, I did not," he
replied. "And I pray with all my heart that you believe me."

"I believe you, Axel," I said without hesitation.

"Meg, will you be my wife?" he said.

"Axel!" I exclaimed.

"My dear, don't answer no immediately. First listen to what I
have to say. I know it is out of the question that you should feel
for me what I feel for you; but we are good friends together, are
we not? We laugh at the same things, enjoy each other's company, both like spaghetti Bolognese and prefer red wine to white.
Not very strong recommendations for spending one's life with
another person, you may think; but from such small beginnings
much may develop. And, Meg, I do love you very much."

"Axel, dear, you're making me cry," I told him.

"Take my clean handkerchief. It hasn't even been unfolded yet."

"Thank you," I said. "I shall look an awful fright if anyone should come in. My nose all red."

"You have an adorable nose," he said. "While you're dabbing your eyes, let me continue pressing my case. As you know, Meg, my chances of succeeding to the big inheritance are almost nonexistent, but I am hardworking and . . ."

"Axel—"

"I have a fine townhouse in Berlin, near to the Tiergarten . . ."

"Please, Axel. Please," I pleaded.

"You don't want to hear any more? Nothing I tell you will make any difference? I play the cello quite beautifully and am very tidy about the house."

I leaned forward and kissed his cheek.

"I am greatly honored, my dear," I told him. "Honored and flattered by your offer. And, though you've made me cry, I do so with a special sort of strange happiness. My dear, you will never know how much I needed someone like you—a thoroughly nice person—to ask me to marry him, this morning of all mornings."

"But—the answer is still no?" he said wistfully.

"I'm sorry, my dear."

"Not even perhaps—at some time in the future?"

I shook my head. "It would be unkind of me to say perhaps when I can see no hope of any change in my feelings," I said. "I am very, very fond of you, Axel."

"But—it's not enough?"

"You know yourself that it's not enough, my dear."

He nodded.

CHAPTER SIX

LATER that morning Esmeralda floated the perfectly appalling suggestion that we women should follow with the men when Philippe's coffin was carried into the family crypt in the evening. Miss Harriet was also present at the time; I had found them together when I called into Esmeralda's sitting room to see what she was doing about luncheon.

"Esmeralda, what a horrid idea," I exclaimed.

"But I'm full of curiosity to see the inside of the crypt," she said. "To think of it—one will see the casket that contains the great George Fanshawe Demaury himself."

"And it's an opportunity that's not likely to come your way again," commented Miss Harriet. "Not unless you're in Venice for another family funeral, that is. The crypt is forever kept under lock and key.

"I was only ever in it once, and that was when my Uncle Charles, my father's brother, died here in 'twenty-five, or was it 'twenty-six? I know I was very young at the time and greatly awed by all the big bronze caskets stacked three deep on their high shelves. Fifteen of 'em there are, you know, and six are still lying empty—waiting for the next six Demaurys who will die in Venice."

"Horrifying!" exclaimed Esmeralda. "But quite fascinating. I shall follow with the menfolk, and I insist on your accompanying me, Meg."

I shrugged. There was no arguing with Esmeralda when her mind was made up; I had learned that from our nursery days. This was the spoiled child who had insisted on waiting up for Father Christmas.

"We'll follow together," said Miss Harriet. "Philippe deserves

that much respect, though I never had any time for him, nor he
for me. I always did say he made a terrible mistake in marrying
that countess creature. Not that I have any objections in principle
to titled folk," she added, with a sidelong glance and a wink at me
—an offering which, to my relief, was unnoticed by Esmeralda.

"That's settled then," said Esmeralda, pleased at having got her
own way as usual. One would have thought that the experience
was so familiar to her as to be taken for granted; but no—she was
preening herself like a peahen at her small triumph.

Her attitude stirred me to make a final point. I said, "I must
say I am very surprised at you, Esmeralda, considering how you
can't abide funerals. I hope you'll not lay the blame at my door if
the experience brings on one of your headaches or an attack of the
vapors. And if it does, I request that you do not faint all over me."

Esmeralda pouted prettily: once having got her way, she was
ever one to be agreeable. "I promise, dear," she said sweetly.

"I am hungry," announced Miss Harriet. "May I make the suggestion that we take luncheon together, here in this charming and
airy room of Esmeralda's? Over a light collation we can have a
good gossip about this and that, do you agree? Splendid. Then be
so kind, Meg dear, as to pull the bell cord and summon a
flunkey."

The servant having appeared, Miss Harriet took charge of the
commissariat and ordered a repast that would have served for a
squadron of hungry cavalry. We would have none of your Italian
fare, she decided, but wholesome English dishes. Green-pea soup
to start with, followed by lamb cutlets ("and let them be lean and
not oversized, my good fellow"); after that a little veal, plain roast
of course, and not frizzled in that horrid batter. I exchanged a
raising of the eyebrows with Esmeralda as the old lady embarked
upon the pudding course: demanded to know what local fruits
were in season, and were there cheesecakes? And was an iced
gâteau beyond the cooks' capabilities?

The poor manservant retired, utterly confused, his brow be-
dewed with anxious perspiration, a long list of Miss Harriet's re-
quirements scribbled upon his starched shirtcuff in mixed Italian
and English.

"Now, what shall we talk about, dears?" said Miss Harriet, relaxing in her armchair by the window and settling the none-too-clean lace cuffs of the unbecoming maroon plush two-piece ensemble that she was wearing in complete defiance of the heat of the day.

I was happy to talk: talking filled the empty silence that led to thinking, and from thought to heartache.

"Do tell us how you fared in your interview with Giles Demaury," I said brightly.

"Yes, what happened?" demanded Esmeralda. "You were on the point of telling me when Meg came in. Was he—pleasant—to you?" There was sharpness in her tones, and I knew the reason why.

"Pleasantness personified," replied Miss Harriet, and her raddled countenance crazed into a thousand lines of good humor, causing a small fall of rice powder upon her corsage. "He could not have been more agreeable. Do you know, he recalled my girlhood delight in sugared almonds—a mild passion that I have never lost. There was a dish of sugared almonds set at my elbow. And a decanter of excellent brandy. I nibbled and sipped as we chatted for hours. Most pleasant. Most pleasant indeed."

Esmeralda shifted irritably in her seat.

"And what did he say about—you know?" she quizzed.

"You know what?" responded Miss Harriet blandly.

"The inheritance?" snapped Esmeralda. "Did he give any indication of his intention toward you regarding the inheritance?"

"He did," replied Miss Harriet. "Yes, I received a very clear impression of my chances."

"And what are your chances, Aunt?" asked Esmeralda.

Miss Harriet smiled. She was enjoying the protracted moment of revelation.

"About the same as your own, dear," she said, inflecting her gravelly voice in a note of false sweetness. "In short—*negligible!*"

Miss Harriet's "light collation" arrived some hours later, in the midafternoon, brought by a small army of servitors. The old lady's demands had clearly strained the palazzo's culinary department to its limits, for all the dishes had been produced from scratch—hence the long delay.

Miss Harriet tasted the green-pea soup and declared it to be excellent, if a trifle overflavoured by the salty ham which had been added as an ingredient. We set to: we were all hungry.

Presently, between mouthfuls, the old lady said, "There is no doubt in my mind at all who is to be Giles's heir."

"Who, Aunt?" asked Esmeralda.

"Why, Bertrand of course," said the other. "Who else, now Philippe has gone?"

"There's Axel von Wuppertal," said Esmeralda sulkily. "He seems to think a lot of his chances."

"I don't rate him very highly in the inheritance stakes," said Miss Harriet.

"Neither does Axel himself," I commented. "In fact . . ."

"In fact what, dear?" asked the old lady, her soupspoon halted halfway to her mouth, the rheumy, kohl-limned eyes fixed keenly upon me.

I recalled the occasion when I had found him inebriated and despairing in the white drawing room, having been told that two others stood between him and his inheritance. But did I have any right to reveal this confidence to my companions? I decided not.

"In fact what?" echoed Esmeralda. "What were you going to add, Meg?"

"Nothing, really," I said feebly. "Only that he told me he didn't think much of his chances."

"It will be Bertrand," said Miss Harriet. "Giles sent for that spoiled brat Helena and her polo-playing appendage, did he not? I've no doubt he despaired at the thought of the fortune eventually passing into such hands as theirs—but it was always a better option than Philippe and his barren countess. No, Philippe alive or Philippe dead, my money has always been on Bertrand. Did I ever tell about the last terrible quarrel between Giles and Estelle? Ah, here are the lamb cutlets. Serve them immediately, fellow. We don't want 'em lying in pools of cold grease."

The serving of the second course taking several minutes, and Miss Harriet's tasting and approving of the wine that accompanied it a few minutes more, it was not till the door had closed upon the servitors that Esmeralda voiced the question which was also uppermost in my mind.

"What was it about—the last quarrel between Giles and Estelle?" she demanded of her aunt. "I never heard a thing about it."

"Ah," said Miss Harriet. "Then you shall, you shall. Mmm, the cutlets are quite delicious. A spoonful of mint sauce would have been perfection, but one cannot expect too much of foreigners. The quarrel—ah, well. There was, as you will both appreciate, a touch of the *opéra bouffe* about the relationship of that couple. The throwing of plates, the exchange of shouted insults in public places. The story of the Russian Ambassador's wife and the up-turned tureen of vermicelli soup I have dined out on for fifty years."

"I can vouch for the truth of that story," said Esmeralda. "My grandfather was present on the occasion."

"He was indeed, dear," confirmed Miss Harriet. "It was your grandfather who placated the poor woman and no doubt averted a sharp exchange of notes between Venice and St. Petersburg. Well, that was the *opéra bouffe* side to the relationship. There was another, less amusing, more sinister side."

She glanced meaningfully at me.

"You mean—Estelle's streak of cruelty?" I supplied.

"Quite so," said Miss Harriet. "Mind you, as I have said many times, I personally found her a kindly woman. She was certainly most kind to me. But the cruelty—there is no doubt that it soured Giles's love for her—and in the end destroyed it."

"Do you really believe that, Miss Harriet?" I asked.

She nodded. "I do, my dear. The buffoonery turned, in the end, to the ingredients for tragedy. It was like a circus, when the clowns give way to the trapeze artist and the laughter dies away in silence as all eyes turn to regard a pair of human beings flirting with death."

"It was like that—with Giles and Estelle?" I asked.

"Twice in a furious rage she tried to kill him," said Miss Harriet. "I learned that from my father, and it was common knowledge in the family. Less well known are the facts of her faithlessness toward him. Not only did she take lovers, but she taunted him with her infidelities. He forgave her many times—as many times as she repented and was contrite, begged him to forget and take her back—but at last she went too far for forgiveness."

Too far for forgiveness! I seemed to hear, in my mind, the voice of the old man on the upper floor of the palazzo:

Sometimes her cruelty was irreversible!

The arrival of the next course, and Miss Harriet's protracted dalliance with the sauces, the accompanying vegetables and the fresh wine, made for an intolerable delay. When the servants had again departed, Esmeralda and I burst out almost in unison:

"And what happened in the end, Miss Harriet?"

"Tell us about their last quarrel, Aunt!"

The old lady, who, as was her custom, had removed her false teeth and laid them by her plate while eating, nibbled rabbit-like upon a mouthful of roast veal before replying. We waited with restless impatience, the food disregarded.

Presently she said, "It took place here, in Venice. By that time their quarrels, both public and private, had estranged them from Society. No one either invited them out or accepted their invitations. I say no one—I mean no one of any quality. Those who came to the Palazzo Demaury, toward the end, were the riffraff and hangers-on of European and American society: the remittance men, the ne'er-do-wells, the cheats and gamblers, women who were no better than they should have been, men of the same kidney.

"Every night this place rang with the raucous sounds of their merrymaking, not infrequently interspersed by the noise of violent quarrels. The palazzo achieved a dubious reputation for orgies that rivaled the excesses of the Renaissance princes. And in the heart, the center of all this, the figures of Giles and Estelle, quarrelling as always.

"There was one among their most frequent guests—I will not mention his name, but he was an Englishman of the highest birth, yet far gone in depravity—whose reputation was such as to exclude him from setting foot under any other roof in Europe. Indeed, it was only by Estelle's whim that he was received even here, for Giles detested and despised him. And it was this—creature—who brought about the final quarrel between the nineteenth century's most talked-about couple. Can I press either of you to the last slice of veal? No? Then I will have it myself, for I cannot abide waste.

"I think—I speculate because I do not have all the details—I think it likely that Giles may have set in train the terrible sequence of events that I will now relate. The witnesses to the events, you see, were not people whose word could be relied on, even when sober—which they most certainly were *not* on that occasion. But it is certain that something out of the ordinary must have dragged from Estelle's lips a most astonishing announcement."

"And what was that?" asked Esmeralda, round-eyed.

"She declared that she was with child," said Miss Harriet. "And that the libertine Englishman, whom Giles so detested, was the father."

"No!" breathed Esmeralda, and I gave an involuntary cry of astonishment.

"As true as I sit here," said Harriet. "That part of the story is undisputed. She made the declaration in public, before their guests, before the kind of people who could be relied upon to shout such a prime piece of scandal from every rooftop in Venice and beyond. But worse follows—and it is here that you will see what I mean when I say that Estelle went too far for forgiveness.

"Next day she retracted it all. Again, before witnesses, she declared that she had lied about her liaison with the Englishman. That—and the child—were all lies, she said, blurted out on the spur of the moment, for no other reason than to wound her husband. That is why I say that Giles must have greatly incensed her, to produce such a result."

"How could she—how could anyone—be so cruel to a person they loved?" I asked.

"She would have had no forgiveness from me," declared Esmeralda. "Not if I had been in Giles's shoes."

(*Sometimes her cruelty was irreversible!*)

"Nor did she," responded Miss Harriet. "Oh, he may have paid it lip service when she protested her contrition. That same night they departed together to the Lido, for all the world like a newly-wed couple bound upon a honeymoon. There they had a champagne supper and danced till the small hours, the cynosure of all eyes: she in the full flower of her radiant beauty, he so handsome, one of the most distinguished men of his generation. Both together again in perfect amity. Alas for amity!"

"That was the night that . . ." began Esmeralda.

A chill shiver ran down my spine.

"It was after three o'clock in the morning when they set off back to the city," said Miss Harriet. "Their private gondola awaited them. It was said afterward that the gondolier expressed some doubts about the weather; advised his master that it would be wiser to wait till dawn light so that he could better judge the state of the waves in the middle of the lagoon. Giles would hear none of it. Told the fellow that he would row them across at once or find himself another master on the morrow. The rest of the tragedy is public knowledge: at dawn Giles was washed ashore, more dead than alive, and Estelle and the gondolier were presumed to have been washed out to sea on the tide—lost forever. But public knowledge was deficient in one significant item of information."

I said, "What was that, Miss Harriet?"

"The fact that neither Estelle nor the gondolier could swim," said the old lady. "As to the latter, it is not unusual for men of the seafaring sort to lack this accomplishment."

"I don't see anything particularly significant about that," said Esmeralda. "If they couldn't swim, it's no wonder they drowned."

"Nor is it surprising that Giles survived," said Miss Harriet blandly, "for he was a swimmer of some renown in his college days. But these two circumstances, taken into consideration, have puzzled and intrigued me down the years. Recently—indeed, as recently as the day before yesterday—I made certain inquiries."

"What inquiries, Miss Harriet?" I asked.

The old lady rummaged in her reticule and brought out a small notebook bound in red velvet, to which was attached a silver pencil.

"I inquired of a gondolier," she said. "It's all here in my commonplace book: the questions I put to him and the answers he gave me. Listen. 'Question: Could a determined man deliberately capsize a gondola? Answer: It would be the simplest thing imaginable. Question: Being filled with water, would the gondola nevertheless not float, being constructed largely of wood? Answer: It would retain sufficient buoyancy to remain afloat—just. But it would offer no life-giving support to its former occupants.'"

We stared in concerted horror at Miss Harriet as she replaced her commonplace book in her reticule and, having finished her veal, put her false teeth back in her mouth.

The menfolk had departed on the funeral procession across the Grand Canal. It was a repetition of Peter Chalmers' obsequies, but without the rain; Philippe Demaury's took place in the glowing sunshine of the early evening. He was due back from the church at seven o'clock—a final journey that would end in the family crypt.

No doubt to fortify herself against the possible onset of one of her headaches, Esmeralda announced that she would have a quiet rest till the return of the funeral party. I was left alone in her sitting room with Miss Harriet, who, after her shocking speculations, had taken on a new and sinister dimension in my mind.

"You don't *really* think that Giles Demaury punished Estelle for her cruelty by deliberately drowning her?" I asked.

"I will say to you, my dear Meg, what I have said to you on a previous occasion," replied the old lady. "There is what has been called the Demaury streak—the love of self, money and power. Should any of these three be put in hazard, your Demaury will lie, he will cheat, he will fight, and—in some cases—he will kill to preserve it. It is possible for me to believe he killed his wife because she threw his love for her back into his face—an act of calculated cruelty that not only destroyed the love he had for her, but also threatened what was even more important to him, a Demaury: his own self-esteem, the love he bore for himself. I do not say it with certainty, but I do say that it is *possible* that Giles deliberately overturned that gondola."

I shook my head in puzzlement and looked out the window, across the Grand Canal to the city in which the Demaury family had for so long enjoyed honor, prestige, riches. How could any one of them risk all that with an act of callous murder? And yet, if Lorenzo was right, someone—and almost certainly a member of the clan—was doing it at that living moment.

Forget Lorenzo: banish his name from one's mind . . .

Frantically, I sought for a question: something to start the old lady talking again, to keep my attention distracted from the hurtful thoughts of my hopeless love.

"But surely, Miss Harriet," I said, "what you call the Demaury streak is a very rare phenomenon. In your own case, for instance—why, it would be impossible—absurd—to contemplate you doing anyone ill for love of self, money, or power."

She remained silent for longer than I liked: indeed, I thought that I had unwittingly offended her, for she sat for a while with her head bowed, looking down at her hands—small, white hands they were, with swollen veins and knobbly joints at fingers and wrists. And when she looked up again, I saw that she was crying.

"I'm sorry, Miss Harriet . . ." I began.

"Dear Meg," she said in her grating voice—so unpleasing to the ear, yet so curiously sincere in tone and timbre. "My dear, you have no cause for sorrow. That you have unwittingly touched a chord of memory and made me cry with the recollection is not entirely a matter for regret. Even my sadness is not unmingled with joy."

"Joy mixed with sadness," I said. "I know what you mean."

"You know because you are in love, my dear," said she. "It is the burden that lovers have had to bear since time began. I loved once. Now you would hardly believe that, would you? Poor ugly old spinster Harriet in love. No—don't give me any reassurance, Meg. I am poor and old, and I was never beautiful. 'Plain little Harriet'—that was what my mother called me."

"People—people who should know better—can be so cruel," I said, but she was not listening to me. Her washed-out blue eyes were far away in scenes of memory long gone.

"He was younger than I," she said. "The handsomest man I ever saw in my life. A soldier, fresh from India. The Bengal Lancers. How the gels swooned to see him in his regimentals. I never thought I had the slightest chance, but he danced with me all night at Lady Delaney's charity ball. 'Miss Harriet,' he said, 'I have never enjoyed an evening so much. It is as if I had known you all my life.' I fell in love with him there and then."

"I know the feeling," I murmured, reaching out and taking her hand. "Suddenly to realize that one has become part of another human being."

"We rode together in the Row," she said. "We went to theaters, parties. My mother could scarcely believe it. That plain little Harriet was being courted by one of the most eligible bachelors in London, and long after she had been consigned to the shelf. Oh, how Mother looked at me with a newfound respect." She laughed —it was a bitter laugh.

I saw a fresh tear gathering in the corner of her eye.

"Don't speak of it any further, Miss Harriet," I murmured. "You will only upset yourself."

"We went to Kew," she said. "I wore a sprigged muslin, carried a parasol of the same material. He wore a striped blazer and a boater with a bright ribbon. We sat side by side in the Orchid House and he said to me, 'Harriet, how does a fellow go about proposing marriage to a girl?' I said—after taking a deep breath, to try and check the wild beating of my heart—I said, 'Well, it's really quite simple. You simply take her hand in yours and say the words—straight out, like a man.' And then he said . . ."

Her voice died in a sob.

"Miss Harriet, please . . ."

"Then he said, 'Do you mean, like this?' And he took my hand in his. I said, 'Yes. Now you simply say the words, straight from the heart.' At that moment, someone walked past, and he gently released my hand. And then—quite simply—he broke my heart."

"Oh, my dear," I murmured.

"He said, 'Harriet, what should I do without you? You are like a sister to me. I'll remember your advice—so sincere and straightforward, just like your dear self. Wish me luck this evening, little sister. With luck, I shall be an engaged man when next we meet.' And then he kissed me on the cheek. Like—like a brother."

She broke down completely, and I put my arm about her thin shoulders.

"Don't take on so, dear Miss Harriet," I begged her.

"He married a great beauty," she said brokenly. "She accepted him at once, of course. And, do you know, Meg? I could not bring myself to hate him for breaking my heart, nor her for taking what I dearly would have wished for myself. We are not all bad, we Demaurys. There is some good, even in the worst of us."

The promise of a fine evening was broken by storm clouds that blew in from the west. The return of the funeral procession was heralded by sheeting rain, and every umbrella that the Palazzo Demaury could muster was pressed into service to escort the mourners from the gondolas into the portals, where we women-folk waited. There were four of us, for Miss Harriet, Esmeralda and I had been joined by Helena Brayne. We stood, black-veiled, with lighted candles in our hands, as Bernard Demaury preceded the coffin into the echoing archway. Hat in hand, his few strands of hair plastered to his domed skull with rain, Bernard looked older than his years. After the bearers came Axel, who flashed me a brief smile of recognition. Then Rupert Brayne, who appeared bored and resentful at having been dragged through the rain be-hind the coffin of one of his wife's relations. He was followed by the various entourages. Mr. Obadiah brought up the rear: I presumed that he was representing his master at the obsequies.

Lighted candles were handed to them all, and with a bow to Bertrand Demaury, Obadiah took the lead and motioned to us to follow him. Thus was Philippe Demaury brought to his final resting place.

The way lay along a narrow, stone-built tunnel that ran from a dark corner of the patio and right under the whole bulk of the palazzo. At the end of it, a short flight of steps led up to an iron-barred door of ancient appearance. This, Obadiah unlocked with a massive key. The door creaked open when he lifted the heavy latch. One by one, we filed in.

The inside smelled of dankness. By the light of our flickering candles I could see green mold plastered on the pillars that supported the roof, and the flagstones were wet and slippery beneath my feet.

We came to another door, which was unlocked. Inside was the family crypt of the Demaurys.

It was a circular chamber of no great size. Indeed, the funeral party—we must have numbered twenty or so, including the bearers—fairly filled the space that surrounded a raised dais upon which the coffin was slowly laid.

I looked about me, and experienced a sensation of awe to see that the circular walls were lined with three tiers of stone shelves, on which stood massive bronze caskets embellished with heavy scrollwork, each bearing an oval plaque upon which, in most cases, names and dates were limned in gilded lettering. I read the one nearest me:

James Henry Demaury
Obiit 4th June, 1841

And, next to it, a name to conjure with: the great founder of the family fortunes:

George Fanshawe Demaury
Obiit 19th September, 1817

The coffin having been placed on the dais, the four bearers withdrew, leaving the principal members of the family surrounding it. Esmeralda nudged my elbow.

"What happens now?" she whispered.

I shook my head. "I have no idea," I whispered back.

As if in answer to her question, Bertrand Demaury gave a preparatory cough and said, "Ladies and gentlemen, I should tell you that the coffin will lie here overnight, on the catafalque. Tomorrow workmen will lift down one of the caskets—it is a considerable task, requiring ropes and sheerlegs—and lay the coffin within it, afterward replacing the casket on its shelf."

"That's what they did with Uncle Charles, my father's brother," said Miss Harriet in a hoarse stage whisper. "I remember it well. That's him over there—do you see the name?"

Bertrand cast her a disapproving glance and went on: "There is no more to be said. The last rites have been performed, but I have no doubt that you will wish to pay your final respects to the departed, so we will stand in silent prayer for a few minutes."

In the stillness that followed, I heard the slow drip of water on stone, Miss Harriet's labored breathing behind me, the beating of my own heart. I tried to assemble some suitably pious thoughts relating to the man whose remains lay in the draped coffin before us, but nothing would come. I could only see a white-faced creature scrabbling for a handhold in the water below—and I deliberately shut out the image. I glanced covertly toward Bertrand Demaury, standing opposite me, head bowed and eyes closed. What was he thinking of? I wondered; he who had been roundly accused by the frantic widow, and toward whom the finger of suspicion was still firmly pointed. Was it so? Had he really caused Philippe's death? Were the bowed head, the closed eyes, a mask to hide the countenance of a murderer?

The damp crypt grew stifling hot with candle flame. I could see a haze of steam rising from the rain-soaked shoulder of the man in front of me. Somebody coughed and shuffled his feet.

And Esmeralda chose that moment to faint!

She slid sideways, slowly, a moan on her lips. I steadied her before she could fall, and Axel von Wuppertal gathered her in his arms.

"I have her," he murmured. "Let's get out of here and into some fresh air."

They parted to let us through, me leading, with Axel and his limp burden following. We took Esmeralda down the corridor and across the patio to the morning room, where Axel laid her upon a sofa, whereupon she immediately opened her eyes.

"Oh, dear," she said weakly. "Did I have an attack of the vapors?"

"You did," I replied. "Just as I had anticipated. Furthermore, you swooned all over me. Esmeralda, you really must learn the limits of your capabilities. Funerals are not for you, my dear."

"And now I've one of my heads coming on," she wailed, pressing a slim hand to her brow. "Do you think you could carry me up to my room, Axel?"

"You are quite capable of walking upstairs, with a little assistance from me, dear," I said unfeelingly. And I gave Axel a knowing nod. "Don't worry. I'll see her to bed."

Axel seemed loath to leave and threw me a longing glance.

"Will you not join me for supper, Meg," he murmured, "after you have put the patient to bed?"

"Not tonight, Axel," I said. "Thank you, but I'm rather tired."

"What are you two muttering together about?" demanded Esmeralda peevishly. "I do hate people who mutter. And my headache's getting worse by the moment."

"Come then, my dear," I said, taking her arm and helping her to rise. "Bed for you."

"Good night, ladies," said Axel. "I will see you tomorrow." The remark was seemingly addressed to both of us, but the look and the message were all for me. My heart went out to him in compassion. If he loved me as he said he did—and I had not the slightest reason to doubt him—I knew well enough how he was feeling.

"Yes, tomorrow," I said. And I smiled at him.

But the new dawn was destined to bring no time for dalliance with an unrequited love.

I was summoned from my bed by an urgent knocking. It was Mr. Obadiah, and the factotum of the palazzo was quite insistent. The police were here, he told me. And Prince Lorenzo insisted on seeing me immediately. I needed no second bidding.

It was eight o'clock. By eight thirty I had bathed and dressed and was running down the stairs, two at a time, my eager heart running two steps ahead of me. Obadiah had said Lorenzo was in the morning room. I paused when I reached the door, waited till I had somewhat composed myself before I went in. The mere sight of him, standing by the window, his back to me, set my heart pounding anew.

"Good morning, Prince," I said.

He turned. The expression on his face made me catch my breath with alarm.

"Please shut the door, Miss Gaunt," he said.

"What's the matter?" I asked. "What has happened?"

There was a tray of coffee things on the table. He poured out two cups and motioned to me to be seated.

"Drink this," he said. "You will need to be fortified. I am afraid that I am about to impose upon you a most distasteful task. In short, I am requesting you, if you will be so kind, to break the news to Mrs. Bertrand Demaury and her daughter that he—their husband and father respectively—is dead."

"Bertrand Demaury—*dead?*" I stared at him unbelievingly. "But I was with him at the funeral only last evening."

Lorenzo nodded. "Of that I am well aware, Miss Gaunt," he said.

"But—how?"

"The wife has been sent for," he said. "As has been her custom since their arrival in Venice, she sleeps aboard the yacht, which she prefers to the palazzo. The daughter, Mrs. Brayne, has yet to be called. It was presumed by all concerned that the dead man slept here in the palazzo last night. Such, however, was not the case." His marvelous gray eyes looked down at me reflectively, as if weighing up my fortitude. "I regret having to tell you this so early in the morning, but it has to be done. Can you bear to hear the rest?"

"Yes," I whispered, far from sure that I spoke the truth.

Lorenzo strode over to the window again and looked out. I was able to gaze upon him in unconcealed admiration, mingled with dread. Black-clad, as ever, he loomed magnificently against the morning light that was reflected back into the room from the glistening waters below.

He said, "At six o'clock this morning, a party of workmen arrived here with sheerlegs, ropes, and various tools and appliances to enable them to place the coffin of the late Philippe Demaury in its designated casket within the crypt. These men were given some breakfast in the kitchen, after which they proceeded to the crypt, carrying their gear with them. Miss Gaunt, I would give much to spare you all this."

"Please continue," I told him. "I'm quite strong-minded, I promise you."

"Arriving at the outer door of the crypt," he said, "they found it locked, with the key in place. This is what they had been led to expect. But, upon opening the door, they found—"

Greatly dreading, I prompted him. "Yes, Prince—they found—what?"

"They found Bertrand Demaury," he said. "He was quite dead,

with a candle lying close by. It is clear that the candle fell from his hand and was extinguished."

"You mean, he was locked in the crypt?" I cried. "Locked in there—*all night?*"

"The police doctor has given me a preliminary report," said Lorenzo. "Demaury died sometime before midnight. Of heart failure brought on by—shock."

"Shock?" I exclaimed, suddenly appalled.

He nodded. "The condition of the deceased man's hands—the fingernails—indicate that he spent some considerable time and effort in trying to—to beat and claw his way out of the crypt."

"Locked in there!" I breathed, horrified. "Locked in that awful place. In the dark. Fighting to get out. Screaming—"

"Miss Gaunt, I never should have told you this!"

"I was asleep long before midnight," I said. "And during that time he was fighting to get out of that awful place. All alone. An ill man. Dying of fright in the dark!" I buried my face in my hands, fighting in my mind to keep out the image that burned before my eyes.

I felt Lorenzo's hands on my shoulders, and it was like the touch of fire.

"It is all over now, Miss Gaunt," he said. "He is at peace. And now the living must be served."

I opened my eyes, looked up into his.

"Yes," I said. "His wife and daughter. Of course. You want me to break the news to them."

"Without telling them—the details that I have given to you, of course."

"Of course."

"Simply that he died of heart failure. He was, as everyone knows, prone to these attacks. It could have happened at any time."

"Only—it happened in the crypt," I said, watching his eyes.

"Yes."

"How did he come to be locked in the crypt, Prince?"

"I do not know, Miss Gaunt. But I shall find out."

"You think that he was locked in deliberately, don't you?"

"Yes."

"By the same person who caused the death of Philippe Demaury?"

"Yes, Miss Gaunt."

"And by the same person who armed the Borgia goblet and killed Lord Peter Chalmers?"

"Miss Gaunt, you read me like a book."

Lorenzo gave me an entirely free hand in the matter of breaking the tragic news to the dead man's wife and daughter. Mindful of Helena's unflattering estimation of her mother's character, I doubted if my news, however tactfully delivered, would do any other than send the poor woman into hysterics. It then occurred to me that it might be best to tell Helena first, in the hope that her summation of her own character might be so far from the truth that she would surprise even herself and reveal, in grief and adversity, the fortitude that she had never had occasion to need in her pampered upbringing. After all, I thought, she bore an impossible marriage with quite remarkable courage. Who knows?—there might be unsuspected depths of strength in her. Enough, perhaps, to reach out and strengthen her mother. Yes, I decided—first I would break the news to Helena. She might then prefer to go herself to her mother.

In the event, it happened quite differently.

Obtaining directions from Obadiah as to the whereabouts of the suite of rooms that Helena shared with her husband, I set off upstairs upon my daunting task. On the way, I met Rupert Brayne coming down. He was wearing his impeccably tailored riding-out clothes and was smoking a cigarette—a habit I abhor. His haughty gaze flickered over me for an instant, then he gave me a brief "Good morning, ma'am," and went on his way.

My mind was made up on the instant.

"Mr. Brayne, I would like a word with you!" I said sharply.

He halted. Turned. Looked up at me with an expression of annoyance. Clearly, a man who was not accustomed to being peremptorily addressed by a nobody.

"Ma'am, whatever your business, it will have to wait," he said. "I'm due over at the Lido."

"You won't be riding out at the Lido today, Mr. Brayne," I retorted quietly. "Not unless you are the most unfeeling man who ever breathed. And I can't believe that—even of you."

His eyes opened wide at that.

"Madam, have you taken leave of your senses?" he demanded.

There was a balcony leading off from a half-landing near where we stood. I pointed to it. "Come out here, Mr. Brayne," I told him. "Sit down on one of those seats and compose yourself. I have something to tell you."

For an instant I thought he would refuse: turn on his booted heel and continue down the stairs without deigning even to give me the scant courtesy of a refusal; but curiosity, and something else—a sudden realization, perhaps, that the insignificant Miss Gaunt was not the nobody he had reckoned her to be—made him stay. Motioning me to precede him, he went out onto the balcony, waited till I had seated myself, and then sat down. From his waistcoat pocket he took out a gold half-hunter watch, which he opened and laid on the arm of his chair.

"I have a gondola awaiting me at the steps, ma'am," he said, "and it will so remain another ten minutes, at the end of which time I shall depart in it. Tell me what you have to tell me. You have ten minutes."

I steeled myself for a bold thrust to pierce the guard of his insufferable male arrogance.

"Mr. Brayne," I said, "do you love your wife?"

The dark eyes flared with surprise; his chin went up.

"That is a most improper question, ma'am," he said.

"Why so?" I asked. "I find it perfectly reasonable, and simple enough to answer. Indeed, your wife volunteered the information without my asking. She loves you—do you know that, sir?"

"I—I—is that what you have to tell me?" he asked, confused.

"Not all I have to tell you," I replied. "There is more. But—first—will you answer my question, please? Do you love your wife? It has a bearing upon what I have to tell you, and believe me, what I have to impart is very grave."

I nearly lost him then. I think he was within an ace of rising to his feet and leaving me. And then his angry, confused eyes wavered and were directed toward his hands—lean, horseman's hands. When he spoke, his voice was husky and strained.

"Miss Gaunt, it is common knowledge that I married for money," he said. "You may ask them at my club back home in Boston, at the Royal Yacht Squadron in Cowes, in the gentlemen's smoking rooms of every smart hotel in Paris, Berlin, Rome. I am something of a laughingstock in all those places—and many more.

"I was bought, ma'am—purchased—for a marriage settlement. That is common knowledge. That is what the world thinks."

"And is it true?" I asked.

He shrugged. "The bald fact is true. I possessed a name, a place in Society. But I had no fortune. The Demaury marriage made good the deficiency. And now I am a rich laughingstock."

"And Helena—what of her?"

He gave no sign of surprise at my using his wife's first name, but replied, "Helena is a very sensitive person. She was not unaware of the looks that were thrown our way when we mingled together in Society, the silence that fell over a gathering when we entered, the sly whispers behind fans, the mocking eyes that were rolled in our direction, the hum of cruel comment that followed our departure."

"And so you no longer mingle together in Society?"

"As much by Helena's wish as by mine, I assure you," he replied.

"Not even to Murano?" I asked quietly. "Would the simple glassblowers of Murano have known that you married for money, and have mocked you both in consequence?"

He met my gaze. It suddenly struck me that I had seen the expression before—somewhere, just beyond the edge of my remembrance.

"That was a genuine lapse of memory, Miss Gaunt," he said. "And I have regretted it ever since."

"You explained that to Helena?" I asked.

He shook his head. "When things go wrong—badly wrong—with a marriage, there are some explanations that die on the lips. Helena simply would not have believed me."

"I think she would have believed you," I told him. "Or, at least, I think she would have *wished* to believe you."

"You think that—truly?" he asked.

"Yes, I do," I said. "Now will you answer my question—do you love her?"

He did not reply for a few moments, and in that time I remembered where I had seen the expression on his face: it was the same hungry, yearning look that Helena had worn.

"The bald fact of my marrying for money is true," he said. "But I would have married Helena if she had been a pauper's daughter. Now, I don't expect you to believe that. The world will never believe that, no matter how much I protest. And things have gone so badly wrong with our marriage that not even Helena believes it any more."

"But you believe it?" I demanded.

"Why, yes, of course," he replied without hesitation.

"Then, Mr. Brayne, you have an opportunity to give Helena your strength and your love at a time when she is going to need it as never before in her life," I told him. "You are going to be able to sustain her—and help her to sustain her mother—as never before. I believe that out of a great evil is going to come a great good. For both of you."

And then I told him about his father-in-law's death. Omitting nothing.

My encounter with Rupert Brayne took place around nine thirty. By eleven o'clock, he was escorting his wife and mother-in-law from the Palazzo Demaury to the yacht *Semiramis*, to bury his murdered father-in-law at sea, and then proceed home to America. I did not intrude upon their grief with farewells, but watched from the window of the morning room as the gondola shaped a course toward the Dogana; saw how he held both women's hands; saw the splendor in Helena's eyes, outshining her tears.

After that the palazzo became a turmoil.

Passing through the patio on my way upstairs to see Esmeralda, I came upon piles of baggage that were being carried down and deposited by the servants; and upon inquiring, I was told that the guests were leaving. News of the latest tragedy had swept through the great mansion like the whisper of a plague. The palazzo had become a place of death, and no one wanted any part of it.

Esmeralda had been told. I found her already up and dressed, though she had declared that she would spend the day in bed. Her lady's maid had given her the dreadful news with her midmorning breakfast tray.

"I'm not staying here to be murdered!" she cried. "Where have you been, Meg? Why are you never around when I want you?"

"I've been rather busy," I told her. "Talking to various people."

"It couldn't have been important!" she snapped.

"It was all fairly important," I said.

"In the end I had to send for Axel," she said. "I'm leaving at once, of course. It's quite clear that somone is trying to kill us all —all the Demaurys who are likely to get the inheritance. Well, I shan't be here to be slaughtered like a lamb. Axel has gone to the Hotel Danieli to secure me a suite of rooms for the night. I—that is, we, you and I—will leave for England first thing tomorrow."

"Leave Venice?" The very thought of it was like a stab to the heart. Leave Lorenzo?

"Of course!" she shrilled, her baby-blue eyes wide and staring. "You don't think I could rest easy within a hundred miles of this place, do you? We would have gone this very day, but I sent Axel to the railway station and he came back with the news that there isn't another sleeping compartment to Dover till tomorrow morning. I shall spend tonight in terror of my life."

At that moment there came a knock at the door. Esmeralda gave a shriek of alarm.

"Who is it?" I called.

"Axel."

I let him in. He smiled to see me.

"Well, did you get me a suite?" demanded Esmeralda.

"Yes, I did," he replied.

"With a bath and running hot and cold water?"

"Yes."

"And a sitting room?"

"Yes, there is a very handsome sitting room, Esmeralda."

"And a room for Meg?"

"Yes."

"Well, you can take me there," said Esmeralda. "I shall go now."

Axel gave me a discreet wink. "Very well, Esmeralda."

She jammed a hat pin firmly through her bonnet and neatly rolled chignon of golden hair, and picked up her reticule.

"Come, then," she said.

"But what about your things?" I asked, gesturing round the bedroom. Like every living quarter that Esmeralda occupied for more than a few hours, the place was littered with articles of discarded attire, while scent bottles, items of maquillage, hair tongs, cascades of hairpins, powder puffs, and pieces of jewelry overspilled every table. And I knew that the dressing room next door was piled high with crumpled, discarded linen—not to mention the three large cabin trunks and eight hatboxes full of clothing not yet used.

"You will attend to my things, of course," she said with some surprise. "Who else? Get that stupid girl who's been acting as my lady's maid to pack everything. And see that the minx doesn't steal any of the jewelry. Then arrange for it all to be brought over to the Danieli and join me there. Come, Axel."

He gave a shrug of helplessness and followed after her. A minute later, he was back.

"Meg, I've something here for you," he said.

He held out his hand. I was shocked to see a small pistol made of dull blue metal lying in his palm.

"For—me?" I exclaimed.

He nodded. "Not to alarm you, Meg, but I think you should have it for your protection while you are in this place. It is quite simple to operate. See—you depress this catch, and the trigger can be pulled. There are six bullets in place, and they will fire for so long as you continue to pull the trigger."

"No, Axel—no!" I said, waving the thing away.

"You will not take it?" he said. "Meg, I beg of you—for your own protection—just take it, even if you have no intention of using it, save to frighten an intruder."

"No!" I cried. "I hate guns."

"Not even if I remove the bullets? See—I take them out. The pistol is now only for show, to unnerve anyone who might wish to harm you."

"No one is going to harm me," I told him. "Axel, I am going to supervise the packing of Esmeralda's things and my own, and then I am coming to the hotel. It is broad daylight, Axel. There is no one in the Palazzo Demaury, or the whole world, who has any cause to harm me. Now, will you please go and leave me to sort out this mess? Go, my dear, before Esmeralda comes back to find out what's become of you."

He left. I shut the door behind him and leaned against it, closing my eyes and drawing a deep breath. The prospect of our imminent departure from Venice completely unnerved me. How should I exist without seeing Lorenzo, if only occasionally? Even to know that he lived and breathed under the same patch of sky was enough to sustain me. I knew what would happen to me when we arrived back in England: there would then begin the long and empty journey through the years without him. I would become an old maid like Miss Harriet: locked in a prison of memories, with only the grave as my release.

A distant clock struck the hour, and was joined by others. The sounds jolted me back into reality. There was much to be done, and the doing of it would fill my mind—which was a blessing.

I pulled the bell rope to summon the maid, but without waiting for her I set to, to make some inroads upon Esmeralda's scattered belongings. I was still at it a quarter of an hour later—and no sign of the maid. I pulled the bell rope once more and resumed my task.

When the hour struck again, I was still at it. And still no maid. The bedroom by that time was in some sort of order. I had packed the clothing away in a trunk, and the bits and pieces into Esmeralda's vanity box. Pushing back a stray lock of hair, I remarked to myself that I had missed luncheon and was hungry. Moreover, the light was failing, it was oppressively hot, and I felt in need of a bath. At that moment a flash of lightning lit up the shadowy bedchamber, and it was immediately followed by a crash of thunder from overhead. And then the rain poured down outside the window.

I looked out. The Grand Canal was deserted save for a few craft which hastened through the rain-splashed water.

The storm continued. It grew darker. I lit a candelabrum to see my way inside the dressing room, which was windowless. It must have been four o'clock or later by the time I had finished my lonely task: everything put away in a trunk or hatbox, and everything labeled. It only remained for me to gather up my own traps.

I went out into the corridor, which was unlit and shadowy. It occurred to me to wonder why the servants had not thought to provide any illumination—as they had been in the habit of doing during all the bad weather we had experienced in the city, when the skies had been so dark. On my way to the main staircase I passed a narrow flight of steps that was used by the servants, and there I heard the sound of footfalls descending. Prompted by curiosity, I paused to see who it might be. Esmeralda's maid, perhaps, come in answer—in exceedingly belated answer—to my repeated summons.

It turned out to be my own maid, the child Assunta. She was dressed in street clothes, with a kerchief over her head and tied under her chin. After her came a middle-aged man carrying a tin trunk. Her eyes opened wide to see me.

"Oh, *signorina*, what will you think of me?" she said.

"Why, what have you done—what's the matter?" I asked.

Before she could reply, her companion addressed her in voluble Italian, indicating me. She replied in the same language, and with equal force. When the exchange had finished, she returned her attention to me.

"This is my father," she explained. "The news is all over Venice that another *signor* has died. Peoples is saying that the Evil Eye has come to the palazzo. My father, he has come to take me away with all the rest."

"All the rest?" I cried. "You mean—all the other servants have gone?"

She nodded vigorously. "*Si, signorina,*" she said. "All is saying that they will not stay here with the Evil Eye. I must go now, *signorina*, or my father will be angry and beat me. Please forgive. *Addio, signorina.*"

They clattered off down the next flight of steps and along a corridor below. I heard a door slam shut behind them. And then there was silence.

Like rats abandoning a dying ship, the inhabitants were fleeing the Palazzo Demaury. Esmeralda had gone. The remainder of the guests had likely gone. The servants were fleeing.

Was I, then, alone in the mansion—alone in the house of death, where dwelt the Evil Eye?

Panic seized me. Quickening my pace from a walk to a run, I sped down the long corridor toward the staircase, my footfalls sounding perilously loud and revealing upon the marble-tiled floor.

It was then I heard a thin and wavering cry: coming from behind one of the doors which I had just passed. It sounded like a summons for help.

I paused irresolutely. Was it a trap? I do not reckon myself to be a brave person, and I would have given anything to have turned and run. Run, fool, I told myself. There is nothing there for you but peril. Anything—anyone—could be waiting for you behind that door.

Then the call was repeated, and I recognized the voice.

I opened the door and looked inside. A small lobby led directly into a bedchamber. Though the shutters of the inner room were half-closed and the sky outside as dark as night, I could dimly perceive a small figure lying upon a huge tester bed, gray hair spread against a white pillow. I remembered that I had been in that apartment before.

"Miss Harriet, is it you?" I called.

"Meg, oh, Meg, what a blessing you have come," she replied feebly. "I have been lying here, ringing the bell, but no one answered me."

I went in to her. There was a box of vestas on the bedside table, and a candlestick. When I made to take out a match and light the candle she gave a small cry of protest.

"No light!" she said. "I couldn't bear for you to see me as I am —without my paint and powder. I can't face the world without my paint and powder, Meg. And my hair all in rats' tails."

"Let me do your hair for you, Miss Harriet," I said.

"Not now, my dear," she said. "I'm too tired. I can't imagine why I should be tired, for I slept like a babe all last night. The contented sleep well, Meg. They sleep very soundly, do the contented."

"And you are contented?" I said, amused. "Well, I'm glad to hear that, Miss Harriet."

"Sit down, Meg," she said, pointing to a seat close by the bed. "Sit down, for I have much to tell you."

I obeyed her. "Now, what have you to tell me, Miss Harriet?" I asked.

"Concerning the inheritance, my dear," she said, "what would surprise you most—about the outcome, I mean?"

"You mean—which of the Demaurys do I think least likely to succeed?" I said.

"Yes. Yes. Which of us?"

"I really don't know," I admitted.

She clicked her tongue impatiently. "Come now, gel. Of all the Demaurys and their adherents, which of 'em do you think the most unlikely to succeed?"

There came a roll of thunder. It seemed farther away than the last. Perhaps the storm was passing, I thought. But it was still as dark as night.

I searched my mind and said, "Well, I suppose I can be counted as an adherent, being related to the Demaurys by marriage. And of all the people who came here, I would guess that I have no chance, no chance at all."

Again the old lady gave an impatient click of the tongue, and a dismissive gesture of her thin hands. "Of course, of course," she said testily. "You are not even under consideration. I speak of the principal Demaurys and their immediate relations: the younger offspring, the in-laws, the—old and unconsidered . . ." She made a significant pause. And I knew what was expected of me.

"Why, Miss Harriet," I said, "I suppose that, of all the Demaurys here, one would count you as being the least likely to succeed to the inheritance. I mean—as you yourself have told me—Giles Demaury has never liked you, ever since childhood."

In the gloom I saw her thin mouth pucker in a toothless smile, and knew that I had seized upon the answer for which she had been fishing.

"Quite correct," she said approvingly. "And that is exactly what everyone thinks. But everyone is completely wrong!"

A crash of thunder rattled the window frames. I strained my eyes to read the expression on her countenance. It crossed my mind that she might be delirious. I decided to humor her.

"Why don't you have a little nap, Miss Harriet?" I said. "I have to pack my things and arrange for someone to deliver them, along with Esmeralda's, to a hotel. We're all leaving here, did you know? Would you like to come with us? I'm sure it can be arranged. Have a nap, do, and I'll wake you up as soon as I've . . ."

"You don't believe me, do you?" she said, breaking in on my remarks. "You think I've gone soft in the head. But it's true, you know, I'm to succeed."

"If you say so, Miss Harriet," I said placatingly. "Now, close your eyes and . . ."

"The doctors tell me I'm very ill," she said. "But it's all lies. That fool doctor in Cambridge, he said I might die at any time if I wasn't careful. Told me to give up drinking brandy. Humph! I'll drink as much brandy as I choose, and I'll still outlive *him*. Yes, I expect to live for years yet. Strange, though, that I'm not feeling at my best at the moment. But I'll be better soon."

"Of course you will, Miss Harriet," I said. "Of course you will."

Her thin hand stole across the counterpane and slid into mine. It was like touching a dead bird: paper-dry, cold, almost fleshless.

"When I die, Meg, it will all be yours," she said. "I've made my will. Made it before I left England. Everything—the Demaury inheritance—will be yours."

"Miss Harriet!" I exclaimed. "You *can't* have done such a thing!"

"You are the daughter I never had, Meg," she whispered hoarsely. "If the dream of my life had come true—if *he* had asked me instead of another—you would have been my child."

"What are you saying?" I cried.

The ghost of a hand tautened on mine.

"He wasn't a Bengal Lancer, Meg," she said. "I kept the secret from you then, but you must know now. He was a sailor. A Commander, Royal Navy, no less."

"My father!" I exclaimed.

"He was the most wonderful person I have ever known, Meg," she said. "If I had not loved him as I did, I think I would still have regarded him as a man above all men."

"Oh, Miss Harriet," I breathed. "What can I say?"

"I was prepared to hate her, your mother," she said. "The

Demaury streak, you know. And then, quite by chance, I met this beautiful young woman at a tea party in Mayfair. We were introduced and sat chatting together for some time. I had already decided that I wanted this delightful person as a friend, when someone said that she was engaged to Commander Dick Gaunt. And then it was too late to hate her."

"You—became friends?" I asked.

"We met from time to time," she replied. "I first saw—the two of them together—when your mother's sister married James Demaury. By then the hurt had lessened. They were, of course, the most glorious couple. My admiration quite quenched any jealous resentment. But I never did overcome the awful sense of—loss."

I saw a tear trickle down the lined cheek. And she closed her eyes and winced, as if in pain.

"Don't talk any more, Miss Harriet," I said. "Rest."

"Then you were born," she said. "And soon after came news that—he—had died in the West Indies. I flew to your mother's side, to offer what comfort I could. But it was no use. She had lost all reason for living. I understood. If I had once lived in the great light of his love, I could never have existed without him."

My own tears were falling: I felt them splash upon my hand, still clasping hers.

"I don't remember either my mother or my father," I said. "And, do you know, Miss Harriet?—that is what hurts me most. After the wonderful things that people have told me about my parents—never to have known them."

"Yes, yes, you were no more than a baby when you were orphaned," she said. "It was I who persuaded Roland Demaury to take you in. Worst day's work I ever did in my life. All was well till that Esmeralda came along. From then on you were naught but an unpaid skivvy. Oh, you were educated well enough. Clothed and fed. But that Esmeralda. Hateful creature. The way she has treated you through the years. The way she treats you now. You, Meg—who might have been my own daughter, if only—"

She broke off as a paroxysm of coughing racked her thin frame. Helpless to aid her in any way, I could only hold her hand and wait for her agony to cease. When it did, I could see, even in the gloom, that a terrible change had been wrought upon her. There was not a vestige of color in her face, which had taken on the appearance of a skull, with the strained skin stretched tautly across the bones. Her breath was labored, and her voice scarcely above a whisper when she spoke to me again:

"I shall get better, Meg. Meg, where are you?"

"Here I am, Miss Harriet," I said, gently squeezing her hand.

"Stay with me, Meg," she said. "I shall be better soon. Then we can go away together. The fortune, it's all to be mine, you know. Every penny. And when I'm gone, it will all be yours. You'll be rich, Meg. Rich beyond belief."

"Don't say any more, dear," I told her. "Rest yourself."

"That Esmeralda," she said. "Wicked, like all the Demaurys. I sent her that adder, you know. After that dinner party. The way she treated you. Like an unpaid slavey. The way she treated that other poor gel—humiliated her in front of us. I sent the adder. Wish it had bitten her. Heh!"

I stared down at her, a slow finger of horror tracing the whole length of my spine. Involuntarily, I made to draw away my imprisoned hand, but her grip tightened and held me fast.

"Miss Harriet . . ." the words choked and died on my lips.

"The doctors are all fools," she whispered. "I shall be better soon. Where shall we go to, Meg? Shall it be Monte Carlo? Would you like that, eh?"

"Yes," I said.

"Are you there, Meg?"

"Yes, I'm here, Miss Harriet."

"Don't leave me. I'm very frightened," she said. And then I think she breathed my father's name.

And then she died.

The storm had abated when I left the chamber of death, having closed Miss Harriet's eyes and drawn the edge of the sheet over her face. I walked in to the staircase, and paused there, listening to hear if there was any life or movement in the great mansion.

Nothing.

I made to ascend the stair.

Wait—what was that?

It came quite clearly from below: the slow padding of bare feet on the tiled steps. Someone was coming up toward me.

I called out, "Who's there?"

No answer. But, worse than that, the footsteps stopped.

"Who is it?" I called again.

Still no reply—but the padding of bare feet on tiles recommenced, more slowly than before. Whoever it was had decided to approach me with stealth. The thought struck me with sudden terror. Turning, I bolted up the stairs, two at a time, my heart pounding.

When I reached the next landing, I paused to listen—but not for long: he—whoever it was—had now become my pursuer; the padding footfalls were coming up at a run!

Retreat became a headlong flight, with no thought but to win myself free from my pursuer, in consequence of which I suddenly realized, when I had gone some distance farther, that I had passed my own floor and was now ascending to the upper stories of the palazzo and heaven knows what perils.

With a pounding in my ears, panic-stricken and near to collapse, I came at length to the top of the staircase. There was an open door at the end of a short passageway. I raced toward it and through the door, slamming it behind me. I breathed a silent prayer of relief, to find my fingers closing on a key. I turned it in the lock, and laid my head against the cool woodwork.

There came a roll of thunder, distant this time. The storm must have gone by. A shaft of thin sunlight played across my hand. Looking round, I saw that I had entered a high-ceilinged chamber with shuttered windows down two sides. There were no furnishings save for a dark picture in a gilded frame on the far end wall. It was the portrait of a woman. On a sudden impulse of curiosity, I approached it.

The artist—and he must have been a painter of considerable skill—had depicted a woman in a scarlet crinoline gown of the early part of the century. Startling against the redness, one slender white hand trailed a lacy handkerchief, and a small monkey in a short jacket and a pillbox hat sat gravely by the woman's skirts.

The monkey!

I knew then who the subject of the picture was. Raising my

eyes, I looked up into the painted representation of Estelle Amor's face.

It was a proud face. High-browed, aristocratic. With the look of a Spanish princess. Raven-black hair fell in careless abandon upon splendid white shoulders. Haughty eyes stared down at me and found me wanting. Eyes that were capable of contemplating cruelty. My gaze wavered before them.

This, then, was the splendid creature whose life and career had blazed like a comet across the early years of the century; the other half of a romance which was spoken of in the same breath as that of Heloise and Abelard, Tristan and Isolde, Guinevere and Lancelot. This was the woman, also, who—if the word of dead Miss Harriet was to be believed—had perished out in the lagoon by the machinations of the husband and lover whom she had so gravely wronged and so often. While marveling at the beauty of the face above me, I conceded that its owner could well have been capable of all the acts with which she was credited.

I was jolted out of my contemplation by a sound from behind me. Alarmed, I turned to see that one half of a double door at the far end of the chamber was slowly opening. Of the hand that turned the latch, there was no sign. It opened inward and was still. All beyond it was in shadow.

The open door, since no one issued through it, could only have one meaning: it was an invitation to me to enter the room beyond. It was not an invitation that I welcomed with any enthusiasm.

I was remarkably short of options: I could either obey the summons or stay where I was. Since I was unarmed and helpless (in that moment, how I wished that I had accepted Axel's offer of the pistol!), the gesture of remaining was a mere futility. Whoever had caused that door to open was calling the tune. If I refused the invitation, if I did not enter the far room of my own free will, I might well be—fetched.

Taking a deep breath, I summoned up the tattered remains of my fortitude and walked slowly down the length of the chamber, toward the open door. As I drew closer, I could see that someone —it looked like a woman, by the silhouette—was seated at the far end of the room beyond. Another five paces and I picked out a splash of redness in the gloom. When I reached the door and passed through, I was able to observe, with mounting alarm, that it was indeed a woman—and that she was wearing a scarlet crinoline, a counterfeit of the one in the painting. Hardly had I realized the fact, and before my mind had come to terms with the implications, when I came abreast of a man standing just behind the door, his hand on the latch.

It was the gardener and sometime gondolier of the palazzo. My glance fell to his bare feet, and I knew who had pursued me up the stairs. The man smiled at me pleasantly enough, bowed slightly, and went out, shutting the door behind him.

I was alone with—the woman in scarlet.

The windows of the room were all shuttered, as in the chamber where the picture hung. By the thin daylight that shone through the cracks, I made out the shape of the raven-dark hair that tumbled about her shoulders, but the face was in deep shadow.

I approached her, the name trembling on my lips. It was unbelievable, absurd, fantastic. And surely not true.

"Estelle Amor?" I whispered.

There came a low laugh from the figure in the chair. She leaned forward slightly, so that her profile was caught in a beam of light from a crack in one of the shutters. It was the face of an old woman; but there was the same haughty look that I had seen in the portrait. One white hand went up and took hold of the raven tresses, pulled at them, drew them away till I was staring in growing realization at a bald head with a feathering of white down.

Under the imperious nose, the thin-lipped mouth parted in a smile of amused mockery.

"Yes, I am Estelle. You are now a party to my secret, my dear. Which is that for the last sixty-odd years the world has known me as Giles Demaury."

CHAPTER SEVEN

"GIUSEPPE tells me that the palazzo is empty, servants and all," said Estelle Amor. "Even Obadiah has deserted me. Well, he will not be missed. As for the Demaurys—" she waved a thin hand with a gesture of contemptuous dismissal—"I could not find it in myself to wish anything but ill for that accursed brood."

I found my voice. "Miss Harriet died in her bed a short while ago," I said. "I was with her at the end."

"Did she then?" was the reply. "Then there will be no more killings."

"I think you are right," I said.

"She killed them all, did you know that, child?"

"I guessed as much," I said.

"She made a deathbed confession, perhaps?"

"No," I said. "I think she might have done so, if she had had the time. She confessed to—something quite disgusting. And it set me thinking that anyone who could do such a thing was capable of almost anything."

"It is the taint of the Demaury blood," said Estelle Amor. "She seemed such a delightful child, and I loved her very dearly. And then, one evening—would you believe it?—it was during a reception we were holding at Morley's Hotel . . ."

"The monkey!" I exclaimed.

The marvelous blue eyes widened with surprise.

"You have heard the story?" she said. "That is curious, because I never breathed a word of the truth to a soul, but supported the child's lie—which was that the poor little creature slipped and fell of its own accord."

"I—I don't understand." I stared at her.

"The child must have been insanely jealous of my affection for the monkey," said Estelle Amor. "I had no idea, of course, that she felt for me with such a passionate intensity. I went out toward the balcony and was witness to her picking up the monkey and throwing it to its death. I was shocked. Horrified. The more so when Harriet—who had no idea that I had seen it all—threw her arms about me and tearfully informed me that the little creature had slipped and fallen. I kept my counsel—said nothing. One does not destroy a small child because of one transgression, however appalling. But I never trusted Harriet Demaury again."

I said, "She told me that it was you who threw the monkey to its death."

The old lady drew breath sharply. "Did she say that? Then she was even more pernicious than I would have believed. I summoned her to see me the other day, you know. For no other reason than to reassure myself that she possessed all the worst traits of the Demaurys in full measure. It was then I became convinced that she had somehow had a hand in Philippe's death, and when I heard of Bertrand's end, I knew that I had not been mistaken. To put it crudely, Harriet was killing off all the most likely candidates, in the belief that she would remain as the only possible Demaury to whom I would leave the inheritance. Little did she know that I would far rather have bequeathed the fortune to charity than that she should have touched a penny."

It was my turn to be surprised. "But, ma'am," I said. "Miss Harriet told me only a short while ago, when she was dying, that she was the one who would inherit. She was quite convinced, I promise you."

It was very still in the room. Estelle Amor had leaned back in her chair, and her face was in deep shadow so that I could not gauge her expression when she replied:

"I cannot imagine how Harriet Demaury could have received such an impression. As I have said, she was the last of the Demaurys to whom I would have left the inheritance. Indeed, knowing them as I do, and feeling about them as I do, I have decided that the inheritance will not go to a Demaury."

Intrigued, I could not resist asking the question that immediately sprang to my mind—in all innocence.

"Then—who, ma'am? Oh! I'm sorry. I had no right—"

Estelle Amor leaned forward so that her face—pink-skinned, and wrinkled all over like a well-kept old apple—was in clear view. And her eyes twinkled with a youthful fire.

"You have every right to ask, Margaret Gaunt," she said mildly. "And I will give you the answer. The one who will inherit is— *yourself.*"

The sky outside had become dark again. I had pleaded with her, begged for reasons, denied that I had any right, told her again and again that I did not want the inheritance. She had listened to none of it. With the bland detachment of the very old, she had waved it all aside and had merely asked me to pull the bell cord and summon the gardener, Giuseppe. Giuseppe came promptly, padding barefoot to the summons; lit the candelabrum that stood upon the table close by the chair where Estelle Amor sat. The warm candlelight played flatteringly with her striking features, and I was put in mind of the beauty in the picture frame next door.

"That will be all, Giuseppe," said she.

"*Si, signora,*" said the gardener, bowing and departing.

"Giuseppe and you are the only two living people who know my secret, child," said Estelle Amor. "I have never revealed it to Obadiah, who is a person of very low quality. Giuseppe, I can trust. To him I entrusted the task of searching your belongings, along with those of the other guests, as soon as you arrived. My apologies. In a person's baggage lies the key to a person's life. From an inventory of yours I inferred that you are poor, thrifty, industrious, faithful, and chaste. All excellent qualities."

I could not help but smile. "And by what means did you deduce that, ma'am?" I asked.

"Simplicity itself," she replied. "As to your poverty: the paucity of your belongings told all; that you are thrifty and industrious was clear from the way—as Giuseppe described to me—that all your clothing is neatly darned and patched. Your faithfulness to your mother's memory is demonstrated by your retaining the quite expensive fob watch, which, as I have pointed out to you on the previous occasion we met, could well have provided you with your freedom."

"You spoke of my being chaste, ma'am," I prompted her.

"Giuseppe was well instructed by me in the art of prying," she said bluntly. "And I told him to pay particular attention to love letters, photographs, and other souvenirs of romantic attachment. He found none in your baggage. By this I inferred—pray correct me if I am wrong—that, prior to your arrival in Venice, you have had no romantic connections with any man. Correct?"

"That is true, ma'am," I admitted.

"But no longer true, as I am led to believe?"

"Ma'am . . ." I faltered.

"You have formed a romantic connection in Venice," she said. It was not a question, but a bald statement of fact. I was completely confounded, and when I tried to frame an answer, she waved me silent, saying, "No, listen to me. To begin at the beginning, my original intent was to summon all the Demaurys here and—before finally passing the entire inheritance to a charity—see if there was not one among them who was worthy to inherit. I even interviewed Bertrand Demaury's daughter and her husband, and I must say that, as a young married couple, they made a most disagreeable impression."

"But they truly love each other," I interposed. "And I am sure that her father's terrible end has brought them together."

"I'm glad to hear it," she replied. "As to whether they receive any of the inheritance: that is now entirely up to you. It is all yours—or will be when I have gone—and you may dispose of it as you choose."

"But, why, ma'am—*why* have you picked me?" I asked her. It was a question I had put to her more times than I could count. This last time I was to have my answer.

"I have spoken before of my very profound admiration for your parents, Margaret Gaunt," she said. "Upon meeting you, I immediately recognized that you had inherited their excellent qualities. One thing in particular struck me very forcibly about you."

"And what was that, ma'am?" I asked.

"It concerned that wretched creature Esmeralda," she said. "You will recall that she contrived a spectacular entrance and greeted me with a vulgar ostentation of most transparent insincerity. I, who do not bear fools—or knaves—gladly, dismissed her with considerable curtness. You, miss, did not like it."

"I thought your action unnecessarily cruel," I admitted. "I'm sorry, but there it is."

The thin lips parted in a smile. "I am known to be cruel," she said. "Indeed, I have already admitted it to you. What struck me forcibly was the fearless way you leapt to her defense: the look of anger that you threw in my direction. And then the compassion with which you comforted her."

I shrugged. "Anyone would have acted so."

"To a creature such as she? To a pampered, unfeeling minx who has kept you in virtual slavery all these years? I do not think many would have acted as you did, child. No Demaury, certainly. Any Demaury would have delighted in her discomfiture."

I stared at her wonderingly. "And for *that*, you are offering me the inheritance?" I asked.

"It began as a caprice, merely," said Estelle Amor. "There and then that very night, I said to myself, 'That child is the best option that I have: better than any charitable institution, better than all the Demaurys put together. Why not leave everything to her?' And the more I pondered it, the more convinced I became that my caprice was based upon a profound truth. If, as I believe, the possession of enormous wealth is a source of power that can be turned either to great good or to great evil, it followed that the daughter of two people for whom I had a profound admiration would be a likely candidate. Presently, I sent for you. I tried and tested you. And I found in you everything that I had hoped to find."

"Your kindness overwhelms me, ma'am," I murmured.

"I am not consistently kind," she replied tartly. "I may say I did not approve of your accompanying young Von Wuppertal on that sightseeing tour. Shortly after, I sent for the gentleman and implied to him that his chances of inheritance were next to nothing."

"Poor Axel," I said. "He got very drunk with disappointment."

"I'm not surprised to hear it," she said. "Weak, like that father of his. Mark you, he's one of the better Demaurys. Has he asked you to marry him yet?"

"Yes," I said, surprised.

"And you refused, of course. Did you tell him that you were in love with another?"

Astonished, I could only stammer, "Ma'am, I don't know how you—"

She said, "I know because Harriet Demaury told me when I sent for her, and, since she spoke of you with what appeared to be genuine warmth and affection, I had no reason to believe that she lied. You are in love with young Giolitti-Crispi, is that correct? No call even to answer me, child: it is written on your face and in your eyes. When one has known great love—as I have—one recognizes it immediately. Love, of the profound and lasting sort, such as I have known—the sort that illuminates life and transcends death—is unmistakable in others."

Greatly affected as I was by her words, I was emboldened then to put the question that I had thus far hesitated to utter:

"Was it for love that you assumed the role of Giles Demaury for all those years?"

The wrinkled old head bowed. Her voice, when she finally answered me, was broken and strained with a sorrow that sounded beyond bearing.

"Not for love," she said, "but for the other side of the coin. What I did, what I have carried on all these years, has been done for hate."

She asked for water, and I poured a glass from a carafe that stood on a table by her. She took a few sips and then closed her eyes. Presently, she was snoring quietly. I tiptoed to one of the windows and opened a shutter part way. Far below, the gray-blue water of the Grand Canal reflected droplets of light from the low-cast afternoon sun that had reappeared from behind the rain clouds. The canal was crowded with boats: all jostling to and fro, packed with people returning home after a day's work. My thoughts flew to Lorenzo: when should I see him again? What would he say when he learned that the killer of the Palazzo Demaury was no more?

The snoring ceased. The figure in the chair stirred.

"Where are you, Margaret Gaunt?"

"Here, ma'am." I returned to my seat. The blue eyes fixed me unwaveringly.

"I restore my energies with sleep, whenever it comes upon me," she said. "And I now feel strong enough to answer your question more fully. No—do not protest—I promise you that, though the telling of it will be painful to me, it is something that I have longed to speak of for over sixty years.

"I have already confessed my great failing: the streak of cruelty that Giles Demaury found so hard to accept. It is possible—indeed likely—that you have heard one or other of the garbled versions of the final and terrible quarrel that took place here. Well, I will tell you what really happened.

"For some time, our violent quarrels, our scandalous behavior to each other and to our friends, had cut us off from Society. We had only the hangers-on: the sort who would go anywhere, suffer any insult, for the sake of free hospitality. One such person—a man of considerable wit and charm, though totally worthless—I found amusing, as creatures of his sort are frequently amusing, in small doses. Giles detested him and finally removed him from our guest list.

"One night we held a dinner party. I had wished to cancel it at the last moment, and for a very special reason: to my delight, to my utter joy, I had only that afternoon visited my doctor and received the confirmation that I was with child. With the intention of our spending a quiet evening together, when I could break the wonderful news to Giles—who I knew would be as overjoyed as I—I begged my husband to call off the dinner party, but he would not hear of it. Indeed, he was surly and preoccupied—like a man who is nursing a grievance. I had a premonition of trouble. Nor was I mistaken.

"That night, over the dinner table, when everyone present had drunk too much champagne, my husband, whose ill-temper had been further inflamed by wine, accused me of having taken a lover. And he named the man—the amusing and worthless cad of whom I have spoken.

"All conversation around the dinner tale immediately ceased. I guessed with what amused expectation they all awaited the usual outcome of a quarrel between Estelle Amor and Giles Demaury: the screams and imprecations, the plate-throwing, the tears and protestations, followed by the passionate reconciliation. I looked about me: at the debauched and useless creatures with whom we had come to surround ourselves; at my own husband, his face flushed with drink and anger, scarcely better than the worst of them. And I sought for a weapon to smite him—and found it.

"Instead of the screamed denial, I calmly gave him the lie that this man was indeed my lover. I saw my shaft strike home as his jealous suspicions—which had been no more than suspicions—suddenly became harsh reality. Relishing the hurt that I had inflicted upon him, in my cruelty, I craved to cut him yet more deeply. So, before all that company, I said the most foolish, the most cruel and senseless thing I have ever uttered, or am now ever likely to utter in my life: I told him that I was with child by that man.

"Margaret Gaunt, you must realize that as love and hate exist, the greater the love, the greater the hate. I offer this as the only explanation for my lie, and the retraction that I made soon afterward. Yes, the morning after, I told Giles it was not true. I told him publicly, before the same worthless creatures who had heard the lie. I thought he believed me; I told myself he believed me, for there was no shade of expression, no nuance of emotion, of his that could ever escape me—I told myself.

"That night we dined and danced together at the Lido. I repeated to myself over and over again that this man loved me with a passion that mirrored my own. We were legends in our own lifetimes. Our romance was already part of the folklore of the civilized world. But I had forgotten, you see, that the opposite side of the coin from love is the imprint of hate.

"As love begets love, so does hate beget hate. In the early hours of the following morning, as I lay choking and gasping on a lonely beach where providence had cast me up, I went through exactly the same experience as Giles Demaury: all my love, my boundless and passionate love, turned into a terrible and all-consuming hate.

" 'Die, the both of you—you and your chance-brat!'—those

were his last words to me. That was the curse he shouted at me as he overturned the gondola in that night of storm!

"I heard it as the waters closed over my head. When I fought my way to the surface again, he was still shouting—but with mortal terror. The gondolier, whose life he had callously thrown away as a necessity of destroying me, had seized upon Giles in his panic, and they drowned together before my eyes.

"I shall never know how, or by what means, I came to safety. I think I may have ceased to care whether I lived or died, and simply allowed myself to be carried on the current—limp, unresisting. And so I was saved. And lived to hate the man who had hated me enough to want to destroy me.

"In the dawn light, with the hate surging within me, I stumbled over the threshold of a hovel belonging to a fisherman and his wife: a young couple who removed my wet clothes, wrapped me in clean rags and put me into their only bed. I took pneumonia after my ordeal. And I—lost the child.

"The couple nursed me to health. Years later they had a son who grew up to become my faithful Giuseppe. His parents died long since, but I shall be forever indebted to them. It was with their help and connivance that I became Giles Demaury, recluse of the Palazzo Demaury. Free to work my revenge upon that accursed brood, of whom Giles, with his ruthlessness and his instinct for murder, was a typical example.

"Giles had most elaborate plans for the continuation of the Demaury empire in the event of his death. By taking over his life, I set all those plans to naught. It was the only way: what chance would a weak woman have stood sixty years ago in a cutthroat international business like Demaury's? Things will be vastly different for you, Margaret Gaunt: the coming century will see the emancipation of women from the thralldom of men.

"As Giles, I was able to issue orders, mold the Demaurys to my will. To my triumph, I discovered that I had a genius for high finance. Within two years I understood every branch of the Demaury enterprise on both sides of the Atlantic, and was taking seventy-five percent of all profits. In sixty years I had them all in the palm of my hand, so that I could bring them here, weigh them, and find them wanting, let them tear each other to pieces—

and then confound them all by giving everything to poor, thrifty, faithful, chaste and industrious Margaret Gaunt."

"I can't accept it—I won't! You must leave the inheritance to a charity, as you had intended."

I strode up and down the chamber before Estelle Amor. She watched me impassively, her splendid old eyes never leaving my face.

"You will serve my purpose as well as any charity," she replied calmly. "Having been as poor and thrifty as a church mouse all your life, you will not squander the fortune. I don't doubt that the bulk of it will go to charity. I shouldn't wonder if you defied my intentions and gave some to various of the Demaurys whom you think to be worthy: young Von Wuppertal, perhaps, and Bertrand Demaury's child and her husband. That is your business. I respect your opinions and have complete confidence in your judgment."

"Thank you for the compliment, ma'am," I said stiffly.

"You are welcome, miss," she responded. "Only, I beg of you, don't be huffy and petulant with me. It doesn't suit your style. And what you have in considerable quantity, Margaret Gaunt— what makes you uniquely suitable to inherit a great fortune—is the elusive and ineffable quality of your style."

I stopped in my striding to and fro, as if transfixed, and stared at her in alarm.

"Ma'am, you have been talking to Prince Lorenzo!" I exclaimed.

"Indeed I have," she said good-humoredly. "Indeed I have. The Prince was here, at my invitation, only the other day. We spoke of many things. We also discussed you at some length, and he gave me his summation of your character, which, you will be pleased to hear, was entirely favorable."

I was putting out a foot to tread on dangerous ground. I hesitated for a brief moment—and trod:

"You didn't tell him about—about—"

"About your feelings toward him? Would I so presume?"

"Of course not, ma'am. I'm sorry. And did he . . . ?"

"Did he give any indication of his feelings toward you? No, my dear. Apart from the observation about your style, he revealed nothing. Giolitti-Crispi, you must remember, is a policeman, and policemen are adept at dissembling. By a flicker of his eyes, a brief change of expression, he may, indeed, have betrayed himself. But if he did, it escaped my poor old eyes. No, I am sorry, but I can be of no help to you. Do I take it that you are doubtful whether your affections are returned?"

"The prince shares his mother's opinion," I said, "that people of widely differing social classes should never marry."

"Does he, now?" she said. "Well, that poses something of an obstacle to your hopes. You are, of course, the daughter of a British naval officer, and connected with a family of considerable commercial and artistic repute; but I fear that these qualifications weigh very lightly against a title that dates back to the Carolingian empire. Still, when he learns that you are heiress to a tremendous fortune, his prejudices against marrying into the lower orders may be somewhat shaken."

I stared at Estelle Amor; she stared back at me. Neither of us spoke for some time.

I said, "It wouldn't make the slightest difference to Prince Lorenzo."

"Of course not," she replied. "I did not seriously imply that it would."

"Or to his mother," I said.

"Particularly his mother. The Princess Giolitti-Crispi, as I understand, is so divorced from harsh realities that in all her born days she has—in common with most of the ancient Italian nobility—never seen or handled money. That is all left to servants."

I said, "But they are very poor. Except that they reside in a splendid palazzo, surrounded by Titians and Tintorettos and Tiepolos, they would hardly have enough money to live on were it not for Lorenzo's salary as Chief of Police."

"This I have heard also," said Estelle Amor. "Indeed, it is common gossip in Venice, accepted by everyone save—I am sure—the Princess Giolitti-Crispi."

Hesitatingly, by easy stages, I sought the gaze of those marvelous eyes.

"What shall I do, ma'am?" I asked her.

The old lady reached out her hand and laid it on my arm.

"Love knows no shame," she said. "Follow your love fiercely, and do as it demands. If it offers any chance at all for you to win Giolitti-Crispi, take the inheritance. It may do you no good with him, no good at all. If your pride prevents you from taking it, so much the worse for you. You may lose him for that very reason. On the other hand, you may not. But you will never know—and you will regret it all your life. It will be a question mark that will haunt your days."

"You believe so deeply in love—after what you have been through?" I asked her.

She drew a deep breath and said, "I have loved, and I have been loved. That is all. Nothing else matters. Have I answered you?"

"Yes," I replied.

She made a small, fussy gesture with her hands. "My dear, I am growing tired," she said. "Giuseppe tells me that Esmeralda has moved to a hotel. Go and join her. This is no place for the young, for the living. Have no worry for the remains of Harriet Demaury: Giuseppe and his wife will do what has to be done, and she will be laid to rest in the family crypt. Come and see me again, Margaret. We shall not meet many more times in this life. Kiss my cheek."

I stooped and kissed her. Her eyes were already closing in sleep, and as I quietly opened the door, the recluse of the Palazzo Demaury was snoring gently.

On her arrival at the Hotel Danieli, Esmeralda had succumbed to a violent attack of headache, so that poor Axel had had to secure a doctor to attend her, and had had to remain with her till she slept, so nervous was she of being left alone.

He greeted me on my arrival at the hotel and invited me to join him for dinner, but I declined, pleading tiredness. I then took him to one side and told him of the death of Harriet Demaury, and of my conclusions about her guilt. His honest, candid eyes opened wide with shock as my tale unfolded. When I had finished, I charged him with the task of contacting Lorenzo and repeating to him everything I had said. This he promised to do immediately. I then rose and firmly bid him good night.

Axel had taken care to see that my room was one of the finest in the hotel, overlooking the end of the Grand Canal, with San Giorgio Maggiore standing like a white sentinel upon its islet opposite. I disrobed, bathed, and, putting on my peignoir, I sat in the window seat while all Venice went to sleep, and lights went out, one by one, on the quays and in the houses across the lagoon, and the moon rose above the domes and towers of that most serene city. And I turned over in my mind the disturbing events of that crowded day, particularly the death of Harriet Demaury, surely the victim of her own frailties, cursed with the Demaury taint of which she had often spoken so bitterly.

I thought of Estelle Amor, for over sixty years the prisoner of her own fate, self-condemned to a life of solitude and memories.

And then my mind turned to Lorenzo and the great love I bore for him. Sweetly comforting, the thought of it lulled me to drowsiness and from drowsiness to a deep and dreamless sleep. When I woke, the moon had gone down, and one single light moved slowly across the lagoon, borne upon a gondola that was slowly shaping its course into the far darkness. I waited and watched till it died in the night; then I laid myself upon the bed and slept till midmorning sunshine crept across the room and warmed my hands and arms.

As light follows darkness, as the rainbow brings promise of blue skies after storms, so, upon my awakening, I experienced a sense of emergence from gloom and heaviness. It was a feeling that was quite unaccountable, for the really important question in my life had not been resolved, and I should have been in a state of deep anxiety about my prospects with Lorenzo. But, curiously, I was not.

So I arose, put on my old skirt and blouse, did my hair in a bow at the back, told myself in the mirror that all was bound to come out well in the end, and went in search of some breakfast.

There was no sign of Axel and Esmeralda, nor of any of the former guests of the Palazzo Demaury. I took coffee and some crusty, crisp bread in the breakfast room, was engaged in conversation by an elderly Englishman of military bearing who was occupying the next table, and had just exhausted all possible variations upon the topic of the Venetian weather, when I became aware of a portly figure in blue moving purposefully across the room toward me. It was the police sergeant. He carried his cocked bicorne hat under one arm, and in his other hand he bore a posy of summer flowers with a frill of paper lace around the edge. Bowing low, he presented the posy to me.

"*Buon giorno, signorina*," he murmured through his soup-strainer mustache.

"Good morning, Sergeant," I responded. "How very kind of you. They smell quite lovely. But what brings you here?" I hoped I knew the answer to my question.

"*Il principe*, he begs you to call upon him, *signorina*," said the sergeant. My heart leapt, and I knew that it was the joyful anticipation of this summons that had accounted for my waking with a feeling of elation.

"Now—at once?" I asked.

"When the *signorina* is ready. There is no hurry," he assured me.

I never finished a cup of scalding-hot coffee so quickly, nor left so large a piece of bread uneaten on my plate. To the elderly English gentleman of military bearing, I wished a "good morning" of such sprightly gaiety as to cause his monocle to fall from his eye and dangle at the end of its ribbon upon his astonished chest. Treading on air, I walked out of the breakfast room with my sergeant of police bringing up the rear.

The boat and crew were waiting at the hotel steps; the men drawn up as for inspection, their oars pointing skyward like guardsmen's muskets. I exchanged greetings with them all, and the sergeant handed me to a seat in the stern, where a plump cushion had been provided. We set off.

To my surprise, we headed straight across the lagoon, leaving the isle of San Giorgio on our right. Ahead, beyond a string of small islets, lay the long, low profile of the Lido.

"Then we are not going to the Palazzo Giolitti-Crispi?" I queried of my sergeant.

"No, *signorina*," he replied, smiling somewhere beneath his great mustache. "*Il principe* is at the Villa Mimosa, which is on the Lido."

I nodded, smiled, shrugged my shoulders, and sniffed at my nosegay. What matters where I next saw Lorenzo. Near or far, the happiness was going to be almost too much to bear. A small fishing boat went by, laden down with its catch, bound for the markets of the Rialto. A small boy and a white dog stood on its prow. The lad waved, and I waved back. And so, at length, we came to the Lido.

The sergeant secured an open hackney carriage from a rank, helped me in, and took his seat opposite me. We clattered slowly down a rutted, tree-shaded road lined with sleepy houses behind high walls all overhung with hibiscus and bougainvillea, till I saw ahead, over the shoulders of our driver, a line of illimitable blueness that was the Adriatic.

Close by the seafront, the sergeant gave an order, and we turned in between high marble gateposts and up a winding driveway flanked by a high thicket of hibiscus overtopped by clumps of white lilac and flame-colored rhododendron, till we came in sight of a villa of white marble, with a colonnaded portico and roof of terra-cotta pantiles surmounted by a copper cupola with a weather vane. It was a small building, but beautifully proportioned, so that I cried out with pleasure.

"What an adorable place!"

"Is the Villa Mimosa, *signorina.* Was built by the father of *il principe. Signorina* will be pleased to descend?"

Lorenzo—tall, and black-clad as ever—descended the steps from the portico to receive me. Grave-faced, he bowed over my proffered hand. I thought he looked tired, and my heart went out to him.

"It was good of you to come," he said. "What I have to disclose to you were best done in privacy. Did you have a comfortable journey?"

"Yes," I said. "The sergeant and his men are so kind and friendly. I was presented with a nosegay."

Lorenzo smiled, and some of the tiredness seemed to fall away from him. He motioned me to precede him up the steps and into the villa. When we were out of the sergeant's earshot, he said,

"Miss Gaunt, I have to tell you that you have become the darling of the Venetian Police Department. Even Sergeant Bernini, who is the faithful husband and father to a wife and eleven children on the isle of Burano, is quite bowled over by your charms. Is it too early in the morning to tempt you with a glass of light wine, or would you prefer coffee?"

"Neither, thank you. I have just breakfasted," I replied.

He paused, turned to me. I was struck by the gravity in his steady gaze.

"Have a coffee," he said. "You will need something to sustain you in the ordeal that lies ahead of you. I mean it seriously."

"Ordeal?" I asked. "What ordeal?"

We had entered a marble-tiled hallway, at the end of which was an open door that led into a place of cool greenness. Lorenzo gestured for me to enter what proved to be an oval-shaped conservatory constructed of glass and delicately wrought ironwork in the modern Gothic manner. The waxen leaves of tropical climbing plants rose ceiling-high, and the scent of exotic blooms lay delicately upon the air. Lorenzo waved me to a seat that was placed before a marble-topped table in the center of the conservatory. He remained standing.

"I will explain," he said. "Upon receiving your message by way of Herr von Wuppertal, I went immediately to the Palazzo Demaury. As you know, the guests have all departed; indeed, most of them are by now on their way home. It is of no consequence: I shall not need their evidence. The case is closed. The killer is no more."

"Harriet Demaury?"

He nodded. "You are quite correct in your assumption, Miss Gaunt. That feeble old lady was responsible for the deliberate murder of all three men."

"Of Peter Chalmers also?" I asked. "But why him?"

"All is explained," said Lorenzo. "Upon arriving at the palazzo, I was conducted by the gardener Giuseppe to the bedchamber where the old woman lay dead. There I made a search of her belongings and found the answer to all our questions. It was a very simple matter. Upon opening her reticule, I found—this."

He held up a small notebook bound in red velvet, with a silver pencil attached to the spine by a thin chain. I recognized it at once.

"Miss Harriet's commonplace book!" I exclaimed.

"Just so," said Lorenzo, laying it deliberately upon the table before me. "And a most uncommon commonplace book, as you will discover. You see, Miss Gaunt, because of our past collaboration on this case, and because you are intimately concerned in the tortuous workings of the murderess's mind, I have decided that you must know all. You must read it."

My hand reached out to touch the worn cover of the small book, faltered, and avoided it.

"Must I?" I asked him.

"I think it is necessary," he said quietly. "I will leave you now, but will send in some coffee for you. You will find it a most—disturbing document. But it must be read."

A bow, and he was gone. I watched his tall figure disappear through the doorway, heard his footfalls fade away down a corridor. A door opened and closed, and then I was alone with Harriet Demaury's commonplace book.

Nerving myself, I opened it at random.

. . . luncheon with the rector's widow, who is a tremendous bore, but keeps a good table (inherited shares in S. African diamond mines). Gave me recipe for v. excellent ginger pudding: ½ lb flour, ¾ lb suet, ¾ lb moist sugar, 2 large teaspoonsful grated ginger. Shred suet v. fine. Mix in flour, sugar, ginger. Stir well. Butter a basin and put mixture in *dry* (this is the secret). Boil for 3 hrs.

I imagine that Estelle will send for me when she feels her end approaching, and reveal her "secret"—while at the same time telling me that she is leaving everything to her dear Harriet, her "little treasure." I shall not let her know that on the only occasion I have seen her, 30 years after Giles's death, I instantly penetrated her disguise, and was the only member of the family to do so. The all-seeing eye of childhood fixes forever in the memory every nuance of manner and gesture. . . .

I skipped over several pages. Immediately following upon a recipe for making raspberry vinegar, my eye was caught by my own name leaping up from the page.

I think I could not abide it if Meg greatly favored her mother, either in character or appearance. Happily, she is all her father (and might still have been had I been her mother —and who would have wished her to be a Demaury?). Well, when I have inherited, I will open my heart to her. She shall come and live with me. Afterward she shall have every penny. . . .

The disjointed comments—interspersed with notes on amusing remarks she had overheard, names and authors of books she had been recommended to read, and innumerable cookery recipes— were sprinkled with occasional dates. With their aid, I was rapidly brought to the latter half of the strange book, and a grotesque entry:

I have just heard that he is dead—and good riddance to that highborn libertine who sought to bring ruin to my darling Meg. No one saw me work the mechanism of that Borgia cup (as my Uncle Charles had been unwise enough to show me all those years ago) and place it on the table in front of Lord Peter. I nearly died—or screamed out a warning and betrayed myself—when my darling picked it up. But happily she did so by the safe handle and immediately passed it to him. . . .

My flesh crawled in the horror of reliving that scene in the light of the knowledge that lay within the hideous little book. Driven by a frenzied curiosity, I skip-read several more pages, till I was attracted by the sight of other familiar names.

Though I believe I know Estelle's intentions toward me, I must take no chances. Bertrand and Philippe being my only possible rivals, I determined to set them at each other's throats. Sent Bertrand a note about Philippe's involvement in the Panama business (I had it from Lady G———, who is intimate with the De Lesseps). I think Bertrand would have killed him for me, had I not noticed the gap in the rails. Asked Philippe to bring me a brandy to that quiet part of the deck. One small push was all that was needed. . . .

Immediately following that shocking admission, there came a note of her being summoned to the recluse on the top floor. On her return, Miss Harriet confessed to feeling "unnerved." Was she mistaken in her confident belief that she would inherit? she asked herself. Estelle had now sent for Bertrand's daughter and son-in-law. Was it then to be Bertrand after all?

I read on, wincing with nausea.

. . . it was easily done. I trailed far behind the others, complaining of my rheumatism. Bertrand gave me his arm. At the outer door of the crypt, I told him I had left my reticule behind and would he please fetch it? (I had not brought my reticule.) After I had shut and locked the door, I waited to hear him come back. Faintly, through the thick door, I heard his screams. . . .

There was much more toward the end: repeated reassurances to herself that all was well, that the inheritance was secured for her and—the phrase made my gorge rise—her "darling Meg." She mentioned, also, Lorenzo, but with circumspection, as if that dreadful commonplace book, in which she had calmly and dispassionately recorded the means by which she had destroyed three human beings, had been no place to be indiscreet about her "darling Meg's" possibly hopeless love for a scion of the Venetian aristocracy.

Over and over again, I leafed through that record of an old and unattractive woman's struggle to reach out of a lifetime of neglect and disappointment and claw her way to love and affluence. If the child is, indeed, father of the man, the sad case of Miss Harriet went a long way to support that contention. The jealous and self-seeking impulse that had caused her to hurl the little monkey to its death from the high balcony was that same murderous impulse which had led her to obliterate her relations Bertrand and Philippe.

But—and this was what disturbed me most—the killing had not been solely for her own self-seeking. Always, in that book, my name was invoked: it was for the sake of "my darling Meg" that she had dreamed and schemed—and had finally murdered—for the inheritance. And the murder of Peter Chalmers had been all for my sake. An "unselfish killing"—hideous thought.

After a long time, I laid the book aside and was surprised to see that sometime during my strange ordeal—a glance at my fob watch told me I had been absorbed for an hour and a half—someone had brought me a cup of coffee. It stood at my elbow, and was now stone-cold.

Sick at heart, I rose and went out of the cool and soft-scented conservatory of the Villa Mimosa, into the hallway. There I found my sergeant, the portly, mustached Sergeant Bernini—who was so bowled over by my charms, despite his wife and eleven children on the isle of Burano—standing stiffly to attention, his cocked bicorne under his arm. Hastily, I wiped the residue of tears from my cheeks and smiled at him.

"Where can I find the prince, Sergeant?" I asked him.

"Follow me, please, *signorina*," said that worthy fellow. He had not gone five paces across the hallway before he paused and looked over his shoulder. "The coffee, *signorina*, it was hokay, yes?"

"It was excellent, Sergeant," I assured him. "Only, I was not very thirsty."

He threw me an embarrassingly adoring glance, shrugged his broad shoulders, and continued on his way, bringing me at length, by way of a long corridor, to an archway that gave out onto a balustraded terrace roofed by dense vines, upon which hung clusters of the largest and blackest grapes I have ever beheld.

Lorenzo was standing at a far corner of the terrace, a long telescope to his eye, looking out to sea. He lowered the instrument and met my gaze.

"Well, Miss Gaunt?" he said.

"You were right," I said. "It was indeed a most disturbing document."

"But you agree that it had to be read—by you?"

"Yes," I said. "It makes everything very clear. In a way, Miss Harriet was a very honest person, you know. She never made any secret of what she called 'the Demaury streak.' I should have remembered that it was she who said that there are—were— Demaurys who would kill."

Lorenzo nodded. "Such a one was Giles Demaury," he said. "As we also learn from the commonplace book."

I glanced at him warily, this man that I loved, remembering that he was also a policeman.

"Did you not know Estelle Amor's secret before you read the book?" I asked him.

"No," he said. "But you did?"

"I learned only yesterday," I said. "And, do you know, the odd thing is that Miss Harriet guessed that Giles Demaury must have tried to kill his wife; indeed she told me so, and Esmeralda Demaury with me. What she did not tell us was that the murder plan had gone awry and that it was Estelle who survived."

"I saw the person I have always known as Giles Demaury only a few days ago," he said. "And it never crossed my mind—as it never crossed my mind on the past occasions when we met—that she was a woman."

"An actress also," I reminded him. "But tell me, Prince—"

He glanced at me shrewdly as I hesitated.

"You are going to ask me perhaps if I am intending to take any official action regarding Estelle Amor?" he said. "As, for instance, arresting her for imposture, perhaps—is that what you have in mind, Miss Gaunt?"

"Yes," I admitted.

"I think no," he said. "There has been no fraudulent deception of the kind that would stand up in an Italian court of law. In Italian law, Estelle Amor is entitled to succeed to her husband's fortune, entirely and without restraint. As, indeed, she is entitled to bequeath that fortune to whom she pleases."

I allowed myself to take a very deep breath and to exhale it slowly, meanwhile watching his dark profile as he gazed unconcernedly over the balustrade and out to sea.

"As a matter of fact," I said, "she has offered to leave the fortune to me."

Not by so much as a flicker of an eyelash did he betray the slightest surprise or interest.

"Indeed, Miss Gaunt," he said politely. "May I proffer my congratulations?"

"And I have decided to accept the offer," I said.

"It would have been extremely imprudent of you to have declined," he said. "Ah, here comes Sergeant Bernini with a flask of our excellent red wine of the country. Do please be seated, Miss Gaunt. Thank you so much, Bernini. That will be all. To your very good health and fortune, Miss Gaunt."

He raised the glass to me and I somehow summoned up a brave smile. Inside, I was all tears. I had never really believed that my coming into a fortune would make the slightest difference to Prince Lorenzo Giolitti-Crispi's intentions toward me. But it had been lovely to whisper it into my pillow.

"You will be returning to England soon, I don't doubt," he said.

Now we were to have polite small talk. We would sip our wine. He would offer me another glass, which I would refuse. Then he would—presumably with much relief—hand me over to Sergeant Bernini's care, to escort me back to the city.

"Esmeralda Demaury is indisposed at the moment," I said, "but she will doubtless wish to go home at the earliest opportunity."

"And you will accompany her?"

"Of course," I said, genuinely surprised. "I am her companion."

"Of course," he said. "Of course. Is the wine to your taste?"

"It is excellent," I said. "What a truly lovely villa this is. The sergeant tells me it was built by your father."

"Indeed, yes," said Lorenzo. "And I will recount to you a quite amusing story. My father lost a considerable amount of money in the Monte Carlo Casino one night in the winter of 'eighty-seven, and was reduced to borrowing his cab fare back to his hotel from the doorman of the casino—a picayune amount, a few francs merely. 'Do you know, *monsieur*,' said the doorman to my father as he handed him the money, 'you are the fifth gentleman who has borrowed from me tonight.' My father, who saw signs and portents everywhere—like all inveterate gamblers—seizing upon the mention of number five, immediately returned to the *salles privées* and placed his cab fare *en plein* on five."

"And won?" I asked.

"Not only won," he said, "but won no less than four times in succession, thereby turning my father's few francs, by successive multiples of thirty-five, into a very considerable fortune. With which he built the Villa Mimosa. Oh, and he repaid the doorman."

We both laughed.

"How are your family?" I asked. We had half finished our glasses of wine. I was more than ready to go; the small talk was becoming quite intolerable, and I was terrified that somehow, by word or gesture, he would move me to tears.

"My mother is well," he said. "And my sister—my sister is to be married."

I glanced at him in surprise. "Indeed?" I said.

His face told me nothing. Again, I remembered that he was a policeman.

"You are slightly acquainted with the gentleman in question," he said. "Signor Alfredo Zucchi."

"The carpenter," I said.

"The same."

"I—I hope they will be very happy," I said in a small voice.

"And so do I, Miss Gaunt," he said. "As I believe—as I have belatedly come to believe—that they will."

"You have somewhat changed your views, Prince," I said.

Placing his half-empty wineglass on the small table that stood between us, Lorenzo got up and walked over to the balustrade, where lay his telescope. Putting the instrument to his eye, he scanned the shoreline. He then laid it down and turned to me.

"My views, Miss Gaunt, remain unaltered," he said. "What has happened is simply this: prompted by a hint from yourself, I have delved rather more deeply into the life of Alfredo Zucchi.

"You were quite right to suggest that there are good carpenters and bad carpenters. On inquiring, I found that Alfredo Zucchi is one of the former. In my inquiries, also, I learned that there are carpenters whose dedication to their craft is a way of praising God. Such a carpenter is Alfredo Zucchi.

"My inquiries into the nature of carpenters broadened into an inquiry into the nature of men, Miss Gaunt. A policeman, you must know, does not see the best aspects of the human state in his work. More sinners than saints come a policeman's way; he learns a certain cynicism, a way of looking behind the deceiving smile and questioning the easy answer. He learns to have doubts.

"I had forgotten that there are men whose smile hides nothing, who answer with honesty, pay their bills, walk upright, and fear no one; who are loved by all and have been so loved all their lives, from childhood. To my joy, to my very great joy, Miss Gaunt, I learned that Alfredo Zucchi is such a man. And I have you to thank for pointing me toward the truth."

I felt my eyes prickling with tears. This was what I had feared: Lorenzo had penetrated my defenses and touched my heart. I blinked vigorously and looked away.

"I—I am glad to have been of assistance," I murmured weakly.

"You have been of very great assistance, Miss Gaunt," he said. "But, as I have pointed out, my views on the disparity between my sister and her intended have not altered. Knowing Giovanna as I do, and learning about Alfredo as I have, I believe that they will rise above their differences of class. I believe that theirs, indeed, is a union that was fashioned in Heaven."

If he had looked closely, he could not have failed to see that the tears were coming to my eyes quite uncontrollably. Fortunately, the part of the terrace where I was sitting was in deep shadow from the overhead vines. I sought desperately for a brief question, something I could trust myself to deliver without betraying a telltale tremor in my voice; something to get him talking again, to keep his attention diverted while I got control of my emotions once more.

"When—when is the wedding to be?" I asked.

"As soon as can conveniently be arranged," he replied. "My mother has yet to be told. That will pose a few problems, but I think I can convince her that the world will not end because a Giolitti-Crispi is marrying a commoner. I shall point out that we are fast approaching the twentieth century and a new spirit is in the air. I shall soften the blow by reminding her that Alfredo is even poorer than we are."

"How will that soften the blow?" I asked, puzzled.

"Why, imagine my mother's shame and humiliation if Giovanna was marrying for money," he said. "Or simply if she *appeared* to be marrying for money."

My mind was racing with a thousand new thoughts . . .

"Would that be so awful?" I demanded. "For a Giolitti-Crispi to be thought to have married for money?"

"My mother would think so."

"And you, Prince—what do you think?"

The inheritance! Estelle Amor had induced me to accept the inheritance by suggesting that it might influence Lorenzo in my favor. "Love knows no shame," she had told me. "Follow your love fiercely. . . ."

Lorenzo said, "You ask me what I think, Miss Gaunt. Well, I will try to answer you honestly. As far as Giovanna is concerned, I think it would be a matter for some regret if she married for money and not for love. On the other hand, if Alfredo, with whom she is making a love match, had been a rich man, I think it would have been a matter for some rejoicing. My mother, as I have said, would think otherwise."

"I see," I said, greatly relieved.

"Not quite, Miss Gaunt," he said quietly. "You have only had half of my answer. For a woman—be she a Giolitti-Crispi or not—to make a love match with a rich man is entirely suitable. But for a man—any man—to marry a rich woman is to put himself in an impossible position."

"Oh!" I exclaimed.

"Quite impossible!" he repeated vehemently. "In my philosophy, the man must be the breadwinner or he is nothing. The disparity between a poor man and a rich wife outweighs any other, be it disparity of age, class, religion, race. Poor man, rich wife, is a recipe for disaster!"

"But, if there is love . . . ?" I faltered.

"No love could possibly survive under such circumstances," he said. "The man's pride, his self-respect, would constantly be affronted. The wife's esteem for her husband would gradually become eroded. Love would fly out the window. Oh, Meg, I have made you cry, and I would not have done that for the world."

His hands reached out and took mine. The expression in his wonderful gray eyes told me everything.

"You already knew about my receiving the inheritance," I said.

"The person I knew as Giles Demaury told me," he admitted.

"That would have been—before I received the invitation to dine at the Palazzo Giolitti-Crispi?"

"The day before," he said. "I had to see you again, though I knew that the inheritance made it impossible for me to aspire to winning you."

It was music in my ears. I closed my eyes and imagined that I was dreaming. When I opened them, his face—his beautiful, grave, wise face—was still there.

"You lectured me about unsuitable marriages," I reminded him. "Any faint hope I might have entertained regarding you was squashed quite flat."

He said, "I was thinking aloud. Telling myself that your fortune had placed an insurmountable barrier to my hopes. Meg, I had no idea, no idea at all . . ."

Hands clasped, we stood and looked into each other's eyes, and the world moved.

"How am I ever going to learn to live with you?" I asked him. "You are quite impossible."

"I shall not resign my position as Chief of Police," he said. "As the first Giolitti-Crispi in a thousand years to make his living by honest toil, I am not to be bought with mere money."

"You most certainly will not resign," I assured him. "As a woman who has lived all of her life by other people's grace and favor, I shall greatly esteem a marriage partner who is willing to toil while I spin."

He put his arms about me, and it was like standing on the threshold of a great truth.

"The matter of your inheritance . . ." he began.

I laid my fingers across his lips, but only briefly.

"Tomorrow," I said. "Let's talk about that tomorrow."